T0209752

TREASURES OF THE HEART

QUEST FOR THE SIMPKINS' GOLD

DONALD MUTTER

WESTBOW
PRESS®
A DIVISION OF THOMAS NELSON
& ZONDERVAN

Copyright © 2020 Donald Mutter.

All rights reserved. No part of this book may be used or reproduced by any means, graphic, electronic, or mechanical, including photocopying, recording, taping or by any information storage retrieval system without the written permission of the author except in the case of brief quotations embodied in critical articles and reviews.

This is a work of fiction. All of the characters, names, incidents, organizations, and dialogue in this novel are either the products of the author's imagination or are used fictitiously.

WestBow Press books may be ordered through booksellers or by contacting:

WestBow Press
A Division of Thomas Nelson & Zondervan
1663 Liberty Drive
Bloomington, IN 47403
www.westbowpress.com
1 (866) 928-1240

Because of the dynamic nature of the Internet, any web addresses or links contained in this book may have changed since publication and may no longer be valid. The views expressed in this work are solely those of the author and do not necessarily reflect the views of the publisher, and the publisher hereby disclaims any responsibility for them.

Any people depicted in stock imagery provided by Getty Images are models, and such images are being used for illustrative purposes only. Certain stock imagery © Getty Images.

All Scripture quotations are taken from the King James Version.

ISBN: 978-1-9736-8189-2 (sc)
ISBN: 978-1-9736-8187-8 (hc)
ISBN: 978-1-9736-8188-5 (e)

Library of Congress Control Number: 2019920701

Print information available on the last page.

WestBow Press rev. date: 12/11/2019

CONTENTS

Preface vii

One 1
Two 11
Three 27
Four 63
Five 71
Six 83
Seven 91
Eight 109
Nine 129
Ten 153
Eleven 173
Twelve 181
Thirteen 187
Fourteen 203
Fifteen 207
Sixteen 217

PREFACE

As the first son born into the Mutter family, surrounded by five girls, I had to occupy my time with fantasies about mystery and intrigue. I imagined myself on some grand adventure, trying to solve an impossible riddle and escaping from an almost certain death. Yet the only dangers were in my mind, and the only adventures were the ordinary ones a boy faces as he grows up. From an early age, I was fascinated with old houses and the mysteries behind the walls of those grand old structures. There was one house in particular just down the road from ours—a house I had heard was haunted! Of course, I found out later on that it was just an old house, and the lady who lived there was just an old lady.

When I sat down to pen the words to this book, my imagination from childhood took over again. This time, however, it took me on the greatest adventure I could have ever imagined. I hope the contents of this book do the same for you as you follow Tom and his fellow teens through the haunted castle and more as they battle unseen forces. I hope this book helps to reveal to you the same secrets that have been revealed to me—secrets that have changed my life and can change yours.

I patterned the main character after my son, who was also a preacher's kid. He, of all people, knew the pitfalls of growing up as a PK, as well as the other hardships all teenagers face in life. I pray this book will help you with your own challenges and in all the grand adventures this life has to offer. God bless you.

ONE

As Tom rounded the corner of the old, weather-worn, dilapidated building at the edge of his street, the one-eyed monster stared up at him. Tom froze in his tracks for what seemed like an eternity, pondering what his next move would be and thinking back to the event that had caused his sudden hesitation.

But it wasn't a one-eyed monster. In fact, it wasn't a monster at all. It was just the same old mudhole he had slipped and fallen into only two days earlier.

It wasn't just the thought of falling into a mudhole that brought back those troubled memories. It was the fact that Julie Patterson, his one and only, had been there when it happened.

Thomas Lee Parker was like most fourteen-year-old boys going through that awkward age. He wanted to be a man, and he'd let his parents know more than once that he was growing up, whether they liked it or not. What made adolescence even tougher for Tom was the fact that his father, James, was a minister. Reverend Parker pastored a church in their hometown of Richfield and had been pastor there for as long as Tom could remember. It wasn't that Tom wasn't proud of his father. He loved his father very much and was proud of him. It was just tough to go through life as a preacher's kid, and he'd gotten into plenty of scrapes at school for being called a PK.

Tom also felt he was too old for that church nonsense. Sunday was the most boring time in the world for him. None of his friends went to church, so they had their Sundays free to run the malls, fish, swim, or just lie in bed until all hours.

It wasn't fair!

Julie Patterson was Tom's one true love—at least the funny feeling in the pit of his stomach told him that each time she walked by. Long brown hair that flowed over her shoulders like a waterfall and the most beautiful deep blue eyes he'd ever seen were part of the reason he was stuck on her. Yes, she was pretty—very, very pretty—but she was nice too.

On that fateful morning, Tom passed by her house, as he always did, and stopped to walk her to school, as he always did. But this would be one walk he would never forget.

"Hi, Tom! Bye, Mom!" yelled Julie in the same breath while rushing from one room to the next, trying to find everything she needed for school. "Be with you in a minute!"

"That's okay. Take your time." Tom was used to waiting. If there was one thing he had learned from his mom and his big sister, Megan, it was that a man always had to wait for a woman, so he'd better get used to it.

There was only one problem with Tom's relationship with Julie; someone else was after Julie's affection. It wasn't just any old someone. It was none other than Toby Miller, the school bully and Tom's archenemy. Toby was a sophomore at Richfield and the star of the Richfield High Falcons junior varsity basketball team. At fifteen, he was older than Tom, and more importantly, he was a lot bigger. He had picked on Tom since grade school, and Tom was getting more than a little fed up. But what could he do? Tom squaring off with Toby would have been like a Volkswagen taking on a tractor trailer. And Tom wasn't about to tell his mom and dad. It was his problem, and he was going to take care of it himself. After all, that was a big part of being a man, wasn't it? Anyway, Toby was going to get what was coming to him someday.

Julie finally made her way to where Tom was waiting in the entrance hall. "You ready?" she asked as she slipped by him and opened the big wooden door leading outside.

I've been ready for ten minutes, he thought with a grin as he followed her down the steps, through the yard, and down the sidewalk on another of their seemingly endless treks toward school.

The day was bright, and the sky was blue, with only a few clouds, which looked like puffs of cotton floating as if God himself were guiding their every move—which he was, according to Reverend Parker. The only traces of the previous three days of continuous rainfall were a few puddles here and there and a slightly swollen Carson's Creek, which still looked as if someone had poured coffee with cream into it. Pine Street was a quiet little part of the Richfield suburbs, with its vast assortment of brick ranches, split-levels, and just plain houses with siding and shutters of every style and color. The houses weren't fancy or expensive, but they were neat and gave the look of comfort and friendly charm—with the exception of the house on the corner where Pine Street connected with Second Avenue.

The Simpkins mansion was the oldest building in Richfield, except for the courthouse. Built in the 1870s, the house was an architectural masterpiece. It dwarfed every other house on the block, and with the huge granite stones in its massive chimney and the marble steps leading up to the great oak door, it looked as if it belonged more on top of a lofty hill somewhere in Europe than on the corner of Second and Pine. The mansion had four huge, circular granite towers that looked like giant rockets with their roofs pointed toward space, as if they were waiting for the countdown to blastoff. But the mansion had been abandoned for more than a hundred years and was in terrible need of repair. A few years back, the city council had talked about restoring the house and making it a historical landmark, but they didn't have the funds to undertake such a task.

The house itself was mysterious and spooky. According to some, it was haunted. Many people had reported hearing strange sounds coming from the north tower on moonlit nights, but Tom had never heard any. It was just someone's wild imagination; old houses always seemed to bring out the worst in people. Besides, the strangest and most interesting thing about the Simpkins mansion wasn't a ghost. It was the legend of the Simpkins treasure.

Joe and Charlie Simpkins were brothers who came out to the Great Northwest from Pennsylvania during the great gold rush of the mid-1800s. Joe was a little bigger than his younger brother, but both were tough, strapping, brawny men who weren't afraid of anything. Legend had it that the boys mined a large portion of the western face of the Rocky Mountains, but for the first few years, they found little gold. As tough and stubborn as the boys were, they began talking of packing up and moving back east with some of the other misfortunates.

But something happened one day that would change their lives forever.

Joe was digging just inside the opening of the mine. As on most of the preceding days, he wasn't having any luck. But suddenly, he heard a thunderous crash that shook the ground under his feet, causing him to lose his balance and fall to the ground, hitting his head on a rock.

When he came to, he found the strength to get to his feet, grab his old mining lamp, and make his way into the center of the mine. There he saw the sight he had expected yet prayed he wouldn't see: the mine had caved in, trapping Charlie. Joe went back to where he had been digging, paying no attention to his pounding head or the huge scratch on his face, and grabbed his pick and shovel.

Digging feverishly, Joe finally cleared away enough dirt to get to his brother, but to his horror, Charlie was dead. He had been crushed by the dirt and rocks of the cave-in. Joe dug away the remaining dirt from Charlie's lifeless body. As he reached down to pick up his only brother, he glanced up to the roof of the mine, where he saw sparkling light reflecting back at him. He lifted his light and stared in amazement at one of the largest veins of gold that had ever been found.

At least that was what the legend said. In his death, Charlie

Simpkins had uncovered the gold strike that was still talked about more than a century later.

Joe had the mansion built in honor of his brother and worked the mine until he found no more gold. One day Joe left the mansion, the mine, and the town and was never seen again. His mysterious disappearance left the whole town talking about what had caused Joe to leave, but more importantly, they wondered what had happened to all the gold. Some said he took the gold with him, but according to the most popular story, he hid the gold somewhere in Richfield and left a secret code of some sort to show where it was. Of course, the code was never found, the gold was never found, and the secret remained a secret to that day.

Tom and Julie walked past the Simpkins house at a slow, steady pace, talking about school and the basketball team—things teenagers usually talked about—when suddenly, Tom heard a sound behind them. It grew stronger until it caused his head to turn. But it was too late.

Toby Miller zoomed by them on his motorcycle, shouting, "Watch it, stupid!" As he rushed by, the sound of the motorcycle startled Julie so much that she quickly moved aside to get out of Toby's way and nudged against Tom's shoulder. Tom, who was walking on the edge of the sidewalk, felt his body losing control of its balance. He had time to twist around and get a glimpse of where he was falling—and regretted it. Getting closer and closer to the horrified look on his face was the mudhole made by the melting snow and all the rain. Tom dropped his books, bracing for the fall. The inevitable was happening, and there was nothing he could do about it.

Splash! Tom went face-first into the mud, water, and slime like a diver doing a belly flop into a pool. Only he was no diver, and this was no pool. Tom's face went through the muddy water and slammed into the ground at the bottom. By that time, the rest of his body had found the mud, and he was wallowing like a pig rooting for some corn in its pen. His nose hurt, and he thought it might be bleeding, but who could tell under all that mud? Anyway, that was not what was hurting him. Tom was glad the mud was covering his face—it covered up the redness he knew for sure was flooding over him, part embarrassment and part anger.

"Are you all right?" Julie was holding out her hand for Tom to take it, but Tom didn't want her to get muddy too. In fact, he wished she would walk away and quit looking at him.

"I think I'm okay" was all he could get out. He knew he must look like a mess, and he was sure that from Julie's viewpoint, it must have been a hilarious sight. But from his angle, it wasn't funny, and he appreciated that Julie didn't laugh.

By that time, Toby, who had seen what had happened, had turned around and was heading back to the scene of the accident. "Aw, is the poor widdle boy all wight?" he said sarcastically as a sneering grin crossed his face. Toby's voice made the hair stand up on the back of Tom's neck—even when it was plastered down by muddy water. "Hop on, Julie, and I'll give you a lift to school." He then revved up the motorcycle a time or two in such a way as to tell Julie, "I'll give you the ride of your life."

Toby had always been kind of a spoiled brat. The motorcycle was just one of a whole list of expensive gifts his affluent parents had given him on his thirteenth birthday. Tom's heart settled down a little bit when Julie looked at Toby with a stern face and said, "No, thanks, Toby. I'll stay here with Tom if you don't mind."

Toby shut off the engine, apparently so Julie—and Tom—could hear what he had to say next. "When are you going to wise up, Julie, and give up on this little pip-squeak? You need a real man—someone who can show you a good time."

Tom started to say something, but he could tell Julie was already worked up and ready to explode.

"Well, Toby, if I find a real man, I'll let you know. But right now, all I see is a spoiled kid who thinks he needs to tell everybody how great he thinks he is. Now, if you don't mind, Tom and I can take care of this little problem, and we don't need any of your brilliant advice!"

"Suit yourself." Toby kicked the starter, and the motorcycle roared back to life. He raced off to school, leaving one angry girl and one mud-caked boy.

"Come on, Tom. You need to get back home and change," Julie told him.

"I'll be fine, Julie; you go on to school, and I'll go home and clean up and meet you there. And thanks, Julie, for what you said to Toby."

Julie yelled over her shoulder as she walked off, "He had it coming, the big loudmouth!"

Tom slipped quietly through the back door of his house. He didn't want his mom to see him like that. The Parker home had a small staircase in the kitchen, leading to the upstairs, with a larger staircase in the living room. Using the back staircase was convenient in situations like the one Tom was in… *I'll just take a quick shower and put on some clean clothes, and maybe I won't be too late for school,* he thought as he started up the back staircase. "So far so good," he whispered under his breath, a little surprised that it was going this easily.

At the top of the stairs, he made a quick right-hand turn toward the hall—and ran into his mom, knocking a basket full of towels out of her hands.

"Tom, what in the world happened to you?" Now, JoAnn Parker was the kind of mom who didn't think things just happened. Her children always had to explain every little detail of what had happened, where it had happened, why it had happened, who had been with them when it had happened, and whose fault it had been.

"Mom, I just fell into that big old mudhole in front of the Simpkins house—that's all. It's no big deal." Tom wasn't in the mood for a game of twenty questions, but he knew his mom.

"Did somebody push you into the mudhole?"

"No," Tom fibbed. Technically, Julie had pushed him in, but it hadn't been her fault, and he didn't want to explain it.

"Was Julie with you?"

"Yes. Look, Mom, I'm late for school; I'll explain it all to you this afternoon," he said, hoping she would forget about it by then.

JoAnn suspected there was more to the story than Tom was telling her, but she decided not to needle him anymore. *He'll tell me when he's ready.* She picked up her clothes basket and started gathering the towels. "Okay, Tom, I just wanted to make sure you were all right. I'll see you this afternoon."

Tom showered, changed, and headed back to school at a quick, steady pace. His mom had written him an excuse, which he needed because he was more than an hour late. Tom wanted her to make up an excuse, but church people were notoriously honest. So when he got to school, he got a couple highly raised eyebrows from the assistant principal and from the principal, who was called in because the assistant principal found his story so hard to believe.

I knew Mom should have made up something. I feel so ridiculous, he thought to himself as he headed toward his classes. It was truly a day that would live forever in his memory.

Well, that had been two days earlier, but as Tom stared down at the mudhole, it seemed to say, "I know you; you took a swim in me just the other day, didn't you?" Tom tried to get those thoughts out of his mind. He had a basketball game to get to. His Richfield Falcons JV squad was playing their cross-town rivals, the Flat Ridge High Cougars. Tom was just a substitute; he got to see some playing time, usually in the fourth quarter, when his team was way ahead or way behind. Toby was the star—everybody knew that, especially Toby. But Tom wanted to be part of the team and do something to help, even though he knew it wasn't much. At five foot four and 120 pounds, he wasn't exactly the ideal size for basketball. But he was still growing, and he had a pretty good jump shot. He could also dribble as well as anyone else on the team. He knew that sooner or later, he would have his day in the sun—he just had to be patient.

The sun was slowly starting to settle behind the snowcapped mountains, so Tom turned his thoughts away from the mudhole and toward the big game ahead of him. As he slowly started moving again, he glanced toward the old Simpkins mansion. *I wonder if the legend is true,* he thought to himself as he glanced up at one of the huge granite towers that seemed to stretch endlessly toward the sky.

As his eyes brought his view back down, he caught a glimpse of the old granite chimney out of the corner of his eye. Was that a flicker of metal behind one of the stones? The sun seemed to be reflecting off something behind the stone, but he couldn't be sure.

The cement had worn away, leaving a small crevice for the light to shine through. No, his mind was playing tricks on him. He was late for the game—it was time to get going. He hurried toward the school so he would be on time, but right now, his mind wasn't on the game; it was on whatever was behind that stone.

TWO

"Where have you been?" Jason Bennett, Tom's best friend, was a great guy, but he was too uptight. He wasn't laid back like Tom was. "The rest of us were here a half hour ago, and we're ready to go out; and here you come in like you're part of the audience."

"I'd say that's all we'll be tonight anyway, Jason. Against Flat Ridge, we'll be lucky if Coach Waters lets us on the court to warm up," Tom told his friend. "Listen, I've got something I want to talk to you about."

"Not now, Tom; you've gotta get on your uniform before Coach gets in here for his usual pep talk, or you're off the team. You know how mad he was the last time you were late."

"All right, Mother," said Tom in his usual laughing tone. He put on his uniform and was seated beside Jason just seconds before the locker room door opened, and Coach Sam Waters walked in.

Coach Waters had the look of a typical basketball coach. He was tall, about six foot three, with broad shoulders; long, slim legs; and an overall physique that showed he had spent some time in the weight room. He was dressed in casual dress slacks and had on his red Richfield Falcons sport shirt with the flying falcon emblem in the left corner, over his heart, which was where it belonged, for Coach Waters's heart was with the Falcons. He had been with the school for seventeen years and had brought the JV basketball program from utter despair to make it one of the top programs in that part of the state. He had been asked several times to move up to the varsity but had always turned down the offer. "No varsity team is worth the program it's printed on if they aren't shaped and molded during their JV years," Tom had heard Coach Waters say at least a dozen times. He was proud of his JV teams, and it showed.

Coach didn't usually have a whole lot to say in his pregame pep talks. Tom figured he didn't need to say much—he'd said enough in practice to make up for it.

"Now, men"—they were men until after the game, and if they lost, they became boys again—"we all know what an important game this is for us. We are tied with Flat Ridge for the district lead, and this is a must win for us if we plan on winning the district and going on to the regionals." The regionals was as far as a JV team could get—there was no state tournament for junior varsity. "Now, Miller, I want you guarding the Branscome kid; he's their best player. We'll start out with man-to-man coverage and see how that works. Martin, I want you to double up on Branscome when he gets the ball. The rest of you help out on coverage, and watch for the open man. Okay, let's get out there and win this one for the Falcons of Ridgefield High!"

With their usual roar, the players jumped up and headed toward the door. Tom and Jason were at the back of the line, where the substitutes were destined to be. As they made their way through the tunnel leading to the gym floor, Tom's mind wasn't on the game. He couldn't stop thinking about whatever was behind the stone in the chimney of the Simpkins house. It probably wasn't anything important, but Tom was a curious young man, and not knowing was driving him crazy!

Jason could tell something was wrong. "Hey, man, what is it with you?" he asked. "This is our most important game of the year, and you're out in dreamland."

"Jason, if you promise to go with me somewhere tonight, I promise you I'll get my mind on the game and keep it there."

"Where are we going?" Jason asked with a puzzled look on his face. He was a curious young man too.

"I can't tell you now. Just promise me you'll go."

Jason shrugged in a sign of surrender. "All right, I'll go—boy, now you've got me so curious about this I may not be able to get *my* mind on the game!"

Their pace quickened as they passed through the open doors and trotted behind their teammates onto the gym floor to the roar and approval of the hometown crowd. "Come on, Jason. Get your mind on the game," Tom said. "Let's go out there and watch our boys beat those Cougars," he said in a sarcastic tone.

The game was pretty much typical of county rivalries. There was some pushing and shoving, and one boy even threw a punch, but no real damage was done. The refs kept the game in relative control, calling a technical foul on each team to show the players and coaches they were still in command of the game.

The score at halftime was 32–30 in favor of Flat Ridge, and Coach Waters was not pleased. "We could be up by ten points if you guys would play like you're capable of. We've got to keep that Branscome kid from getting the ball on the baseline. That's his shot, and he's been killing us from that spot. We're going back to the one-three-one zone defense; the man-to-man isn't working too well. Miller, when they double-team you, find the open man; don't try taking shots with two guys on you. Remember, this is a team game, and we can only win as a team!"

Telling Toby Miller to stop ball-hogging was like telling a fish to stop swimming. When Toby got the ball, he was going to shoot the ball—nobody was going to take his glory away from him.

Coach Waters continued. "Okay, we've still got a half of basketball to play, so let's get out there and win this one for the Falcons of Ridgefield High.

He always says that, Tom thought to himself. *He must think it's the appropriate thing to say—either that, or he can't think of anything any better.*

In the second half, Richfield played a much better game. Toby was still his usual ball-hogging self, but the rest of the team played better defense and kept the hotshot Kevin Branscome from getting his shots from his favorite spots. Even Tom got to play for about two minutes. He didn't score any points, but he made a couple nifty passes to set up some easy baskets. Besides, playing gave his sore butt a little rest and got his mind off that other little matter.

Jason got into the game too, only for about a minute to give Toby a rest. Jason wasn't a bad basketball player. At five foot eight and 145 pounds, he had pretty good size, but he was a little awkward and wasn't much of a shooter. But he loved to play and probably tried harder than anyone else on the team.

Richfield won the game 59–55, upping their record to 16–1 and almost assuring themselves of a spot in the regional tournament. Toby got eighteen points to lead the team in scoring. Coach Waters said he was proud of the team's effort, and he called off Monday's practice as a reward for the win. Tom was glad of that; the practices were the worst part of being on the team.

Tom dressed quickly, trying to stay out of Toby's way. He was still mad about the mudhole incident, and the names he had been called at school helped to add fuel to an already hot fire. Mud Man and the Creature from the Black Mudhole were names he'd been hearing from Toby and his friends for the past two days. *One of these days, Toby Miller*, thought Tom. *Pow! Right to the moon!* He shoved his clenched fist in a hooklike fashion toward the ceiling.

Fifteen minutes later, Tom and Jason emerged through the big double doors leading outside the school with their hair still wet from the showers. Jason was prodding Tom for more information on his big secret. "All right, Tom, what's this all about? Where are we supposed to be going tonight that is so all-fired important?"

Tom looked over his shoulder and then to the left and right to make sure no one was looking. "You know that big old house at the end of our street—the Simpkins mansion?"

Jason hesitated for a minute as if he were afraid to answer. "You mean the one that's haunted?" Jason was kind of a chicken—not that Tom was all that brave, of course, but at least he could watch just about any horror movie ever made. Jason could too—if he didn't mind staying up all night.

"That house is not haunted, Jason. I've lived on that street for ten years, and I've never seen or heard anything coming from that house. It's just an old house—that's all!"

Jason hesitated on his next question too. "Well, what about it?" he asked.

"I want you to meet me at the Simpkins house at eleven o'clock tonight."

This time, Jason's eyes got as big as two golf balls, and he didn't hesitate at all with his next question. "Are you crazy?" His voice cracked, partly from fear and partly from puberty. "Do you mean to tell me that you want me to meet you in front of that spooky old house at eleven o'clock tonight?"

"Now, calm down, Jason, and let me explain." Tom was a smart kid, and smart kids were usually pretty good at explaining why they were about to do something stupid. Tom told Jason the whole story as they walked up North Street toward Jason's house. He told him what he'd seen and said that maybe it was nothing, but it was worth a look.

"But ain't you afraid we'll get caught? What if my parents see me sneaking out of the house, or what if the cops see us prowling around? There are laws against trespassing, you know." Jason wanted to talk his friend out of the plan, but Tom was determined.

"This is Friday night, and the cops will all be patrolling downtown. And you've sneaked out of the house several times— remember last week, when you crawled out the window so you could meet Melissa at Pizza Town? C'mon, Jason. No more excuses. It's only a couple blocks from your house, and I promise to be there when you get there."

Jason saw the look of determination on his friend's face. "Okay, I'll do it, but I'm doing it under protest. Just remember that."

Tom walked on past as Jason turned into the driveway leading to his house. "Just as long as you're doing it." Tom loved the little thrill he got when he successfully talked somebody into doing something he or she really didn't want to do.

By the time Tom got to his house, it was around ten o'clock. His mom and dad had just gotten home from the revival his dad had been preaching all week, and Megan was still at the school, watching the varsity game—or, more precisely, watching her boyfriend, Kevin, play in the game.

"How'd the game go?" his father asked. James Parker was proud of his son, and he was glad Tom was on the team, even though he didn't like to see him miss so many services.

"Oh, we won. How did the revival go?"

"Well, there were two saved tonight," Reverend Parker said with a sparkle in his eye.

Tom could never understand why getting "saved" was so great. How could people be happy about giving up the good times in life and spending the rest of their lives in church? But those fanatics helped put food on the table, clothes on his back, and a little money in his pocket, so he wasn't complaining. Right now, he had more important things to think about anyway.

"Well, good night, Dad. See you in the morning." Tom hurried up the stairs and down the hall to his room. He was glad his dad had allowed him to have a phone in his room. There were times, like this one, when he needed to have his privacy, and using the phone in the living room was like broadcasting his conversations over cable TV. He had one call to make before his rendezvous with destiny. His hands were sweaty and shaking as he picked up the receiver and dialed the number for the house down the street.

"Hello, Mr. Patterson. Is Julie there?" There was something about talking to a girl's father that made a young man's stomach tighten up. Tom had seen many movies about a girl's father hating every one of her boyfriends, and he figured it must be normal for Mr. Patterson to hate him too. But his stomach eased up a little when he heard the sweet, sexy female voice on the other end.

"Hello? This is Julie."

"Hi, Julie. This is Tom. Look, I know it's late, but I have a favor to ask of you."

"What is it, Tom? You sound kinda nervous."

"Can you get out of the house tonight? I need you to meet me in the front of that big pine tree in your yard in half an hour."

"What for, Tom? What's this all about?"

Oh boy, here we go again! Julie was as full of questions as Jason was. "I'll tell you when I get there—do you think you can sneak out without your parents catching you?"

"Sure, I guess so. Okay, Tom, I'll meet you there, but this had better be good."

Tom didn't know if it would be good or not. *Why am I doing this?* he thought to himself. *It will probably turn out to be a piece of chewing gum wrapper that someone stuffed into that crack in the stone. Maybe I should just call the whole thing off. No, I've got to find out one way or another.*

"Don't worry, Julie; it'll be worth your trouble." Tom didn't know whether or not it would be, but he figured he had to tell her that, or she wouldn't go. "I'll see you there in twenty five minutes."

Tom hung up the phone and looked at the clock: 10:20. He hadn't given himself much time, but it would be enough time to get his stuff together and meet Julie.

He moved quickly but quietly from his room to his dad's workshop in the basement. Looking through his dad's tools, he quietly talked to himself, which he always did when he was nervous. "Chisel, chisel, chisel—where on earth is the chisel? Oh, here it is. Now I need a hammer." He wanted a ball-peen hammer, but all he could find was an old claw hammer that looked as if it had hammered one too many nails. He quickly stuffed the hammer into his gym bag along with the chisel and his flashlight and quietly shut the lid on the tool chest. Then, slowly, he turned toward the staircase leading to the kitchen—and met his dad, who had slipped up behind him. His dad had his hands on his hips and a puzzled expression on his face.

"Tom, what in the world are you doing with my tools?"

Tom's eyes rolled up toward the ceiling as he thought to himself, *Man, you'd better think up a good fib and think it up fast.* Tom told a lie only when he needed to get himself out of a jam, and this was as big a jam as there was, so he made up a beauty. "Uh, I need these tools for a school project that me and Jason are working on. I thought I'd get everything ready tonight so we can get started on it first thing in the morning."

James Parker looked at his son for a few seconds. The way he'd told the story didn't sound right, but there was no need to doubt his word—not just yet anyway. "All right, Tom, just remember to put them back where you got them."

"Okay, Dad, I will. I promise." *That was a little too easy,* Tom thought to himself, but he didn't have time to analyze his dad's response. He had an appointment to keep.

By the time he got back to his room, he was ten minutes from his appointment. He knew he would have to hurry but at the same time make sure his family was unaware of what was going on. He slung the gym bag across his shoulder, opened the window, and climbed out onto the branches of the big old oak tree.

"What a terrible place to put a tree!" Tom had told his parents when they'd moved into the house on Pine Street. He had been only four at the time, but he'd been old enough to know that he didn't want any old tree blocking his window. But ten years later, he had changed his mind. The tree was his escape hatch—a way of getting out of the house when he didn't want his family to know he was leaving. Its massive trunk and huge limbs pointing in every direction were sturdy enough to hold Tom—and probably two hundred more kids his size.

Tom moved slowly from one limb to another, taking care to hold on tight to whichever limb he had hold of at the time. When he was nine, he had fallen out of that same tree and broken his arm, and that memory told him to be careful.

Upon finally reaching the bottom, he gazed through the kitchen window to make sure no one was watching. His mom was in the kitchen, fixing a snack, but her back was to him, so it was easy to move past the window and across the yard. He turned the corner of the house, moving out of the shadows and into the light of one of the many streetlights on his block, when he noticed a car pulling into the driveway.

"Oh, this is just great!" he whispered to himself.

Kevin was bringing Megan home, and Tom knew they would stay out in the car for a few minutes to neck—they always did. He knew he would have to take an alternate route through the backyard and past the Martins' place before he could double-back to the sidewalk and on to Julie's house.

I just hope I can get there before she comes out, he thought as he detoured over the Martins' fence. "It's a good thing the Martins' don't have that pit bull anymore, or I'd be dead meat."

He made his way through the wet grass of the Martins' yard without anybody noticing—at least he didn't think anybody had noticed—and before long, he was on the sidewalk, hurrying along. His short, skinny legs moved faster and faster as his feet pounded out an increasing rhythm on the concrete sidewalk. The quarter-mile jog seemed like a ten-mile run to Tom. *I just know I'll be late, and Julie's going to kill me*, he thought, running faster and faster, his breath puffing out spouts of steam from the frosty air.

Finally, after what seemed like an hour, he was able to slow down, and he came to a stop at the old pine tree.

"Good. She hasn't come out yet," he said to himself.

"That's what you think!" A slim, shapely figure emerged from the shadow of the pine. The expression on Julie's face said it all: he was late, and she was mad. "Tom, do you know what it's like to stand out here in the middle of the night by myself? I could have gotten picked up or mugged or even worse by the time you got here."

"I know, Julie, and I'm sorry." Tom was always apologizing—he never seemed to do the right thing at the right time.

"Well, what's this all about?"

"Can I tell you as we walk? We're late as it is."

"Walk where? Where are we going?"

Tom finally got Julie to walk with him, and he told her the strange tale—then she got mad again.

"What! Tom, do you mean to tell me that you got me to sneak out of my nice, warm house into this cold night air to go with you to some stupid old house to move a stupid old rock, all because you saw something shiny behind it? Are you out of your mind?" Julie was trying to talk quietly to keep from waking up the neighborhood, but it was pretty hard to be quiet when mad.

"C'mon, Julie. Just this once. I have a hunch that it's something important. Maybe it's the Simpkins gold!"

"Aw, Tom, you don't really believe that stupid old legend, do you? Don't you think that if there was any gold, somebody would have found it by now? This is crazy—I'm going back home."

"Please, Julie, go with me just this once." Tom knew he was getting desperate—he was begging. "If you go, I won't ask you for any more favors as long as I live." He looked at her with sad puppy dog eyes.

How could I say no to that? Julie thought to herself. "You win, Tom; I'll go with you."

When they finally arrived at the Simpkins mansion, Jason was already there. With him was Melissa Stewart, a perky little thing with short brown hair and sparkling brown eyes that twinkled when she smiled—and she was always smiling. "I knew you'd be late, so I brought Melissa," Jason said.

"How did you know I'd be late?"

Jason was surprised Tom would even ask such a question. "Because you're always late."

Tom couldn't argue with that.

"Well, let's get this over with so I can get Melissa back home before her parents know she's gone," said Jason.

Melissa, never liking the role of the helpless female, smiled at

Jason. "Are you worried about getting Melissa back home or about getting Jason back home?"

Jason gave her a funny look but didn't reply.

Tom turned to face the other three with the look of a surgeon about to perform an operation. "All right, Julie, I need you to hold the flashlight. Jason, you can help me move the stone after I get the cement chiseled out. Melissa, you stay close to the curb so you can let us know if anybody's coming. Okay, let's go."

The great stone chimney was built on the north side of the mansion, facing Second Avenue. Each stone had been cut from the granite in the surrounding mountains and brought to the location by horse and wagon. Tom estimated that each stone weighed about 150 pounds, including the one they were going to have to move to get to whatever they were trying to get to.

The cement was worn from the elements but was still hard to chip away, and Tom was working up a pretty good sweat even in the cold night air. Julie moved the light from Tom's hammer and chisel just long enough to shine it through the gap in the stone. The light of the flashlight bounced back to her, and with a look of amazement, she turned to Tom and Jason and said, "There's something in there all right. I can't tell what it is, but it's something shiny—that's for sure."

Melissa was getting bored as the watchwoman. "I wonder what's taking them so long." Her eyes scanned the territory from left to right and front to back. Nobody was stirring. She'd seen two dogs, a cat, and a possum but no sign of the cops—or any other human being, for that matter.

As her eyes glanced across the yard, she saw the big mudhole running along the edge of the sidewalk. "That must be the mudhole I heard about at school," she said to herself. Being an eighth grader meant missing out on some of the upper-class stories, but she'd heard about the great mudhole incident, as had every other student, teacher, coach, janitor, cafeteria worker, secretary, and principal and anybody else associated with Richfield High School.

Her gaze was suddenly interrupted by an approaching vehicle. Melissa hurriedly ran to the side of the house where her friends were and yelled softly, "Hey, you guys, someone's coming!"

At the sound of Melissa's warning, Tom stopped chiseling, Julie doused the light, and Jason quit what he was doing, which was nothing, and ran around the side of the house with Tom, Julie, and Melissa hot on his tail. They made it just in time—they hoped.

"Be quiet," said Tom. "I'll look around the corner and see who it is."

There was no such thing as a corner on the Simpkins house. The four round towers circled what would have been the corners in such a way that you had to walk two-thirds of the way around the tower to look around the corner. Tom eased around the tower, making sure to keep his back and the back of his head firmly pressed against the cold, rough granite. He finally reached the spot where he could see the road—unfortunately, a spot where he could be seen—and watched the vehicle pass. It was a red Jeep, and based on its rate of speed, it was unlikely anybody in the Jeep had seen them.

He eased back around the tower to where his friends were. "Do any of you know anybody who drives a red Jeep?" None of the group recalled anybody who owned such a vehicle. "Well, it's gone now, so let's get back to what we were doing and finish this up."

The four didn't notice that the Jeep had turned down Park Boulevard and pulled off the road with its lights turned off.

Tom worked as hard as he could, chiseling the cement away from the huge stone. Finally, he got as much cleared away as he felt he would need, so he turned to see where Jason was.

"He went to check on Melissa," Julie told him. "He'll be back in a little while."

Tom was surprised Jason had enough nerve to walk around that spooky old house by himself in the dark. Melissa was the brave one. If they ever got married, Melissa would be the one going downstairs with a ball bat in her hand while Jason cowered under the bed if they heard a burglar. That was the main reason Tom wanted Melissa watching the road—he knew she wouldn't be scared out there by herself.

Jason finally made his way back. "Are you ready?" he asked. Seeing the cement cleared away from the stone, he had his answer.

Tom grabbed the upper corner of the stone, and Jason grabbed the lower corner. It was hard for both boys to get into such a tight space, so pulling on the old granite stone was a muscle-stretching exercise. "I haven't strained this much since I tried to bench-press two hundred pounds during football season," Jason said as he tugged and pulled with his teeth clenched and veins popping out in his neck.

"C'mon, Jason. Just a little harder—I think I felt it budge," said Tom.

Julie had the light positioned where she would be able to see behind the stone as it was moved. It was moving! At first, it moved slowly; then, as the cement loosened its grip, it moved easier and with less effort on Tom and Jason's part, until there was about a five-inch gap between where the stone used to be and where it was now.

"That's enough," said Tom.

"Thank heavens," said Jason. "I thought my arm was going to come out of its socket."

Julie was straining her pretty blue eyes, trying to see what had made all this trouble necessary. "I can see something shiny, but I still can't tell what it is," she said.

"Well, reach in there and get it," said Tom.

"You reach in there and get it—I'm not sticking my hand in there."

Tom didn't want the rest of them to know it, but he too was afraid to stick his hand into the opening. But there was only one way to find out what the thing was, and if that meant risking his hand to get the thing out, then it was a risk he was going to have to take.

Slowly, he put his hand through the gap in the rock, feeling his way inch by inch through the unknown regions behind the chimney, until his fingers touched something cold and hard. It felt like a flat piece of metal.

"I've got it!" he said excitedly as he drew his hand out much faster than he had put it in.

As Tom drew the object out and the light of his flashlight shone upon it, all eyes were glued to their amazing discovery—except for Melissa's, of course. She was still in the front, keeping watch and wondering when the treasure hunters were going to finish up and get out of that place.

Melissa was braver than most teenage girls, but that place gave her the creeps—and the shadows moving in the bushes across the street didn't help matters much. *It's just my eyes,* she thought to herself, hoping the thought would calm the terror gripping her heart—but it didn't. She'd had about all she could take for one night.

Peering around the edge of the west tower, Melissa saw her friends gazing at whatever they had found. "Hey, when are you guys gonna get this over with? I've got to get back home before my dad finds me missing, or I'll be grounded for the rest of my life!"

Tom motioned for Melissa to come join the rest of them, and she quickly scurried over to the edge of the chimney.

What Tom held in his hand was not a chewing gum wrapper—but it wasn't a treasure of gold either. It was a small, flat piece of metal about two inches wide and six inches long. It looked like the plates tacked up on the office doors of doctors or lawyers.

"I knew it. I just knew it!" Jason said. Even In the darkness, Tom could see the redness of Jason's face. "I come out here in the middle of the night, trespass on someone's property, and just about strain my guts out moving a stupid rock, and for what? The plate off the school library! Girls, I don't know about you, but I'm going home. Indiana Jones here can do some more exploring if he wants to, but I'm calling it a night." Jason Bennett was a pessimist in every sense of the word.

Tom thought of a good comeback to his friend's rash statement, but he didn't use it. "Hey, guys, look at this. There's writing on this plate!"

It wasn't exactly writing—not in sentence form anyway—but something was engraved on the plate. Tom lowered the beam of the flashlight to more clearly make out the inscription:

Cell-15 R-10 Up-4 Lay Up

"Lay up? Oh wow, Tom, you've really got something there. I suppose Joe and his buddies played a lot of basketball while he was hiding the gold, and *lay up* is part of his secret code. I'm sure he would have enjoyed the game a lot more if basketball had been invented back then!"

There Jason went again, shooting his mouth off. Why couldn't he look at things the way Tom did?

"Maybe *lay up* refers to something else besides a basketball term," Tom said. "We don't know what kind of language they used back then. Maybe a layup was a block layer or something like that."

Julie had been relatively quiet all that time but felt she needed to somehow gain control of the situation. "Look, guys, it's twelve thirty in the morning. Now, I suggest we all go back home and go to bed, and we can discuss this tomorrow, okay?"

They all agreed that Julie's plan made sense. Besides, Jason was going to have to come over to Tom's house tomorrow to work on the little "project" he had told his dad about earlier.

Tom stuffed the plate in his shirt pocket and took Julie's hand, and the two proceeded up Pine Street through the mist and eventually out of sight.

Jason and Melissa headed in the opposite direction along Second Avenue, toward North Street, where they both lived.

None of them bothered to look back at the old Simpkins mansion. If they had, they would have seen the light flickering in the window of the old north tower.

THREE

By the time Tom got back to the old oak tree in his backyard, it was almost one o'clock. He and Julie hadn't talked much as they made their way up Pine Street. As they'd walked past the rows of houses shrouded in darkness, whose owners were probably asleep in their nice, comfortable beds and having sweet dreams about the weekend, Tom had been deep in thought about the strange metal object they had found and the even stranger engraving. What did any of it mean?

Julie had brought up the idea that maybe Toby Miller was playing another one of his tricks, but Tom didn't buy that. "Toby doesn't have enough brains to think up something like this," he had told her. He'd made sure Julie got through her bedroom window all right, and then he'd proceeded up the sidewalk toward his own home.

The old oak tree sure was a sight to see. He was tired, sore from all the hammering and pulling, and disappointed. He had wanted that little sparkle he had seen to be just a small corner of a vast storehouse of gold behind the chimney. Before he had left his house earlier that night, he'd kept reminding himself, "It's probably nothing, Tom, so don't get your hopes up." Yet deep down inside, he had gotten his hopes up, and now his dreams were all smashed.

"Well, Tom," he whispered to himself, "don't just stand there feeling sorry for yourself. Get up to bed, and forget it—at least until tomorrow."

He didn't realize just how tired and sore he was until he started climbing back up the big old oak tree. Each time he reached up for a limb to pull himself up, his face tightened. It was as if his arms were telling his brain, "Hey, don't stretch me out like that—haven't you used me enough for one night?"

He finally made his way to the limb adjacent to his bedroom window. By that time, he was exhausted, and he half stepped and half fell through the window, barely getting his arms out in time to keep his head from thudding against the bedroom floor. There were two reasons he was glad he caught himself: one, he didn't want his mom and dad to rush into his room to see what had happened, and two, it was the only head he had, and he didn't think it would function well if it was all busted up.

Slowly, he peeled off his pants, shirt, socks, and shoes—not necessarily in that order—and fell across the bed like a tree cut down by a lumberjack.

"Boy, am I gonna sleep well tonight," he told himself. But he didn't.

When he finally dozed off at around three o'clock, he had some of the wildest dreams he'd ever had. In one, he dreamed that Toby Miller was riding by on his motorcycle with a basketball in his hand. Tom was trying to run away, but his legs wouldn't move. Then Toby threw the ball at Tom, hitting him in the head and knocking him into the Simpkins mudhole. Tom saw gold bars lying in the mud, but every time he picked one up, it turned into a chewing gum wrapper. Then Tom saw Julie standing over him as he lay in the mud, crying, "Get up, Tom! Get up, Tom!"

"Get up, Tom!"

Tom awoke with a jolt.

His mom was standing over him with her JoAnn Parker smile on her face. "Get up, Tom. You don't want to sleep all weekend, do you?"

"What time is it?" He was sure it must be around seven or eight o'clock.

"It's ten thirty. Jason called and said he'd be over in half an hour to help you work on your project."

"Okay, thanks." Tom got lazily out of bed and started to stretch his arms, but he winced and stopped his stretching exercises abruptly.

"What's the matter?" His mom had heard his moaning all the way down the hall.

"Oh, nothing, Mom; I guess I must have bruised my arm in the game last night." Tom didn't like making up stories to fool his mom, but after all, he couldn't tell her the real reason his arms were so sore. And he could have bruised his arm in the game, so he wasn't really lying, was he?

By the time Jason got there, Tom had showered and dressed and was sitting at the kitchen table, eating a bowl of Crunchies. It was a beautiful, sunny day outside. The air was a bit nippy, but it was still warm for a February day. Jason had brought Melissa with him—or rather, Melissa had come along because she wanted to see the secret of the chimney again. Mrs. Parker invited the two into the kitchen, where they sat at the table, watching Tom eat. Tom hated to have people watch him eat.

"Are you two sure you don't want anything to eat? Maybe some cereal or a doughnut?" he asked with milk dripping off his chin.

"No, thanks," they both said with a laugh, which caused Tom to realize his foolish-looking condition and reach for a paper towel.

Jason's laugh soon turned into a serious kind of half grin as he gave Tom the look he always gave him when apologizing. "Look, Tom, I'm sorry about what I said last night." His voice lowered to a whisper as he looked around to see if anybody else might be listening, but Tom's parents were in the living room, and Megan had already left with Kevin for a nature hike. "I just want you to know that I'm with you on this adventure, and whatever help I can give you on this, you've got it."

"The same goes for me too," said Melissa. "Who knows? This may turn out to be a lot of fun." In a town the size of Richfield, which had a population of around fifteen hundred, give or take a vagrant or two, fun and adventure were pretty hard to come by. "By the way, Tom, have you given any thought to what that stuff on the plate means? I gotta say that I'm with Jason on that lay up deal—I mean, I've never heard that term mentioned except in a basketball game."

Tom finished his cereal and wiped the last remaining milk off his chin. "Well, let's forget about that part and try to figure out what the rest of it means. It looks like it might be some sort of code, and who knows? We might just be the ones to solve a one-hundred-year-old mystery."

"And get rich in the process!" Jason's eyes widened, and his face broke out into a broad grin. "Where's the plate now, Tom?"

"I've still got it in my coat pocket—I never took it out after I put it in there last night. Listen, you guys, we have to go somewhere private where nobody can hear us."

"How about your room?" Melissa asked.

"No, my mom and dad are always walking by the door, and those walls are as thin as cigarette paper," he said, using a term he'd heard Grandpa Parker say a thousand times. "I've got it—I'll get the plate and some paper and pencils and meet you two at Tyson's woods in an hour. I'll call Julie, and if she doesn't have company or anything, she can come too. We'll try to figure this whole thing out."

They all agreed to the meeting, and Jason and Melissa said they would get some sandwiches, potato chips, and pop to make it into a picnic.

"Sounds great to me—you know how I love picnics," Tom said as Jason and Melissa strolled off hand in hand. *Ah, young love. Isn't it wonderful?* he thought. Jason and Melissa had a special kind of feeling for each other; he could see it in their eyes.

Tom had the same kind of feeling for Julie, but he wasn't sure how she felt about him. They had fun together and enjoyed each other's company, but to Tom, it didn't seem like the boyfriend–girlfriend relationship he wanted it to be. It was more like an "I'm your buddy, and you're my pal" kind of thing, which was fun during a treasure hunt but not so much on a moonlit night on the front porch swing.

Tom dismissed those starry-eyed thoughts for a moment and headed up to his room. He met his dad at the top of the stairs.

"Well, Tom, where are you headed in such a hurry?"

"Oh, me and Jason are going up to Tyson's woods for a few hours with the girls on a picnic. I'll be back before supper."

"Is that where you and Jason are doing your project?" Mr. Parker asked.

"Project? Oh yeah, the project." *Come on, Tom. You just about gave yourself away.* "Yeah, the girls are going to help us, so we decided to make a picnic out of it." The problem with lying was that you had to keep lying to get yourself out of the last lie, so you needed a good memory—which he didn't have. "Well, I gotta go, Dad, or I'll be late."

Tom hated to give his dad the brush-off, but this was important. He had a reputation for always being late, and that was one monkey he wanted off his back; *I'm gonna make it on time or die trying*, he thought to himself as he picked up the phone and dialed Julie's number. This time, he gave a sigh of relief when Julie picked up the phone.

"Oh, hi, Tom. I was wondering when you were going to call."

Julie Patterson was a freshman who was liked by all who knew her. She was vice president of the freshman class and held offices in a couple clubs. She was one of the top ten in her class in grade point average, but she wasn't one of those eggheads who sat around studying all the time. "I guess that's the reason I like Tom so much," she'd told her dad one day. "He likes to get out and have fun—and so do I." Julie had special feelings for Tom, but she didn't know if he liked her or if he just wanted somebody around in case he got himself into trouble—and he was always getting himself into trouble. Most of the time, it wasn't his fault, however; it was the fault of Toby Miller, the big bully. Julie couldn't stand Toby, but Tom had somehow gotten it in his head that Toby was an old sweetheart of hers. He'd probably gotten that idea from Toby, because he certainly hadn't gotten it from her.

Her thoughts returned to the present when she heard Tom on the other end.

"Hey, Julie, are you listening to me? We have to meet Jason and Melissa in Tyson's woods, so if you're not busy or anything, come up to my house as soon as you can—and bring some pencils and paper."

"Uh, yeah, okay, Tom. I'll be there in ten minutes." She hung up the phone, grabbed her jacket and the pencils and paper, gave her parents a quick goodbye, and headed up the sidewalk toward the preacher's kid's house.

Vince Tyson owned a 120-acre farm on the outskirts of Richfield. Its rolling hills, beautiful meadows, and lush green forests made it one of the most beautiful places on earth—at least Tom Parker thought so. For a kid who had lived in the suburbs all his life, a farm was a paradise. Of course, as someone who'd lived on a farm all his life, Mr. Tyson couldn't see what the big thrill was. But he always got a kick out of all the kids who roamed the hills on many spring, summer, and fall days. His own kids were grown and had moved away. He got to see them some—maybe during Thanksgiving or Christmas—but his grandchildren didn't get the opportunity to enjoy the farm, nor did Vince get the opportunity to watch his grandchildren enjoy the farm. That was the main reason the kids were always welcome on the place—as long as they behaved themselves, of course.

Tom had been coming to the Tyson farm since he was around eight years old. That was the first time he had gone home with Jason. Jason's dad owned the land adjacent to the Tyson farm, and when Tom first had seen that place, his own little house in the suburbs hadn't seemed the same. Jason's family had sold their small farm two years ago and moved uptown—Tom never had figured out why— but Tom and Jason returned every so often to run the hills, climb the trees, play in the creek, fish in the pond, and just get back to nature.

"Megan can drive fifty miles for a nature hike if she wants

to—this is my nature hike," he told Julie as they approached the gate leading to the narrow path that wound its way like a spiral staircase around the hill and into Tyson's woods, his favorite place on earth.

Jason and Melissa were already there when Tom and Julie arrived. They had a quilt spread out on the ground and were in the process of getting out the plates, napkins, sandwiches, chips, and drinks. The middle of February seemed like a silly time to go on a picnic, but it was warm enough—around sixty degrees—so why not have one? Who said picnics were reserved for the summertime anyway?

Tom hadn't been there five minutes before he was up in one of the big old oak trees. Even though he was growing up, he still loved to climb trees. It seemed to him the air was much clearer and fresher in the boughs of those mighty oaks, maples, and sycamores—and besides, in a tree, he could look down at the rest of the world. At Tom's height, he was used to looking up most of the time. It was as if the trees were his kingdom—his sacred place away from the realities of the world, the Toby Millers, and the big sisters of life.

"I would love to be like the Swiss Family Robinson and live in a big treehouse all my life," he told Julie as he reached down to help her make it up the huge trunk of the great oak and onto the first limb.

"No, thanks. I think I'd rather keep my feet planted firmly on the ground." Julie didn't care much for this Tarzan and Jane stuff, and she was scared of heights, so it wasn't long before she was back on the ground, helping Melissa with the sandwiches.

Jason finally coaxed Tom out of the tree, and they all sat on the quilt for about two hours, eating, drinking, and talking, mainly about the metal plate.

"First of all, let's start with 'Cell-15.' Do any of you have any idea what it might mean?" Tom asked.

"Well, a jail has cells; maybe he buried the treasure under the jail," Melissa said.

"The only problem with the jail theory is that our own Richfield Municipal Jail has a grand total of four cells," said Jason. "I know because me and my dad had to go there on New Year's Day to bail out Uncle Bobby after he got arrested for being drunk and disorderly at the Palmers' New Year's Eve party. I counted the cells then."

"Well, a battery has cells," said Julie, "but the only thing is, I don't think batteries were around back then."

"No, I don't think they were either—besides, batteries only have about six cells, don't they?" Tom asked with a disappointed look on his face. "Oh, we're never gonna figure this thing out. You're probably right, Julie; this is someone's idea of a joke—something to get us running around on some wild goose chase."

Jason gave Tom a look of surprise that his friend would make such a statement. "Well now, I can't believe my ears. Is this my friend, the eternal optimist, speaking, or have aliens invaded his body and turned him into a quitter?" He bit down on his second sandwich and reached for his third bag of chips and his second soda. "Tom, there has always been one thing about you I have admired, and that is your stick-to-your-guns attitude. The fellow I just heard talking doesn't sound like my friend Tom. You had me believing there was something to all of this, and now, when you get me and the girls believing it, you start doubting it yourself. Come on. Let's solve this code and find this gold or whatever there is to find! If we don't try, we'll spend the rest of our lives wondering whether or not we could have been filthy rich!"

Tom couldn't argue with a statement like that. It sounded as if his mind and Jason's mind had switched places momentarily. Jason was lifting everybody up, and he was letting them down. Well whatever happened, he was glad to get his own mind back—what he had said earlier didn't sound right coming out of his mouth. "You're right, Jason," he said. "I don't know what came over me."

Julie spoke up in an uncertain tone—the way people talked when they wanted to say something but didn't know how everybody would take it. "I've got an idea, but I'm not sure you're gonna like it."

Jason finished his lunch finally and reached for his dessert—a candy bar. "What is it, Julie? Right now, we'll be willing to listen to anything."

"Well, Joe Simpkins lived in that house right up until the day he left, right?" she said, and the other three giggled at the way the remark sounded, but they all agreed; as far as they knew, Joe had lived in the Simpkins mansion until the day he disappeared. "And we found this plate," she said, holding up the flat object, "inside the chimney of the house, right?" Again, they agreed, still wondering what she was getting at. "Well, it looks to me like whatever secret is behind this code on the plate should be found somewhere inside the house!"

Tom's and Melissa's eyes lit up, but Jason's face turned as white as the paper Julie had brought to figure on. "Oh no," he said, "you're not gonna get me into that spooky old house. I almost had a heart attack last night just being that close to the outside. There's no way I'm gonna go into that house. Unh-uh! Not me!"

Tom thought to himself, *Well, if our minds were switched before, they're back in the right place now.* This sounded like the old Jason he knew and loved. "Julie's right, Jason; if we want to figure this out, that old house is the best place to start. Can you all slip out tonight, or would you rather wait until the first of the week?"

"Why do we have to go at night? We could find it just as easily—maybe easier—in the daytime." Chicken-hearted Jason was at it again, trying to talk his friends out of something when he knew he couldn't.

"Jason, do you realize how much traffic is on that street during the day? No, it'll have to be at night, and the sooner the better," Tom said. The two girls agreed. By then, their curiosity had overcome whatever fears they'd had before. They couldn't wait until the first of the week—it had to be tonight.

Melissa said she'd bring Jason, even if she had to drag him. "Bring your hammer again, Tom," she said. "You know that old house is boarded up, and we'll have to pry some of those loose boards to get in."

"I might need a crowbar for those boards, so I'll bring one of those too," Tom said. "I'm sure my dad won't mind—especially if I don't tell him."

By the time they had packed everything up and left Tyson's woods, the sun was beginning to sink slowly behind the Rocky Mountains. As Tom watched the sunset, his thoughts returned to yesterday evening, when that same sun had sunk behind that same mountain, just as it had for thousands of years. But on that fateful Friday evening, it had left a little flicker—a small reflection of itself behind an old granite chimney—that had sent these four small-town high school students traveling down a path to the unknown—unknown riches, unknown danger, and unknown adventure. What secrets, if any, were hidden inside that house? The four didn't know, but they were going to find out, for it had always been there in the mind of man to explore the unknown and find out what was behind it all. Whether it was a musty old house or the vast expanse of the universe, man had always had the need to know.

By the time Tom got back to his house, it was almost dark. The four had agreed to meet at the Simpkins mansion at eleven o'clock again that night. Tom would bring his tools, and the rest would bring their flashlights—they wanted all the light they could get. That meant Tom would have to make another trip to his dad's workshop in the basement—a task he didn't look forward to. His dad had always been particular with his tools, and he had gotten several good tongue-lashings for losing some of them while working on his bike. He knew he would have to get the crowbar and the other stuff while his dad was gone. With his dad at the revival, getting them wouldn't be too much of a problem.

That revival couldn't have come at a better time, he thought to himself. James Parker only preached a few revivals during the year; he was mainly a pastor—and a good one at that. The Richfield Community Church had grown under Reverend Parker's pastorate from a congregation of fewer than thirty to a church attendance to date of more than one hundred. Reverend Parker was always modest about the accomplishment.

"God gets all the credit and all the glory for the way this church has grown," he had told his congregation on numerous occasions.

Tom couldn't understand why God had to get all the credit—after all, his dad and mom had done most of the work. In his way of looking at it, God was taking what his dad deserved—and it wasn't fair! Reverend Parker had tried to explain to his son about being humble and giving God the praise for what he helped people to do, but Tom was stubborn. He just couldn't understand a God like that—which was part of the reason he didn't like church much.

Tom came through the back door of his house just in time to meet his mom going out. In her hand she had the most delicious-looking apple pie he had ever seen. His mouth watered as he looked at the scrumptious dessert. His mom made apple pies that melted in your mouth. She made her pies from scratch with fresh apples. He could just see himself sitting down at the kitchen table with a big slice of that pie—with ice cream on it—and a tall glass of cold milk to wash it down.

By the time he came to his senses, though, JoAnn Parker had said her hellos and goodbyes and was out the kitchen door. "Hey, Mom!" Something in his heart told him he wasn't going to get any of that pie, but he thought he'd try anyway. "Who's the pie for?"

"Oh, Tom, the widow Powers is sick again."

The widow Powers is always sick, he thought, *and she's always getting stuff that Mom won't take the time to make for us.* "Well, didn't you make two pies so I could have some?" he asked.

"I'm sorry, Tom; I only had enough ingredients for one. I'll have to make you one later. Look, I have to get this over to Mrs. Powers and get back in time to get ready for church—you know how your father feels about being late." With that, she continued on her journey to give that poor old sick woman the gorgeous pie Tom was dying for.

"That's another thing about this church business—those church people are always getting *my* food!" he muttered under his breath with a scowl as he slung his jacket over a chair in disgust.

Just then, his dad walked into the kitchen and gave him a puzzled look. "What's wrong?" Tom's dad could always tell when something was bothering his son—of course, this time, it wasn't hard to see, with Tom slinging his clothes around.

"Oh, nothing, Dad. I just would like to have had a piece of that apple pie—that's all. Dad, why are we always giving stuff to people? I mean, like that pie or the wood you cut and took to old man Somers last week. Poor people seem to eat better and live better than we do because we're always giving everything we have away."

Reverend Parker looked at his son with kind eyes—the eyes of a man of God. "Tom, this may be hard for you to understand, but every time we give something away, whether it's our time, our money, or our apple pies, we are actually giving to ourselves." He was right—Tom didn't understand, but he allowed his dad to continue. "You see, Jesus gave us several principles to live by while he was here on this earth, and one of those principles is found in Luke 6:38 (KJV). Here. Let me read it to you."

His dad had his Bible—or his Sword, as he called it—handy. He opened the Bible up and read the verse: "Give, and it shall be given unto you; good measure, pressed down, and shaken together, and running over, shall men give into your bosom. For with the same measure that you mete withal it shall be measured to you again." Reverend Parker closed the Bible, laid it on the table, and proceeded to explain to his young son what Jesus meant. "You see, Tom, the reason we have been blessed all these years is because we help others. The principle Jesus showed us here is that the more you give, the more you'll receive. I have applied that principle to my life since I became a Christian, and it has never failed for me or for this family. Tom, Jesus Christ gave his all for us, and all he asks in return is that we give to one another. There are some people in this community who would go hungry if it weren't for people like us or other good people in the community helping them. God has blessed us abundantly, and if we can't share in those blessings, then what kind of people are we?"

Tom thought to himself, *A whole lot richer than we are right now.* He then looked at his dad in such a way as to tell him he'd heard enough. "Yeah, okay, Dad, I guess you're right; I sure would like to have had a piece of that pie, though." He got up, picked up his jacket off the chair, and headed up the stairs to his room. "I hope you all have a good meeting tonight!" he yelled back over his shoulder.

"It'd be better if you were there," his dad said.

"Sorry, Dad. I can't; I've got to finish up some homework." He did have homework, so this time, he wasn't actually lying, although it only took him fifteen minutes to do it.

Tom stayed in his room until his dad and mom left. Megan returned from her hike, and she and Kevin went to the revival, much to the delight of their dad. That was just like a big sister: doing things for their mom and dad just to make her little brother look bad. Well, he didn't care. She could become a missionary if she wanted to—at least that would get her out of his hair for a while.

Tom waited until everybody was out of sight of the house before stirring from his room. Then he quickly went down to the basement and got the tools he would need for that night's adventure. "Boy, I hope this doesn't become a habit," he said to himself. He didn't like slipping around behind his father's back, but it was a lot easier than trying to make up a story to explain why he needed all of his dad's tools. His last story almost had gotten him in trouble anyway. He still couldn't think of a good project to do with Jason in case his dad questioned him about it again.

This time, he found a bigger hammer, which he hoped would save him a lot of sweat and strain. He stuffed it into his gym bag along with the crowbar and an old Boy Scout shovel just in case and headed back toward his room. This time, he was going to leave earlier, and since he figured Megan and Kevin would be out front necking again, he'd go directly over the Martins' fence and double-back. *That ought to get me there on time*, he thought.

He still had about three hours to kill before breaking out of his prison, so he decided to fix himself a snack and take one more look at the plate before his folks got back. He fixed his specialty: a ham sandwich on white bread with lettuce, tomato, and mayonnaise; a bag of chips; and a glass of iced tea. He called it his specialty because it was the only meal he knew how to fix.

The house seemed kind of lonesome that night, like someone who had lost his or her best friend. As Tom headed up the stairs to the second floor, each step seemed to creak and groan as if saying to him, "Don't step on me tonight; I don't feel like taking any more abuse." He didn't like being alone. At times like this, he felt a little bit like Jason. *What if something happens—a fire or something like that? Or what if somebody breaks in? What will I do then?* The thoughts kept creeping into his mind, but he quickly dismissed them. "Oh, Tom, you're growing up—don't be such a scaredy-cat," he mumbled to himself.

By the time he reached his room, he was feeling better. The thoughts were gone, and now he could concentrate on his sandwich and, more importantly, the plate.

Cell-15 R-10 Up-4 Lay Up

"What does all this stand for?" Tom couldn't figure it out. He studied it from every angle. He examined it from front to back and back to front, and he even started in the middle and worked both ways, but each time, he reached the same roadblock. After more than two hours of looking, figuring, studying, and probing, he finally threw his hands up in the air. "Oh, I give up; I guess we'll have to wait until we get to the house to see if this means anything."

Suddenly, a terrible sensation swept over him. *The house!* They were actually going to go inside the Simpkins mansion! In the ten years Tom had lived in Richfield, he had never gone inside that house, not even in the daytime, and that night, in about an hour, he was going to go into that Castle of the Ghosts, as it had been called on occasion. Was the house really haunted, as many people said? He had never seen or heard anything, but that didn't mean the noises and the ghosts weren't real—others had seen and heard. Tom got an uneasy feeling in the pit of his stomach, and it wasn't from the ham sandwich. He was scared—really scared!

"I guess I've been so busy with everything else that I didn't have time to think about what we're actually going to do," he said to the air—but the air didn't answer.

Tom looked at the clock on the wall; it was almost ten. His parents would be home any minute, but more importantly, he would be leaving in about thirty minutes. *Maybe I should leave a will just in case something happens.* That and other foolish thoughts flooded his already troubled brain.

Oh wow, Tom, that's a great idea, his brain answered. *Maybe you'd want to leave your bike and skateboard to your best friend, Jason—only Jason will probably be killed by the ghost of Joe Simpkins, along with you.*

The sound of a car pulling into the driveway brought Tom out of his trance, and he shook his head a couple times to try to straighten himself out. His folks were home, so he had to make an appearance before he made his disappearance. Making his way to the living room and hoping his mom and dad wouldn't detect his uneasiness, Tom gently tried to calm his unsteady nerves.

"Hi, Mom. Hi, Dad. How did the service go?" He said this only to make conversation with his parents—the revival service was the furthest thing from his mind right now.

Mr. Parker was busy putting his jacket away, so Mrs. Parker answered Tom's question. "Oh, Tom, we had a wonderful service; you should have been there—four people got saved tonight. I can't remember when I've enjoyed a service more!"

Tom couldn't understand it—he could go to the same service with his parents, and they would thoroughly enjoy themselves, while he'd sit there bored out of his skull. It was as if he'd walked through the church doors and into the twilight zone! "How could one group of people have so much fun and others be bored at the same time and in the same meeting?" he'd asked himself time and again.

"Did you finish your homework?" a voice asked from the hall closet. That was just like his dad—he had a mind like a steel trap.

"Yes, Dad, I finished it all." Tom hurriedly said his good nights and slipped back up to his room.

Reverend and Mrs. Parker thought it strange that their son would go to bed so early on Saturday night. "That makes two nights in a row he's gone to bed before eleven," JoAnn Parker said.

"Oh well, maybe he's trying to make a good impression on us—he probably wants a motorcycle like that Miller boy has." James Parker knew his son well, and he knew he had something up his sleeve. He just hadn't figured out what yet.

Tom reached his room, grabbed his gym bag, fixed his bed to fool his parents, and scurried down the oak tree in one swift motion. "Boy, this is almost too easy," he nervously told himself. "Now to get to Julie's house. At this rate, I'll be waiting on her this time."

The dew on the lawn was worse than it had been the night before. Tom made his way slowly across the yard to the fence that separated the Martins' place from theirs. The fence wasn't very high, so it was pretty easy to scale, even for Tom. He made it across with no trouble and quietly started walking across the Martins' yard. Since he was early, Tom was able to walk instead of sprinting the five hundred yards, as he had the night before. He was getting used to this sneaky stuff and had come to the conclusion that this was the life for him. *I might even become a spy like James Bond, slipping around from one country to the next, kissing all the beautiful women, and saving the world from villains.* He was in dreamland again, dreaming as he walked and looking toward the future while forgetting the present.

He had just rounded the corner of the Martins' house, when the present came rushing back to him like a giant tidal wave. Looking out of the shadows and into the light of the streetlamp, he saw it—and then he heard it: *Grrr!* With fangs showing pearly white and its upper lip raised to show all the teeth it had, the biggest dog he had ever seen appeared. He froze in horror, his heart beating so fast he thought his chest would explode. The Martins had pulled a fast one—they had gotten a new dog! And this wasn't just any dog—it made their old pit bull look like a miniature Chihuahua.

If I ever get out of this, I'm talking Dad into voting for that new leash law, he thought. Of course, that wasn't going to do him any good at the present time.

The dog moved closer, never taking its fiery eyes off Tom, its teeth still shimmering in the light. It was eyeing Tom's leg the way Jason Bennett would have eyed a steak dinner. *C'mon, Tom. Do something,* he thought. *If you don't, that elk with teeth is gonna chew you up and spit you out.*

Just then, he noticed it—his one chance in a million. At the edge of the Martins' yard, standing next to the fence separating their place from the McCormicks', was Tom's rescuer: a huge maple tree. The trees he loved so much had been a hideout in his younger years and his escape hatch in his later years. Now, in his moment of life or death, a tree was going to be his savior—if he could get to it in time. Tom knew he couldn't outrun the dog, but with a little head start, he figured he could swing up to the first limb before getting his leg bitten off—maybe.

The beast moved closer to its victim with saliva dripping from its mouth—it seemed to be thinking, *My, this boy would make a tasty snack.* But Tom wasn't about to be a dog's dinner. He turned suddenly and headed toward the tree, running like he'd never run before. The dog, noticing that its meal was escaping, headed after him.

Tom could almost feel its hot breath getting closer and closer. The wet grass flew from the bottom of his shoes like water from a lawn sprinkler, and his breath came in short gasps as his feet pounded across the yard. His heart thumped like a piston in the motor of a race car as he drew closer to the tree. The only problem was, the dog was drawing closer to him.

There it was now, just in front of him—the limb of the big old tree was reaching out like an arm of hope to save him from almost certain death. However, as he jumped up to grab on to the arm of his savior, the dog got there in time to grab on to the leg of its dinner.

Tom used every ounce of muscle he had to pull himself up and away from the clutches of the beast. Fortunately for Tom, the dog only managed to grab hold of his pant leg, so it wasn't long before the fabric tore away, and Tom swung up onto the tree limb and climbed to the next limb up, safely away from his predator.

But Tom's troubles weren't over yet. Ole Lucifer started barking. That was just like a dog—if it couldn't get to you, it'd let everybody know where you were. The back porch light came on, and Tom could see the silhouette of George Martin at the back door, so he knew he had to get out of there—fast!

The limbs of the big maple stretched out over the fence and into the McCormicks' yard, so Tom had two choices: he could either wait on Mr. Martin to come out and try to explain what he was doing up in his tree at eleven o'clock at night—and also risk being shot as a prowler before he had a chance to explain—or make a break for it over the fence. Tom chose the latter for obvious reasons and was over the fence and heading through the McCormicks' yard before the back door had slammed behind Mr. Martin.

I just hope the McCormicks don't decide to get a dog, he thought as he ran toward the meeting place. It looked like he was going to be late again.

He finally slowed down long enough to look at his pants. The dog had ripped off about eight inches of his left pant leg, exposing his calf, which was starting to get cold. There was one thing to be thankful for: the dog hadn't taken any flesh—not this time anyway. "Well, maybe if I show this to Julie, she won't punch my lights out," he said to himself. He was glad he was wearing those particular pants; first of all, they were blue jeans, and everybody wore blue jeans, so Mr. Martin couldn't trace the piece of cloth in his pet's mouth to him, and second, they were his old pants, so he would be able to just throw them out in the trash without his mom becoming suspicious. "If this is any indication of what the rest of the night's gonna be like, I ought to turn around right now and go back home and straight to bed," he said to himself. But he didn't—he kept plodding on, ripped pants and all, down to the Patterson residence and the big green pine where he knew his love would be waiting. Of course, in the mood she'd be in, she probably wouldn't look lovely.

The Patterson house was in Tom's sight now. He had stopped running—he was late anyway, so what good would a couple more minutes make? As he slowly approached the pine tree, he could see Julie in the shadow of its branches, wringing her hands. She was scared, and she was mad—he could see that before he got there. But an idea had formed in his brain—one that should get him out of the verbal abuse he knew was coming. He slowed his rate considerably, and just before he reached Julie, he started limping.

This should work fine, he thought. *Julie will be so busy feeling sorry for me she'll forget how late I am.* He was right.

"Oh, Tom, what happened to your leg?"

"Oh, I'll be all right; I just about got eaten by the Martins' dog—that's all."

"But the Martins' pit bull was run over by a car last month."

"It wasn't the pit bull, Julie; it looked more like a real bull to me. They've got another dog—a killer. If I hadn't made it up into their maple tree when I did, I'd be playing the harp right now—or whatever it is they play down there," he said, looking at the ground with a crooked grin.

"Well, I'm glad you still have your sense of humor; I don't think I could laugh if it happened to me. Do you feel able to go through with this? I'm sure Jason and Melissa wouldn't mind calling it off until later," she said with a look of concern.

Tom was sure Jason wouldn't mind if they called it off permanently. "No, I'm fine—let's get this over with while I still have the nerve. Besides, I don't think I'll be able to sneak out of the house anymore without my parents finding out. My dad's starting to get suspicious already—I can tell." With that, he grabbed Julie's hand—he loved holding her hand—and led her down the sidewalk toward the Simpkins mansion and whatever, or whoever, lurked behind it.

Tom was surprised when they arrived to find that Jason and Melissa were just getting there too. "I'm used to your schedule now, Tom," said his friend. "When you say eleven o'clock, what you really mean is fifteen after." The girls laughingly agreed. Of course, when Tom showed them his pant leg, or what was left of it, Jason snickered a bit but did show some concern. "Boy, Tom, you're lucky you didn't get killed; people with dogs like that should chain them up or something." Then a smirky grin crossed his face. "But I sure would have loved to be there to watch all the excitement."

"Yeah, I bet you would have," Tom replied. It just hadn't been his week. First, he'd gotten a 77 on his English test, then he'd fallen into a mudhole, and now he almost had been torn apart by a dog. *What more could happen to me?* he thought to himself. "Well, come on, guys. Let's get around back and get this over with; we're in plain view right here," he told the others. They all agreed and hurried around to the back of the mansion to make their entrance.

The lower windows and doors of the old mansion had been boarded up for obvious reasons. An old house like that would have been dangerous to all the young kids who played in the neighborhood. It also contained a lot of valuable merchandise, and the town council wanted to keep the burglars out—after all, there was still a program in the works to restore the old mansion if the town ever came up with the money, and they wanted all the original artifacts intact.

When the four teenagers reached the back door, they noticed that not only was the door boarded up, but a padlock had been put on it. "We're not gonna get in this way," said Melissa. They had all agreed they wouldn't need a lookout this time, so all four of them would go in the house. In reality, none of them were brave enough to stay outside by themselves.

"Hey, guys, look over here," Julie shouted softly. The other three walked to where she was standing, under one of the windows on the back side. "Look—a couple of these boards are loose, and the glass in the window is out."

Tom shone his flashlight at the window, and it was just as Julie had said. "What luck—we can get in easily through here."

Jason, as usual, was skeptical. "I don't like this, man; these boards look like they've been pried loose, and notice how all of the glass in the window's been broken out. If it had been busted out by some kid with a rock, there'd be jagged pieces of glass sticking up. It looks to me like someone's been going into this house. Maybe they're in there right now, waiting to kill us."

Tom was getting pretty fed up with his friend right about now. "Jason, you've got to be the biggest chicken ever put on this earth. Now, the three of us are going in; if you don't want to come with us, you're welcome to stand out here and wait. We'll be back out in about an hour—maybe two."

That was all it took. "No, no, I'm going in with you. If we're gonna get killed, we'll all die together."

Now, that's the right attitude, Tom thought. *Die one, die all!* Jason had a real way of looking at life.

Tom figured it would be best for him to go into the house first, and Jason would go last; that way, they could help the girls through if they needed it.

The window was high—over Tom's head—so getting in was no picnic, but with a little help from his friends, he was soon safely inside—although being inside the house was not safe by any means. Tom had tossed his gym bag inside, so the first thing he did was make sure it was still there and still had everything in it. He turned on his flashlight and shone it around to get some idea of where he was. The window he had crawled through led to some kind of library or study. Shelves of old books lined the walls, and in the corner was a massive wooden desk. Cobwebs hung all over the shelves, the desk, and the huge oil lamps on either side of the desk. Yes, sir, it looked like an old house in every aspect.

There had been enough fresh air coming through the open

window to keep the room smelling fresh. The stale, musty air typical of old houses hadn't tickled his nostrils yet—but he figured as soon as he made it into the other parts of the house, the stale air would welcome him.

He brought the beam of his flashlight to the floor, checking to see if any rats were waiting to pounce on him. He saw only one small gray mouse run out from behind the desk, across the Oriental rug, and under one of the bookshelves.

Heading home after a hard day's work, he thought as a smile crossed his face.

His smile quickly left, though, and was replaced with a look of terror. There were two sets of footprints in the dust, leading across the floor to the closed door leading to the other parts of the house. Tom's eyes opened wider, and his mouth hung down as he kept the trembling beam of light glued on the footprints. All sorts of wild questions flooded his troubled mind like a raging river. *Who's been here? Are they here now? Maybe they're killers hiding out. Do you suppose they heard us?*

Tom was just about ready to jump through the window and head for home, when he heard a friendly voice outside the window. "Hey, are we invited to this party or not?" It was Julie.

Tom stuck his head out the window, and they could all see the troubled look on his face. "Listen, you guys, somebody's been in here all right—there are some footprints on the floor."

Jason was terrified at the news, and Melissa seemed troubled, but Julie didn't seem too concerned. "Oh, I meant to tell you all, but I guess I forgot. Dad was talking to one of the neighbors the other day—Mr. Thompson. You know Mr. Thompson, don't you, Tom?"

Looking down from the window, Tom nodded. "Yeah, I know him. What's that got to do with the footprints?"

"Well, if you'll give me a minute, I'll explain."

Tom agreed to shut up so Julie could continue with her story.

"Well, my dad and Mr. Thompson were talking about the Simpkins place, and Mr. Thompson said he'd heard on his scanner that the cops had found a couple hobos staying at the house and had thrown them out. That's probably the reason for the loose boards and the footprints you saw. C'mon, guys. Let's go in. I don't think there's anybody in there now." They all agreed, except for Jason, and since he was outnumbered, he had no choice but to go in with the rest.

By midnight, they had all climbed safely through the window and were standing in the Simpkins library, or the study—whichever it was. They had agreed to stay together; Tom said that if there was anybody in the house, they would have a better chance as a team.

As all the flashlights came on, the four brave crusaders walked slowly across the floor to the door. Tom's hand shook as he reached down and turned the knob. Of course, Jason was shaking all over.

"Man, I don't like this," Jason said, his voice quivering.

"It'll be all right as long as we stay together," said Melissa, trying to calm her man down.

She really liked Jason, even though he was sort of a coward. He was fun to be with and had a great sense of humor. He just needed to loosen up, go with the flow, and not let everything bother him. "I wish he was more like Tom," she'd said to some of her friends, yet she wondered if she would have liked him as much if he was.

The door to the library opened with a huge groan that made them all back up slightly. But as soon as they realized the sound was just the door and not a spook, they proceeded through the door and found themselves in a vast hallway. Beautiful paintings decorated the walls on each side. One was of a clipper ship sailing on the rough and churning sea, and one was of a man dressed in traditional nineteenth-century attire. He was a handsome man but rough looking, with deep-set eyes and a thick, flowing beard that hung almost to his chest. "That's Joe Simpkins," said Julie. "I saw his picture in the paper last year. You remember, Tom—the article about the legend and the treasure?"

Tom nodded without taking his eyes off the face in the painting. *Whoever painted that did a great job*, he thought. It was as if the man in the portrait were looking right at him, trying to tell him something.

"Hey, guys, it's getting late; let's get this over with." Jason was getting a little edgy, but what he said made sense.

They moved their flashlight beams in opposite directions, each one getting a different view of the mansion. Tom's light moved toward the back door, the one with the padlock. To the left of that door was the kitchen—he knew that because the door was open, and he could see the old cook stove in the corner. Jason's light had found a small table about halfway down the hall, with an expensive-looking vase adorning it.

"Jason, you're breaking my hand!" Melissa said as she pulled his viselike grip away from her crushed fingers.

"Sorry, honey. I guess I just didn't notice how tight I was holding on."

"C'mon, gang. There's nothing back here; let's move on up toward the front." Tom was taking charge—after all, he was the one responsible for this treasure hunt, and if anybody was going to lead it, it was going to be him.

Moving up the huge hallway with the flashlights piercing the blackness like four thin strips of sunshine, the brave—well, sort of—adventurers trod toward what they hoped would be great reward yet knew could be great danger.

The huge hallway opened up into the living room like a river opening up when it met the sea.

"Wow!" said Julie. "This room is as big as my house!"

Tom was thinking the same thing. What a room it was! It stretched from one side of the castle to the other—at least sixty feet, he guessed—and was almost as wide as it was long. The ceiling extended at least twenty feet into the air, and hanging halfway from the ceiling was the most beautiful chandelier they had ever seen. Sparkling crystals reflected the light of their flashlights, casting prisms of color onto the walls.

Julie tried to count the candleholders but lost count at twenty-five. "How'd you like to have to light those candles?" she asked Tom.

"How'd you like to replace those candles?" he asked. "All right, we can spread out in here since we'll all be in plain view of each other. Look for anything that could tie into the writing on the plate, and if you see anything that looks suspicious, yell for the rest of us. Got it?"

They all nodded, and Melissa pried her fingers loose from Jason's death grip. Tom went right; Julie went left; Jason went straight, toward the front door; and Melissa searched the middle.

The furniture, the most expensive of its time, was covered with drop cloths. Melissa looked under each one but didn't see anything suspicious. Julie discovered a staircase leading to the second floor but thought it best to wait until the search was over downstairs, so they could all go up together. Jason knocked a vase off one of the tables and broke it, nearly scaring them all out of their wits, but he found nothing that had anything to do with the code.

As Tom moved closer to the wall on his side, his light found the huge fireplace. The granite stones surrounding the fireplace were smaller than the ones lining the chimney, and the soot of a thousand fires covered the stones in an eerie black film. He moved his light above the fireplace and focused it on a painting. This painting was so large that it extended the width of the massive oak mantel—around ten feet, as far as he could make out—and was at least six feet high. "I've seen that before—in our art book at school," he said.

"I have too," said Jason.

Tom turned his head with a start; he hadn't realized anyone was listening.

Jason continued. "That's the painting Michelangelo did on the ceiling of that chapel in Rome."

Jason was right; it was the painting that pictured God, or the artist's perception of God, reaching down from heaven and creating man—at least that was what Tom thought he was doing. Tom shone his light toward the other three. "Well, there's nothing down here.

Are you ready to go upstairs?" Of course they weren't ready to go upstairs, but they went anyway.

The heavy oak boards of the staircase creaked under the weight of the four as they made their way slowly step by step toward the second floor. As old as the boards were, the four knew that one could snap at any minute under their weight, even though the heaviest one of them only weighed 145 pounds. The upstairs of the mansion had three large bedrooms, each furnished with extravagant furniture and decorations. One thing was obvious: Joe Simpkins was no tightwad.

They searched every room thoroughly with the same results: not one clue that matched anything on the plate.

Suddenly, there was a loud crash downstairs.

"Douse the lights!" said Tom in a high-pitched whisper. All four flashlights switched off almost simultaneously. Everyone got quiet. They could hear only Jason's heavy breathing.

"Jason, do you have to breathe so loud?" Tom whispered.

"I can't help it, Tom; when I get scared, I hyperventilate."

"Well, can you do it a little quieter? We want to find out what that was before it finds us."

Melissa grabbed Jason's shaking hand, hoping that would help to calm him down, which it did. Of course, none of them were very brave, not at that moment anyway. But they knew they had to keep their composure. Falling apart wasn't going to help them, especially right now.

"C'mon," Tom said. "We've got to go downstairs and find out who, or what, is down there."

Tom took Julie's hand, Julie took Melissa's hand, and Melissa already had Jason's hand. Together they eased down the hall with their backs and heads sliding against the wall as they went, until at last they made it to the great oak staircase.

Kneeling down, the four crept slowly down the stairs, trying to conceal themselves behind the banister. The sculptured rails of the banister didn't hide them completely, but at least they weren't in plain view, which made them feel safe, even if they weren't. The huge living room was almost totally dark, with the exception of a few faint beams of light from the streetlamps outside shining through the cracks in the boards. Tom was terrified, but he knew he had to keep calm for the sake of the others; after all, he was the leader, though it was a role he would have gladly given up right about now.

Slowly, they worked their way to the bottom of the stairs. "Jason," Tom whispered. "Come here; I might need your help." Jason reluctantly made his way from the back of the line, his favorite spot in times like that, and knelt beside Tom. "Jason, if somebody's in here, we may have to fight our way out."

"B-B-But what if it's something you can't fight?" Jason wasn't losing it; he'd already lost it—his mind, that was.

Tom let that remark go; it wasn't worth a reply. "Now, Jason, I'm going to ease my head up over the newel post," he said, referring to the large post at the bottom of the stairs that connected to the banister—all old mansions had one, "and see if I can find out what it is."

"Okay, Tom," Jason replied in a "Better you than me" tone. "If you need me, just scream." At a time like this, Jason was trying to be funny. Tom figured he was cracking jokes to try to hide his fear, but he knew how scared Jason was, and he knew how scared he was, and no amount of humor was going to make him feel any better.

Having to stretch his neck, Tom slowly raised his head up over the post. Starting with the back hallway, he slowly moved his eyes across the room, straining in the darkness to see what he could. Enough light was shining through to make a small sparkle on the chandelier. Nothing was moving—that was for sure. *What was that?*

Tom noticed a figure over by the front door. His heart leaped into his throat, his hair stood up on his neck, and terror engulfed him like an ocean wave. Two red eyes, burning like coals of fire, were looking right at him. He could feel his heart thumping, and beads of cold sweat broke out on his face. This was the end—he knew it! The ghost of old Joe Simpkins was there to destroy whoever had broken into his home—Tom and his three friends.

Jason noticed his friend's sudden transformation from brave leader to drooling zombie. "T-T-Tom, w-what is it? C'mon, Tom. It can't be that bad—can it?" Jason was scared out of his mind, and he hadn't even seen anything yet.

"J-J-Jason, l-look over at the door," Tom replied with a quiver in his voice. Jason raised his head up to where his friend was. "D-Do you see what I see?"

Jason looked in the direction Tom was pointing, saw the fiery red eyes looking straight back at him, and fainted dead away, falling off the last step and landing with a thud on the living room floor.

The creature—or ghost, or whatever it was—didn't move. By that time, Julie and Melissa had raised themselves up to look, and in perfect unison, they let out two gut-wrenching screams.

Tom couldn't take any more of this. *If that thing is going to kill me, I'm gonna get a good look at his face before he does.* He stepped out from behind the post and shone his light directly into the face of the monster—a stone statue of an old army soldier!

The statue's eyes glowed even brighter in the beam of Tom's flashlight. It had two glass eyes—ruby-red glass eyes, to be exact. "Whew!" Tom wiped the sweat off his forehead with the back of his hand and walked over to where the statue stood. A beam of light from the streetlamp outside was shining through a crack in one of the boards at just the right angle to bring the statue's eyes to life. Tom's heart still hadn't slowed down much, but he gathered enough energy to walk back over to the girls, who were trying to revive Jason.

"Jason! Jason, wake up; everything's all right now," Melissa whispered, gently shaking her beloved.

Jason's eyes twitched and then slowly began to open. Suddenly, they were wide open. Jason let out a terrifying scream, and his fists started beating the air.

Fortunately for the two girls, none of the punches landed. By that time, Tom was back, and he grabbed his buddy. "Calm down, Jason; it's gonna be all right."

"But the ghost. The demon—did you get him? Where did he

go?" Jason was so worked up he was about to go out again, so Tom didn't waste any time in straightening things out.

Shining the light at the statue, Tom said, "Jason, there is your demon!"

Just one look was all it took. "Whew!" Now it was Jason's turn to wipe away sweat.

Tom explained to his friend about the fiery eyes to his satisfaction.

"Oh, I saw that statue while I was looking down here a few minutes ago," Jason said. "I don't know why I didn't think about it."

"Well, for our sakes, I sure wish you had!" said Melissa.

Jason's fear suddenly turned to embarrassment. "Uh, you guys won't tell anybody about me fainting, will you? I'd hate for Toby and his friends to get ahold of something like that."

"Listen, Jason," said Tom, "none of us are going to tell any of this to anybody, at least not until it's all over. Besides, fainting is no big deal—I've fainted before." He really hadn't—he just wanted to make his friend feel better.

"Hey, that reminds me," said Melissa. "If nobody is here, what made that crash we heard?"

"I can answer that for you," said Julie. "Look over here." The beam of her light was focused on a big gray tomcat crouched in the corner of the room. Near the cat was a table with a broken lamp lying next to it, and an oil spot was still visible on the rug.

Now that all the excitement was over, the four were ready to continue their search. Of course, Jason was ready to go home and go to bed, but the others paid no attention to him.

"Well, all we've got left is the kitchen, the dining room, the room off the library, and"—Tom held his breath before letting it out—"the four towers." He was getting everything back in order. "We'll save the towers for last if it's all right with all of you." Nobody argued with him on that one; those towers would have made a coward out of the bravest man.

They searched the dining room and the room next to the library—another bedroom. "This must have been Joe's bedroom," said Julie. The room wasn't nearly as fancy or elaborately decorated as the three bedrooms upstairs. This bedroom seemed to fit the mold of a rugged miner, even if he had been rich. Still, they found nothing. All that was left to search was the kitchen.

"Oh, please let it be in here," said Jason. He had made up his mind that if the towers were to be searched, the other three would have to do it. He would rather take his chances down in the living room by himself than go up into those towers.

The kitchen was a symbol of early American cooking. The old cook stove Tom had seen earlier was rusty and broken down. A wood box sat at the end of it, with some old logs still in it. Two cabinets sat against the wall on the far side with their doors open, and a few old pans and broken plates were in plain view. Next to the kitchen was a small pantry full of shelves, and on the shelves were a few old jars, some with fruits and vegetables still in them, although the contents were so old they were unrecognizable. The four searched the kitchen, checking the stove first and moving over to the cabinets, carefully checking everything yet finding nothing. Moving on through the pantry, the four shone their lights over every shelf, checking thoroughly to keep from missing anything.

"Well," Tom said with a sigh, "which tower should we start on first?"

"Wait a minute, Tom; look back here." Julie had found something at the back of the pantry.

"What is it, Julie?" asked Tom as he walked with the others to where she was standing.

Julie had the beam of her light focused on a small door that was only about five feet high and barely visible, except for a small oval-shaped doorknob. "I wonder where this goes," she said.

"Well, there's only one way to find out," Tom said as he grabbed the knob, turned it, and pulled as hard as he could.

Nothing happened. The door wouldn't budge.

"It's stuck," said Jason. "Here. Let me give you a hand."

Both young men pulled as hard as they could on the handle but with no results. The damp air and the passing of time had wedged the little door as tightly against its frame as Lorie Sander's blue jeans were wedged against her frame. But with some help from the girls, the door loosened up before finally popping open, sending all four of them sprawling against the opposite wall.

Finally regaining his balance and composure, Tom picked up his flashlight and walked to the doorway. There were steps leading down into a cold, damp room.

"Wonder what it is," said Jason.

"C'mon, everybody. Let's go down there and see." Tom grabbed Julie's hand, Jason grabbed Melissa's hand, and the four started down.

Creeeak! The steps weren't accustomed to having any weight put on them and sounded out their disapproval. Something about a creaking board always seemed to make a scary situation even scarier, and this time was no exception. The space behind the door had gone so long without fresh air that the four had a little trouble breathing at first.

"Whew, we need oxygen masks down here," said Jason, and the others nodded in agreement.

At the bottom of the staircase was a large room with a dirt floor. It was lined with shelves, just like the pantry.

"I didn't know houses had basements back then," said Melissa.

"It's not a basement," Tom said. "It's a root cellar—I saw one of these in my great-grandpa Parker's house."

"Tom!" Julie said, almost shouting. "Do you think the 'Cell' on the plate could be short for *cellar*?"

Tom got excited—it was the closest thing to a clue he'd heard so far. "It might be, but what does the number fifteen stand for?"

Jason had an idea. "Tom, count the number of steps leading from the pantry to the cellar."

Tom began to count. "One. Two. Three. Four." His excitement grew as he reached the bottom. "Thirteen. Fourteen. Fifteen!" he shouted loudly enough to make the others jump. "This is it—it's got to be!"

Tom's hand shook as he pulled the plate from his coat pocket.

Cell-15 R-10 Up-4 Lay Up

"Okay, we have the 'Cell-15,' we think—now, what does the 'R-10' stand for?"

Melissa spoke up. "If 'Cell-15' brings us down to the bottom of the steps, maybe 'R-10' stands for 'right ten feet.'"

"No, it means 'right ten paces,'" said Jason. "On every treasure map I've seen on TV, they use paces to measure their distance."

Tom walked over to the bottom of the steps, facing in the opposite direction. Then he turned directly to the right, stepped off ten paces, and stopped right in front of one of the cellar walls. The walls of the cellar were made of granite stones—the same kind used in the house, chimney, and towers, only smaller.

"Okay, now we come to 'Up-4.' It's got to mean four blocks up from the cellar floor." Tom's voice quivered. He couldn't believe it—what had been so hard to figure out was now falling into place like magic.

Jason counted up four blocks from the floor, but because of the staggering of the blocks, there were two blocks together in the fourth layer. "Which block is it, Tom?" he asked. Before Tom could answer, Jason saw it. "Hey, look here." He pointed to the block to the right—or, more precisely, to the cement around it. Actually, it wasn't surrounded by cement, as all the other blocks around it were. Joe Simpkins evidently had wanted to make sure whoever solved the code found the right block. "That must be what the 'Lay Up' on the plate meant—Joe laid up this block over the treasure!"

Jason's heart was pounding. Could there actually be a treasure behind that stone? Jason's imagination took over. He could see himself diving into the swimming pool behind his mansion and his parents pulling into the driveway in their new Rolls-Royce and parking next to his Mercedes. "Ah, this is the life! Rich and powerful, having all that money can buy." Of course, Toby Miller was his janitor. "Hey, Miller," he visualized himself saying, "don't forget to clean the bathroom good this time. You didn't do it so good the last time. You'd better straighten up, or I'll get another moron to clean the john." Miller would kiss his feet, begging Jason to give him one more chance.

"Jason!" shouted Tom. "Help me move this stone if you want to find out what's behind it."

Tom had finished chipping away all of the hardened mud around the stone and was getting a good hand hold on one corner by the time Jason came out of his dream and arrived to help. The two pulled and strained, but the stone wouldn't budge. Tom was beginning to think that maybe Joe Simpkins had been a practical joker, and this was his trick rock. He could just imagine Joe laughing heartily while rigging up this joke on any would-be treasure hunters. But his thoughts quickly vanished, and the stone started moving. The kids didn't know that the type of mud Joe had used dried as hard as cement, and this particular stone hadn't been out in the weather for more than a century, as the stone in the chimney had; therefore, it wasn't as easy to break loose as they had first thought it would be.

Inch by inch, the two worked the stone back and forth left to right, straining with every pull to get the cover off and find the treasure behind it. It was getting late now—around one thirty—but the kids didn't notice their watches. They were too busy with what they were doing. They always had been typical, ordinary high school kids living average or maybe even boring lives. Now they were doing something outside the ordinary—something daring, adventurous, and even dangerous!

But right now, their thoughts weren't on danger, adventure, or the chance of getting caught. Their thoughts were on whatever was behind that rock. The adrenaline was pumping, and the excitement was building. Right now, there was no time, no Richfield, no basketball team, no church service—no thought of anything from their average, ordinary lives. For now, the old root cellar was their world, that stone was their championship game, and the trophy lay behind it. All they had to do was win the game—remove the stone—and the trophy was theirs.

"It's almost out!" shouted Tom with a noticeable strain in his voice. "You girls move out of the way; when this thing gets to the edge, it's gonna fall, and I don't want any crushed feet to worry about."

The two girls stepped back only slightly—they didn't want to miss any of the action. "You two just be sure to watch your own feet," said Julie. "You're closer to that thing than we are."

Suddenly, the dirt turned loose of its grip, and the big rock fell, landed on one corner, and started rolling right at Jason. "Watch out, Jason!" yelled Tom, but Jason was quick on his feet and dodged the big rock easily. The old block took a couple more turns and fell over with a thud on the hard dirt floor. Almost instantly, every light turned away from the stone and moved to where the stone had dwelled before being so rudely evacuated.

"See anything?" asked Jason, his voice shaking.

"Not yet," said Tom. "Hey, wait a minute—I see something shiny in there."

"Is it g-gold?" Jason was ready to begin his dreaming again, starting where he'd left off, with Toby Miller kissing his feet and begging for his janitor's job back.

Tom's hand moved slowly through the opening and into the dark crevasses that for many decades had been undisturbed. *Well,* he thought, *here we go again.* No ordinary person liked to stick his or her hand into a black hole without first knowing what was behind the blackness, and Tom was about as ordinary as they came. But again, he knew he had to in order to solve the mystery.

His hand groped through the blackness, feeling for any sign of the treasure. His fingers moved slowly across each crack and ridge in the rock, gently searching for something—anything—to notify his brain that a discovery had been made.

Oh no, he thought, and the other three saw the frown on his face. His hand had touched something similar to the object he had touched only the night before: a smooth, flat metal plate.

"I don't think you guys are gonna like this," he said as he pulled the object from where it had been hidden all that time. "It's not the treasure—it's just another code."

Jason's dream quickly evaporated as reality crashed in around him. "No gold?" he asked in the most pitiful voice they had ever heard.

The group shone their lights through the hole for one more look, but it was obvious the treasure wasn't there. Tom's mind returned to a thought he'd had earlier: *Joe Simpkins was a practical joker!* He was playing games with them. There was no telling how many more of those plates were buried or hidden around that house or perhaps everywhere else in Richfield.

"Well, what's on this plate?" asked Jason with a deep sigh, a sign of surrender. Tom held his light to the plate and read the inscription:

Caroline--In-35 Down-15 L-10 Down for yourselves

"This one's even crazier than the first one. How are we ever gonna figure this one out?" Tom was ready to give up, go home, go to bed, and forget the whole deal—but Julie was not.

"Look, guys, we're in this too far to stop now. We figured out the first code, didn't we? And I think if we work at it, we can figure out this one. So what if we didn't find the treasure this time? Maybe we'll find it the next time—but we'll never find it if we just throw up our hands and quit!"

What a pep talk! thought Tom. One thing he liked about Julie was that she could make the best of the worst situation—except when he showed up late. She'd make the worst of that.

"I agree with Julie," said Melissa. "What have we got to lose? It's not like we've got so much pressing business in our lives that we don't have time to figure this thing out. I say we go for it. All in favor, raise your hand." Every hand went up almost in unison.

Even Jason didn't hesitate this time, to the surprise of the other three. "Why not? I've already figured out what I'm gonna do with my part of the treasure, so we've gotta find it now."

The others laughed at Jason's honesty. They then proceeded up the stairs and through the house to the open window through which they had made their initial entry. Getting out was easier than getting in, and in no time, they were outside in the cold night air.

The bare skin on Tom's leg was getting cold, so the four said their quick farewells, paired off into couples, and quickly went their separate ways to their nice warm homes and their even nicer soft beds.

The red Jeep parked along the sidewalk on Second Avenue about a half mile from the Simpkins mansion roared to life. Spinning tires and throwing gravel, it pulled out onto Second Avenue and stopped right in front of the mansion.

Out of the shadows ran two dark figures. They moved stealthily along the bushes and through the darkness until they made their way to where the Jeep was parked. The two climbed into the Jeep, and with a sudden burst, it sped away into the night.

FOUR

"I cried unto my God with my voice, even unto God with my voice; and he gave ear unto me." James Parker was preaching from Psalm 77:1 (KJV)—that much Tom knew. But the rest of what he said didn't register. For one thing, Tom was so sleepy he could hardly keep his head up in church. For another, he was engulfed in his thoughts about the night before.

"What could 'Caroline' stand for? The other plate didn't have a name like that on it. And what if there are many more codes?" Young Tom never had been good at riddles, and a code was a riddle to him.

As he looked at the plate, he could just hear it laughing at him. "Come solve me if you think you can," it seemed to mockingly say to him. The other three had solved the last code, and it would have to be up to them to solve this one.

"And if we cry unto God, we can have faith to believe that he will hear us and that he will listen to our wants, our needs, our joys, our sorrows—anything at all that touches us, God is concerned with. If anyone here wants to come to Jesus for whatever reason, I can assure you that he is right here to help you. Jesus lived among us; he endured the pain and suffering of the cross. He knows just what you're going through, because he went through it himself. That's why he said in Matthew 11:28 (KJV), 'Come unto me all ye that labour and are heavy laden, and I will give you rest.' If you need Jesus Christ to save you from your sins, please come—the altar is open for you right now."

Two people, a young girl and a middle-aged man, stepped out

and went forward, much to the joy of the congregation. *Two more dummies throwing their lives away*, thought Tom.

After the service, Tom ate a quick snack and hurried over to Julie's house.

"Oh, hi, Tom; come on in." Judy Patterson was one of the nicest grown-ups Tom had ever met—and one of the prettiest too. Beautiful sandy-colored hair flowed down around her shoulders, and deep-set blue-green eyes sparkled when she smiled. It was easy to see where Julie got her beauty from—not that Hank Patterson looked like a troll, but Julie had most of her mother's features.

Hank Patterson was tall, about six foot three, and slim, with dark brown hair, blue eyes, and a dark mustache. He was a common man who worked at the plastics factory at the edge of Richfield. A kind and gentle man who wouldn't hurt a fly, Hank was liked by everybody—everybody, that was, except Tom.

Tom didn't really hate Mr. Patterson; he was just scared of him. Hank never really meant to scare Tom—he liked him. Tom was always polite, saying please and thank you whenever he was around them. He was a nice kid, but Hank was an overprotective father. Julie was still his little girl, and any young man was a threat to his relationship with her, so every time Tom was around, he got a look from Hank—one that said, "If you do anything to my little girl, you'll be in serious trouble!" Judy had talked to Hank about his behavior, but it didn't seem to do any good.

"I'm sorry, honey. I don't mean to scare him. I'll try not to look at him like that anymore," he'd say to his wife. But the evil looks kept coming, putting more fear into Tom's already fearful heart.

"Your dad hates me," said Tom as he plopped down on the side of Julie's bed.

"No, he doesn't; Daddy doesn't hate anybody. He's just trying to protect me—that's all. So have you figured out the code yet?"

"No, I can't make any sense of it at all. Why don't I just give you the plate and let you work it out? I'm terrible at these things."

Tom reached into his jacket pocket, pulled out the old plate, and held it out to Julie.

When she reached out to take the plate, he took her hand in his and looked into her eyes; there was a sincere expression on his face, which was unusual for the freshman.

"Julie, I'm not too good at things like this, but I want you to know how much I care about you. You are a wonderful girl. Pardon me—a wonderful woman. And I really am proud to be a part of your life. As beautiful as you are, you could have your pick of any guy at school, and you picked me." That probably didn't sound very good, but Tom hadn't had much practice at sweet-talking. "And, Julie, well, I guess I'm just trying to say that I really like you—and I have ever since the first grade, when we first met."

Julie couldn't believe her ears; Tom really did like her and not as a pal but as a girl. "Oh, Tom, that was beautiful; I've never had anybody say those kinds of things to me before."

"Not even Toby Miller?" Tom was going to get the topic out in the open once and for all.

"Tom, I'm going to tell you something, and I want you to listen real close to what I have to say, okay?"

Well, this is it, thought Tom. *She's going to dump me and go on to Toby. I shouldn't have told her how I felt—I spilled my guts out to her, and now she's ready to break my heart. Oh well, let's get this over with quick so I can get out of here.* He finally quit thinking long enough to talk. "Okay, Julie, go ahead."

Now it was Julie's turn to hold Tom's hand, and she looked him straight in the eye. "Tom, I don't know where you got your information from, but I want you to know right now that I have never, ever gone out with Toby Miller. I can't even stand the guy. He's rude, arrogant, and self-centered, and he sure doesn't know how to treat a lady. You're the one I want, Tom—not Toby or any other guy. I love the little things you say and the way you make me feel—no other guy makes me feel the way you do. Have I made myself clear, Tom? You are the one I care about. You're the one I want."

Tom could have floated straight through the roof and danced on the clouds right about then. This was it—they had finally gotten their feelings for each other out in the open, and boy, was it ever wonderful! "Oh, Julie!" was all he was able to say. He reached over to Julie, took her lovingly in his arms, and kissed her.

Tom and Julie had kissed before but not like this. Usually, he would give her a little peck when he walked her home from school, or they'd kiss softly while sitting in the auditorium during lunch at school. This time, however, he gave her a deep, affectionate, heartwarming kiss that told her he really did care.

After their lips parted, Julie just sat there on the edge of the bed with her eyes closed and her lips quivering, as if in a daze. "Julie?" said Tom softly.

She awoke from her dream, and a broad smile crossed her face. "Wow! Oh, Tom, that was wonderful!"

The two sat in Julie's room for two hours, talking mostly about themselves, turning loose their emotions and their feelings for one another the way a dam turned loose its floodwaters when it couldn't contain them any longer. The secret code of Joe Simpkins would have to wait—for now.

From that day forward, each knew how the other felt, not only on the surface but also deep down inside. Although Tom and Julie had known each other for nine years, they met for the first time on that warm, wonderful Sunday afternoon—and what a meeting it was!

Julie went to church with Tom that evening. Tom couldn't remember the last time he had actually enjoyed a church service, but he enjoyed this one. It wasn't the beautiful singing or the message delivered by Reverend Parker that caused the good feeling in his heart; it was the beautiful young girl with the long brown hair and the deep blue eyes who held his hand throughout the service. "Oh Lord, if this is a dream, don't let me wake up," Tom said quietly to himself as he lifted his eyes toward the ceiling. He turned to look at

Julie, and as their eyes met and smiles crossed their faces, he prayed once more, this time to himself. *Lord, just let me keep dreaming.*

After church, Tom and Julie met Jason and Melissa at Pizza Town. Jason and Melissa hadn't gone to church, so they had gotten a table and had already ordered the usual—an extra large pepperoni pizza and four soft drinks—by the time the other two arrived.

"Well, how did your Sunday go?" Jason asked, looking at Tom and Julie.

The two looked at each other and grinned. "Oh fine—just fine," they both said together.

Jason didn't notice anything unusual between the two, but Melissa did. *I'll have to have a talk with Julie tomorrow to see what's going on*, she thought to herself.

Jason spoke up again. "You guys thought any more about last night? Man, I never thought I'd ever go into that spooky old house. Did you all get a chance to work on that second code?" Jason asked one question after another, but it was probably best to let him do his talking before the food got there, because when Jason started eating, he didn't have time to do any talking.

"No, I haven't had any time to work on it yet," said Tom. "I gave it to Julie—she can figure these things out better than I can. I do have one idea, though." As all eyes focused on Tom, it was shocking to him that for once in his life, he actually had an idea.

"Well, what is it?" Jason was getting hungry, and when Jason got hungry, he got impatient.

Tom knew the pizza would be out soon, so he'd better hurry up with his idea, or he'd never get it out. "Well, Joe Simpkins is kind of a historical figure in this town, so there should be some information on him at the county library. I say we go over there after school tomorrow to see if we can find anything in the historical records that might tie into this code."

"That's a great idea," said Jason. Tom had gotten it out just in time too, for the waitress had delivered the pizza, and Jason was already digging in.

The four ate and talked for almost an hour, mostly about the code and the mansion. Jason did stop eating long enough to give Tom one important bit of information. "Hey, Tom, did you hear about Eddie Gordon?" he asked with his mouth crammed full of pizza.

"No. What about Eddie?" Tom grew concerned. Eddie was the starting point guard on the Richfield JV team.

Jason finally swallowed his pizza. "He was hiking yesterday somewhere in the mountains and fell off a big rock and broke his arm; he's out for the rest of the season. I guess that makes you the starting point guard for the rest of the season, old buddy!"

Tom couldn't believe it. "You're kidding!"

Jason couldn't answer because he'd refilled his mouth with pizza, but he shook his head—he wasn't kidding! Tom had mixed feelings about that piece of news. Sure, it would be his chance to show what he could do—his big break—and he had always wanted to play a big part in a game, so now was his golden opportunity. But what if he wasn't good enough? What if the Falcons lost in the regional playoffs, and it was all his fault? But more importantly, what about Toby Miller? Tom's responsibility as point guard was to get the ball to the player who was in the best position to score, but he knew that if Toby didn't get his share of those passes—and Toby's fair share was about 90 percent—he'd probably get his face caved in after the game.

Julie broke Tom's train of thought momentarily. "Wow, Tom, I think that's great—don't you?"

Tom nodded and gave the other three a crooked smile. "Oh yeah. Yeah, that's great news—I've been waiting for a chance like this."

Jason slurped the last remaining bit of soda from his glass and waved his index finger in Tom's direction. "You'll do great, Tom; you're a very good basketball player, and now's your chance to prove it. We've got our last regular season game with Lincoln High

Tuesday night, and the regionals start Friday. You and I are gonna do a little extra practicing for the playoffs."

The four finished up the pizza and drinks, paid the bill, and hurriedly left for home. It was getting late, and from the looks of things, it was going to be a busy week!

Tom met Jason at his locker on Monday morning. Julie had already gone to her first class, so the two had a few minutes alone to talk before going to their first period, history. "Jason, I told Julie yesterday that I liked her," Tom said.

"I thought she knew that," Jason said as he popped a stick of chewing gum into his mouth.

"No, Jason, I mean I really told her how I felt, and she told me how she felt. I gotta say it really felt good to get that off my chest. And do you know what she told me about her going out with Toby? She said that she had never gone out with him and that she couldn't stand him. Who told you she'd gone out with him anyway?"

"He told me himself. I should've known better than to believe Toby Miller—he's probably the biggest liar in school." No sooner had Jason gotten the words out than the biggest liar in school walked up behind him.

"Hey, Parker, you're taking over for Gordon, ain't ya?"

There went the hair on Tom's neck, sticking up again. "I don't know, Toby; I haven't talked to Coach Waters yet."

"Well, you're next in line on the guards, ain't ya?"

Tom loved Toby's grammar—it matched his IQ. "Yeah, Toby, I suppose I will be taking Eddie's place. Why do you want to know?" It was bragging time for Toby—Tom could feel it coming.

"Oh, I just wanted to know who was going to be feeding me the ball—that's all. Parker, you just keep the ball coming in my direction, and I'll show you how to win the championship. You got that?"

The thing I like best about Toby, Tom thought, *is his modesty.* He looked at Toby. "I'll do the best I can, Toby—I want to win the championship trophy as much as anybody on the team."

"Look, Parker, the championship trophy is not the one I'm after. It's the MVP trophy I want—and I want you to help me get it. Understand?"

Tom understood perfectly. Toby should have played golf or tennis—a game in which the individual received all the glory and didn't have to share it with anybody else. A team game like basketball didn't seem right for a person whose ego was as big as Toby's.

"All right, Toby, I hear you." That was all Tom could seem to get out. He hated even talking to that boy. What he'd said seemed to satisfy Toby, though, for he turned around and headed for class.

"Come on, Jason, or we'll be late."

The bell rang as the two boys hurried down the long hallway to their classroom.

FIVE

Since Coach Waters had called off Monday's practice, Tom and Jason were able to leave school at a decent hour for a change. The two met Julie and Melissa in the school parking lot, and together they headed out for the Jackson County Library.

The library was located about a mile from the school, so the four had time for a short conversation as they trudged across the parking lot, across Highway 104, and down Fifth Street and turned left on South Boulevard and then right on Colby Avenue. The air was considerably cooler than it had been earlier in the day. After a gorgeous weekend, Old Man Winter was letting everybody know that he was still in control and that springtime would have to wait a little bit longer.

"I hear a big storm's coming this way," said Melissa. "Mom said it's supposed to get here about Wednesday morning." In that part of the country, big snows in the winter were about as frequent as eggs on a chicken farm, so nobody paid much attention to them—they were just a part of life as far as folks in Richfield were concerned.

"I just hope it's not so bad that we can't get our practice in," said Jason. "Tomorrow night's game should be a breeze, but when the regionals start, it's gonna be dog-eat-dog."

Jason was right; Lincoln High School had a grand total of one win during the entire season. Richfield had already beaten them by thirty-four points earlier in the year, so tomorrow's game shouldn't be a problem. Tom was worried about Friday night—that was when the big boys came to play.

Region Three was comprised of four districts, with a winner of each district playing in the regional tournament. Richfield was to represent the Gold Dust District—an appropriate name, considering all the towns in the district were old mining towns. Tom wasn't sure which team the Falcons would be playing—actually, nobody knew yet. Two of the four district championships were going down to the wire, with the champion being decided in the last game of the season. However, one team was in for sure—to everyone's dismay. Undefeated and defending champion Hillside High had beaten Coach Waters's Richfield team in last year's regional finals, and they appeared a good bet to win again this year. Coach Waters had told his players on several occasions that his main goal this year was to get back in the playoffs and beat Hillside.

They'd accomplished part of that goal last Friday night when they'd won their district. But their chances had taken a severe blow with the loss of Eddie Gordon—and the pressure lay squarely on the shoulders of young Tom Parker. Could he take up the slack? Would he fold under the pressure? Did he have what it took to fill in for a player like Gordon? Those and many more questions were being asked around school and around town, yet no one was more unsure of how Tom Parker would do than Tom Parker himself.

"Well, here we are," said Julie.

Tom hadn't heard much of their conversation; he'd been too preoccupied with thoughts about the game. But right now, the game would have to wait. Right now, he had to try to help his friends solve a code—a code people had been trying to solve for more than a century.

Tom took Julie's hand as the four walked up the concrete steps, through the double glass doors, and into the library.

For a librarian, the sight of four teenagers entering a library was enough to make his or her skin crawl. "Oh wow—I've got my work cut out for me this evening," said Sylvia Thompson to herself as she watched the kids walk in. But that thought soon evaporated as she welcomed the four. These weren't average, ordinary, troublemaking kids; these kids looked serious.

Tom walked up to the desk, looked seriously at Sylvia, and politely asked, "Where do you keep the historical records on Richfield?"

These kids not only look serious but also sound serious, thought Sylvia. "What exactly is it you're looking for? I may be able to help you find it."

Julie spoke up over Tom's shoulder. "We're looking for all the information you have on Joe and Charlie Simpkins."

Sylvia was surprised but tried not to show it. "Oh, the Simpkins brothers. You all must be writing a report on this for school—right?"

"Uh, yeah, something like that," said Jason. "Do you have a lot of stuff on them?"

"Oh yes, the Simpkins brothers were important figures not only in the founding of our town but in its growth as well. Most people don't know this, but Joe Simpkins was the town's first mayor—of course, he gave it up because it took too much of his time. I'll tell you he—"

Tom politely interrupted. "Ma'am, if you don't mind, we'd like to read all about that ourselves." Sylvia Thompson had the distinct reputation for being a blabbermouth, and Tom knew if they let her get started, they'd still be there at closing time.

"Uh, sure, okay, let me go back here and see if I can find it all; I think we have it all catalogued." Her feelings were hurt, but that was nothing unusual—to shut up a blabbermouth, one always had to hurt his or her feelings, and Sylvia's feelings had been hurt hundreds of times.

She was gone for about ten minutes and returned with an armload of books, newspaper articles, and magazine clippings. Joe Simpkins was as popular as she had said. "This book here"—she held up a book entitled *The Legend of the Simpkins Treasure*—"should help you a lot. The first part of it gives a biography of Joe and Charlie's life, even going back to where they grew up."

Tom, Julie, Jason, and Melissa gathered up all the documents and proceeded through the library until they came to the first empty table, where they plopped themselves down, took off their jackets, rolled up their sleeves, and went to work. Since they didn't want to risk having anyone see the plate, Julie had copied down all the information and left the plate at home.

"Whew!" exclaimed Jason. "Boy, Tom, I sure am glad you shut Sylvia up; I don't think I could've stood another mouthful like the one she gave me the last time I was here. That woman just doesn't know how to quit talking."

"Oh, she knows how to quit—she just doesn't want to," said Melissa. "But let's forget about Sylvia and concentrate on 'Caroline.' Now, we all know that in solving the last code, we found out what 'Cell-15' stood for and went from there because everything else followed that. I'd say if we find out what 'Caroline' stands for, everything on this code should follow it—right?" The other three nodded in agreement.

Tom, assuming his leadership role, spoke up. "Okay, Julie, you read through this book," he said, pointing to the one Sylvia had shown them. "Melissa, you and Jason go over these old newspapers, and I'll go over the magazine articles. If you see anything at all about the name Caroline or anything else connected with the second code, speak up."

The four sat quietly scanning the books, newspapers, and magazines, studying them carefully to see if there was anything in them that could help in their search. Julie was the first to speak up. "Hey, I think I've found something here."

The rest raised their heads almost simultaneously. "What is it?" asked Tom with a look of excitement on his face.

Julie continued. "Well, look here on page fifteen of this book. The author writes about Joe and Charlie Simpkins growing up in Pennsylvania. But get this." She held the book open and reached it out so the other three could see. "Their father's name was Joseph, and their mother's name was—"

All four shouted out in unison, causing some raised heads and a mean look from Sylvia, "Caroline!"

This was the break they had been looking for. The four went over the page, scanning from top to bottom, to see if it mentioned anything else about Caroline Simpkins that could possibly tie in with the rest of the code. But that was it—just a name.

"Okay, so their mother's name was Caroline. What would that have to do with the code?" Jason asked with a note of frustration.

"I don't know," Tom said. "Did any of you guys see a painting of a woman when we were in the house Saturday night?"

They all shook their heads. "Of course, we didn't go up into the towers," said Melissa. "Maybe something in those towers could help us."

Jason said, "Oh please, let's not go in that house again, especially the towers. We're lucky we haven't been caught, but if we continue to press our luck, we will be."

Jason was turning yellow again, but Tom didn't like the idea of going back into that old house either, at least not until they were sure of what they were looking for. "Look, I hate to say it, but I agree with Jason; we'd better stay away from that place until we find something more concrete to go on. Julie, do you mind taking this book home with you? You can go over the rest of it to see if Caroline is mentioned anymore."

Julie agreed to Tom's request, and since it was just about closing time anyway, the four gathered up their belongings and walked to the counter so Julie could check out the book. They all apologized to Sylvia for their outburst, but Sylvia was more curious than angry. What could be so exciting about the name Caroline? She had never seen kids so excited about a class project before—or was it a class project? There was something mighty strange going on, and she couldn't stand not knowing what it was.

"Did you find what you were looking for?" Sylvia was subtle when it came to prying information out of people; she didn't have a reputation as the biggest gossip in town for nothing. But these four weren't about to talk. They had some sort of secret, and she was dying to know what it was.

"We found some of it," said Julie, "but I'm going to need to take this book home to study some more, so I'll need to check it out."

Sylvia snatched the book out of Julie's hand, punched the card, and handed it back in a not-so-gentle way. They could tell she was mad because she couldn't get any information out of them, and it tickled them to death. The four turned and walked toward the door, laughing as they went—which made Sylvia madder.

As the four walked out the double doors, Jason poked Tom on the shoulder and pointed. "Hey, there's a red Jeep. I wonder who it belongs to."

"I don't know," said Tom. "It looks like the one that went by the mansion Friday night while we were getting that first plate. But there's nobody in it right now, and I'm sure there are at least a dozen red Jeeps in Richfield. C'mon, guys. Let's go home; I've got a lot of homework to do."

The group walked past the Jeep, which was parked along Colby Avenue, adjacent to the library. Tom gazed inside but didn't see anything peculiar; it was just an average, ordinary red Jeep.

They walked together, talking among themselves, until they reached the corner of Second and Pine, where they split up into pairs and went in separate directions. The Simpkins mansion towered above Tom and Julie as they strolled by gazing at its massive structure, as they always did; only now, there was more to the house than there had been a few days ago. Mysteries that had lain dormant for so long were slowly being unraveled by a bunch of kids still wet behind the ears. But these kids were growing up. As a matter of fact, they had grown up quite a bit in the last few days—and before this adventure ended, there would be a lot more growing up to do!

***

"I don't know all those kids." Sylvia Thompson was having a chat with two distinguished-looking gentlemen in three-piece suits. "One of them is a Bennett—Jason is his first name, I think. I used to work with his mother. The other boy is a preacher's kid from over on the south side. I don't know either of the girls. Say, these kids aren't in any trouble, are they?"

"No, ma'am," replied one of the men. "We're just doing a survey on high school kids in America, and we just wanted to use these four as an example of high school life in the Great Northwest. Do they come to the library often?"

"No, I've seen them here only a couple times. They came in here to study some stuff on the Simpkins brothers for a class project—at least that's what they said."

"You act as if you don't believe them, Mrs. Thompson," said the other gentleman.

"Well, it's just that they seemed to get all excited about something they found in one of the books. I mean, kids don't get that excited over class projects—at least no kid I've ever seen, and being a librarian, I've seen plenty."

"What did they do?"

"Well, they were over there studying," she said, pointing to the table where the four had been, "when all of a sudden, all four of them burst out the name Caroline. I thought I was going to have to throw them out, but they calmed down again and went right on working as if nothing had happened. Then, about five minutes later, they came over to the counter and apologized for the outburst, and one of the girls checked out the book they were so excited about."

"What was that book, Mrs. Thompson?"

"Let's see. I have the card here somewhere. Oh, here it is!" She held up the card for the two men to see.

One of the men copied the information onto a small notepad he had taken from his coat. "*The Legend of the Simpkins Treasure* by Ralph Walker," he read to himself as he wrote. "Well, thanks for the information, Mrs. Thompson; you've been a big help."

The two men turned and walked toward the door. Sylvia went back to her duties, all the while mulling over everything in her mind—the four young kids who seemed so interested in the Simpkins brothers and the two finely dressed gentlemen politely asking some pointed questions about the kids. What did all of it mean? Who were those men, and what was so important about the name Caroline? Why had those kids screamed out the name—and in a library of all places? Those and other questions remained unanswered to Sylvia, and it was driving her crazy. She continued going over the library cards, all the while talking to herself and shaking her head.

Meanwhile, the two men strolled across Colby Avenue, got into the red Jeep, and drove away.

***

Megan was helping Tom study for his history test. "Okay, Tom, what years did the Civil War begin and end?"

"It began in 1861 and ended in 1865," he answered.

"That's right. Okay, who was the president of the Confederate States?"

"Uh, Jefferson Davis." Tom knew all this Civil War stuff, but he wanted to go over it one last time to make sure. He wanted to ace this test to pick up his history grade a little. History was the only class in which he was making less than a B average, and an A on the test should pick his grade up from a C to at least a B-. Most freshman boys would have considered a C average in any subject to be great, but Tom did not. It wasn't that he wanted to be an egghead or anything like that. Tom had a good reason for keeping a B average: his dad had promised him that if he maintained a B average until his sixteenth birthday, he'd get him a car. Megan had received a car on her sixteenth birthday, but for her, it had been no sweat. His big sister was not only pretty but also smart, maintaining a 3.75 grade point average throughout high school with little or no effort. That was the reason she was helping Tom. He didn't care much for his big sister—she was too bossy. But she was always willing to help him with his schoolwork—when she had time.

"All right, one last question—I've got my own homework to do. What city was the capital of the Confederacy?" she asked.

Before Tom could answer, JoAnn Parker walked into the kitchen, where they were studying. "Tom, Julie's on the phone."

"I'll get it in my room, Mom," he said as he headed toward the back stairs. "Oh, that last answer is Richmond, Virginia," he barked over his shoulder at the top of the stairs. Megan usually teased Tom about his romance with Julie, but she hadn't said anything yet. "She'll probably wait until I get off the phone and then start on me," he said to himself as he walked down the hallway to his room.

Tom picked up the phone in his room and then waited to hear the phone downstairs being put back into its cradle. "All right, Megan, get off the line! I'm sure Julie doesn't want to talk to you." Listening in on each other's calls was kind of a ritual around the Parker household, but Megan and Tom had gotten wise to each other by now, so getting away with it wasn't as easy as it used to be. *Click.* The downstairs phone was hung up. "Hi, Julie. How's it going?"

The breathless sound of his girlfriend came over the other line. "Tom! Just listen to this. You know how we found out about Caroline being Joe and Charlie Simpkins's mother?"

"Yes, I know. What are you so excited about? Come on, Julie. If you've got something, let's have it." Tom could tell over the phone that Julie was having trouble controlling her emotions.

"Well, Tom, I just found out that the Simpkins boys named something after their mother. Guess what it was."

Tom wasn't in the mood for a guessing game. "Oh, come on. I can't guess—tell me what it is."

Julie drew a deep breath and then spoke as she let it out. "It's the mine, Tom. They named their mine the Caroline after their mother."

Tom was speechless; the news hit him like a ton of bricks. Now it was his turn to wrestle with his emotions. "Well, what do you know?" was all he could get out, but thoughts were churning through his head like balls in a bingo game.

"Tom, are you still there?" Julie was trying to calm her boyfriend down, which wasn't going to be easy.

"Yeah, I'm still here. Julie, do you know where the mine is?"

"No, but the courthouse holds all the old deeds and claims; maybe they still have a copy of the claim on the Caroline. If they don't, I'm sure they have some charts and maps dating back to that time. Oh, we'll find that mine—we've just got to!"

"Yeah, we'll find it. Now, what's the rest of that writing on the plate—have you figured it out yet?"

It was obvious Julie had been doing her homework—in treasure hunting, that was. "Yeah, Tom, the next part is 'In-35.' I'd say that stands for 'in thirty-five paces' from the front of the mine. Then it says, 'Down-15.' There must be a mine shaft that goes down fifteen steps or maybe fifteen feet. The rest of it we can find out when we get there."

"Wow, Julie, this is great! I can almost touch that gold now!"

Julie came back over the line. "Not so hasty, Tom; it may end up being another plate like the last one."

"Well, if it is, I'll just let you work that one out too," Tom said with a laugh. "You know, Julie, you're really something special. Are you coming to the game tomorrow night?"

"I sure am! I wouldn't have missed Friday's game if we hadn't had company, but I have no plans for tomorrow night, except to watch a great guy play basketball."

Tom could feel himself floating again. "Well, I just hope I can keep my mind on the game instead of the beautiful girl in the bleachers."

"Oh, you'll do great—I just know it. By the way, when are we going to get to the courthouse to check up on the mine?" she asked.

"How about Wednesday evening?"

"But doesn't your church have prayer meeting on Wednesday evening?"

"Yes, but I think I can get out of it—I'll just tell Dad that something came up, and I won't be able to make it. He'll understand."

"Okay, Wednesday evening it is. Well, I've gotta go now, Tom; I'll see you at school tomorrow."

"Okay, Julie, bye." As Tom placed the phone back in the cradle, his heart was nearly bursting. There was no greater feeling in the world than being in love—at least up to that point in his life. And Julie was a wonderful girl—most of the time.

Tom sat at his desk for a few minutes, letting all the events of the past few days run through his mind. He thought about the Simpkins treasure and how close they were to finding it. He thought about the misfortunate turn of events that had put him in the starting lineup for the basketball team. He thought about Sunday, when he'd opened up his heart and told Julie his true feelings. Everything seemed to be happening so fast. He felt like a race car driver running in front with nothing but clear sailing to Victory Lane and the winner's trophy. But at the same time, he wondered when somebody was going to throw some oil onto the track and send him spinning into the wall. *I just hope I can stay in the race long enough to find out how it all ends and whether I win or not*, he thought to himself as he got up from his desk, walked (or floated—he couldn't tell which) to his bedroom door, and opened it.

Tom stepped back with a start—there was Megan, smirky grin and all, standing in his doorway. "Well, did you tell little Julie that you love her?" she asked.

Tom had been right; she'd waited for him to come out before starting in on him. Of course, Megan couldn't help herself—there was just something about having a little brother that made her want to pick on him. It was as if it was her duty as a big sister.

"I guess you blew her a few kisses over the phone. Did she tell you she was your buttercup? Or maybe you told her you were her jelly doughnut."

Tom shoved Megan aside without saying a word and headed down the hall. Any other time, the situation would have turned into an all-out war of words, but now Tom was too mature to pay attention to stuff like that.

Megan noticed it too. "Well, it looks like my little brother is growing up; I guess it's time to stop picking on him," she said with a smile, and she strolled down the hall to her room.

SIX

Tuesday seemed to float by Tom like a riverboat in a fog. There was too much on the young man's mind to think about school. He did settle down long enough to take his history test, and since he knew all the answers by heart, he was pretty sure he aced it. But everything else seemed to go by without him even noticing.

Jason just about jumped out of his size-eleven shoes when he heard the news about the plate. The thing that thrilled him the most was the fact that they'd be going into a mine in the middle of the day rather than going into that house in the middle of the night. Both he and Melissa said they'd be happy to go with Tom and Julie to the courthouse the next evening, but Jason seemed concerned about one thing.

"Look, Tom, with all this stuff going on, when are you going to have time to practice? Coach will call off practice if we win tonight—which we should—but we need to get in some practice before the regionals start. I want you to be ready so we can show all those doubters around town just how good Tom Parker really is." Jason seemed more concerned about Tom's future than Tom was.

"Jason, we can ask Mr. Short to open up the gym for us tomorrow night from seven until nine," Tom said, referring to the janitor. "I'm sure he will—and we can get in some good practice then. Okay?"

Jason agreed with Tom's proposal, and the four headed to their next classes, all in opposite directions.

***

Coach Waters sat across the desk in his office with a broad smile on his face and a reassuring note to his voice. "Tom, I want you to just relax tonight and do the best you can; I'm sure nobody's expecting you to come in and be a star, so do your best, and I won't expect any more from you."

The coach had called Tom into his office just before the game—mainly to calm him down. Tom had arrived early for a change, so the two had plenty of time to talk before Coach Waters had to address the rest of the team. "I know you'll make some mistakes tonight—probably lots of them—partly because of nerves and partly because of your lack of experience. If you mess up, don't worry about it—just try to learn from those mistakes. I've always said that the person who doesn't make mistakes is the person who doesn't do much of anything else."

The coach's little talk had helped to calm him down, but Tom was still concerned about one thing. "Coach, Toby told me yesterday to keep feeding him the ball and said he'd take care of the rest."

Coach Waters laughed and leaned forward in his chair, propping his chin up on one of his hands. "Tom, you just get the ball to the open man, and let me worry about Toby. Toby is a good ball player—he could be a very good player if he'd think of this as a team game instead of his own personal glory show. Oh, and one more thing: don't take any shots unless you're open. I don't want you shooting the ball too much—not that I don't think you're a good shooter. I've just dealt with this situation before. I've seen young men come into a game, miss a couple shots, and destroy every bit of confidence in their game."

Tom knew what the coach was getting at. "Coach, you've got nothing to worry about; I'm not going to take a shot at all if I don't absolutely have to."

"Glad to hear you say that. Now, let's get out there and beat those Patriots!"

Tom followed the coach to the boys' locker room, feeling a lot calmer than he had been earlier, and took a seat next to Jason. This was it—his first starting role in a Richfield JV uniform!

The Lincoln High School Patriots hadn't always had a mediocre team like the one that plagued them this year. This year, the Patriots' JV program was suffering. Their best player from a year ago, Scott Walker—Coach Waters's nephew—had graduated to the varsity, while their best player for this year, Eric Combs, had broken his leg in a skiing accident and was out for the season. But the Patriots were determined to pull the upset of the year in their last game, and from the looks of things in the first quarter, they were doing it.

Tom started out badly, throwing his first two passes out of bounds, which got a couple mean stares from Toby as well as a lot of the fans on the Falcons' side. But he settled down midway through the first quarter and started playing the way he knew he was capable of. One smooth no-look pass to Toby for an easy layup brought the crowd to their feet. A behind-the-back pass to Keith Jeffries for an open jumper that tickled the net as it went through seemed to calm down his fears as well as those of the players, the coaches, and even the audience.

However, by the end of the first quarter, the Falcons were behind 14–10. Tom was beginning to relax a little, but Toby wasn't going to give him a chance to relax. He glared at Tom as the two took their seats during the break. "C'mon, Parker. You're not getting me the ball enough! Do you want the worst team in the district to beat us tonight? Just get the ball to me—understand? I'll beat them myself if I have to."

"I wonder if Toby inherited his modesty or if they teach it at the charm school he attends," Jason said to Tom. "Don't worry, man; you're doing great."

Coach Waters wasn't concerned, or at least he wasn't showing it. "Except for those first two passes, Parker, you're doing good. Just find the open man, and get him the ball. Miller, you're going to have to pass off when you're double-teamed. Jeffries, I need for you to move around more. Let's keep the zone defense but put more pressure on the ball. Okay, guys, this is where we crank it up and run these guys off the court. Let's go!" He clapped his hands, the players joined in, and he sent his team back out onto the court.

The second quarter was a different story altogether. Playing hard-nosed defense and good offense, the Falcons turned a four-point deficit into an eight-point lead by halftime. Tom had two steals, which turned into easy baskets at the other end, one by himself and one by Marques Hall. Lincoln High had reverted back to its usual sloppy game, which worked in Richfield's favor.

Now that the game was going their way, Tom had the opportunity to get a breather. As he sat down, he glanced over his shoulder to where Julie and Melissa were sitting. Julie smiled at him and held her thumb in the air as a gesture of her approval. Tom gave her a broad smile and a little wink, letting her know her message was received and noted.

Richfield continued to pull away in the second half. Lincoln just didn't have the horses to keep up with the district champs. When the final buzzer sounded, the score was 61–42 in favor of Richfield. Tom had four points, six assists, and three steals, but more importantly, he'd earned respect from the coaches, the fans, and his teammates—all except for one, that was. Toby was fuming—he'd only scored ten points, one of his lowest point totals of the season. Tom had done what Coach Waters had told him to do: he'd found the open man and passed him the ball. With Toby being double-teamed most of the night, he just hadn't been open that much. Of course, Toby didn't understand things like that; all he could see was the bottom line: he wasn't getting his shots because Parker wasn't getting him the ball. He was going to have to straighten Parker out again, as he had many times in the past.

After Tom and Jason showered and changed, they made their way to where Julie and Melissa were sitting to watch the varsity game. "Well, girls, do you think I'm ready for the NBA yet?" asked Tom with a grin as he sat next to Julie.

"Almost," said Julie, laughing. "You did great, Tom. I'm very proud of you."

"And I'm very proud of you too, Jason," said Melissa, giving him a little peck on the cheek. Jason had played most of the fourth quarter, coming in for Toby after the game was out of reach. He'd scored two points and pulled down two rebounds.

As the four sat watching the game, Toby walked through the gym doors and climbed up the bleacher steps to where his buddies were waiting. Tom's eyes followed Toby as he made his ascent. He knew Toby was mad at him, but for once in his life, he didn't care. He felt that for once, he'd gotten the best of Toby Miller. Toby had picked on him since grade school, and the attacks had continued through junior high and on into high school, culminating with the mudhole incident last Wednesday. But now it was his turn. Tom was getting back at Toby the only way he could: through his pride. But he was sure Toby would retaliate in some way; a person just didn't humiliate Toby Miller and get away with it—especially if that person was Tom Parker.

Toby's eyes caught Tom's stare. *Oh no, he's looking this way,* Tom thought as he turned his eyes away.

"Hey, Parker!"

Tom looked around with a start, as did most of the people on that side.

Toby shook his fist at him. "I'll get you," he said, and then he proceeded up to where his friends were sitting.

"What was that all about?" asked Julie with a look of concern crossing her face.

"Oh, nothing," said Tom, shrugging. "You know how Toby is." Tom didn't want Julie to worry over him, and he figured the less she knew the better. Yet he knew that sooner or later, he and Toby would have to settle things once and for all.

Jason spoke up. "Oh, you know Toby; he has a bad game, and he has to blame it on somebody. Say, you guys, I've got an English test tomorrow, so if you don't mind, I'm gonna head on home."

Melissa left with Jason, leaving Tom and Julie to watch the rest of the game—and what a game it was! Lincoln High's varsity was much better than the JV team, and Richfield's varsity wasn't that great. The teams battled down to the wire before Scott Walker hit a baseline jumper in overtime to win the game for Lincoln.

"Coach Waters ought to keep his relatives in Richfield, where they belong," joked Tom as he and Julie walked home from school. The clouds were rolling in, covering the moon, and the wind was picking up. There was definitely a storm coming; they could feel it in the air.

The two walked slowly hand in hand—or glove in glove—cuddling close together to keep out the cold air and chatting about one thing or another, until they finally made their way to the big old pine tree in the front yard of Julie's house.

"Well, this is where I get off," she joked as she turned to face Tom. She leaned over, kissed him gently, and strolled up the walk and into her house.

Tom watched to make sure she made it inside all right and then trudged on up the sidewalk toward his own home—a lonely-looking figure with his head down, deep in thought, and about to freeze. He'd traveled about fifty yards from Julie's house, when a car pulled up beside him.

"Hey, Tom, can I give you a lift?" It was Kevin Sloan, bringing Megan home from the game. Kevin opened the door of his sports car and pulled the seat up, and Tom crawled into the back. The warmth of the car felt good on his frozen body. Kevin shifted into first gear and gave it gas, and off they roared.

The quarter-mile trip didn't give them much time to talk, but Tom did make one comment: "Hey, Kevin, I'm sure sorry you all lost tonight—man, it was a good game, though."

"Well, we could've beaten them, but they did play a good game, especially that Walker kid; he's gonna have some college recruiters licking their lips by the time he's a senior. Say, Tom, I thought you really played a great game tonight. You surprised me; I didn't think you were that good."

"Well, I just hope I can do well enough during the playoffs; tonight's game was just a warm-up. Friday night is when the real pressure starts. I just hope I'm up to it."

"Oh, I think you'll do great. Say, I can help you if you want me too," Kevin said. His season was over as of that night. The Falcons' varsity had finished third in the district and therefore didn't qualify for the regionals.

"Well, me and Jason are planning on practicing at the gym tomorrow night from seven to nine. I'd appreciate it if you could come out and help us."

Megan, who had been silent all that time, spoke up rather strongly. "Tom, did you forget that tomorrow night is prayer meeting night? Dad's not going to like you missing church to practice basketball."

"But this is important," Tom said. "I'm sure he won't mind this one time. I've got to get in some good practice before Friday, or I'm sunk." He looked at Megan with his brotherly eyes. "And maybe you could help me talk Dad into it, Megan; you've always had a way with Dad—he gives in to you a lot faster than me."

Megan knew a snow job when she heard it, but Tom was right—this was important to him. "Okay, Tom, I'll help you."

By that time, Kevin had pulled his car into the Parkers' driveway. "See you tomorrow night, Tom," he said as he let him out of the car.

"You mean you'll do it?"

"Yeah, I'll help you; it ought to be fun, making a star out of my future brother-in-law." He winked at Megan and drew a funny smile in return. "One thing, though: when you get rich in the NBA, don't forget who your friends are."

Tom laughed. "Oh, I won't. See ya tomorrow night."

It was the one thing Megan had done right: she had found herself a good man.

Tom trudged up the steps and into the house just as the first snowflakes began to fall.

SEVEN

By Wednesday morning, the town of Richfield was covered in a blanket of white. Six inches of snow had fallen during the night, causing havoc and creating schedule changes all over town—and Mother Nature wasn't through yet. An additional six inches of snow was expected before the snowfall ended later that night, according to the trusty weather forecasters.

This time, it seemed the forecasters had called it right. Snow continued to pour like salt from a salt shaker onto an already covered lawn at the Parker house. Jackson County schools were closed that day, bringing an unexpected but welcome vacation for many school kids—except for a certain preacher's kid.

"Man, this is gonna put a dent in my schedule," said Tom to himself, disgusted at the way things were going. Tom Parker normally would have been doing backflips off the coffee table upon hearing news of a school closing. But why did it have to be that day, of all days? He had so much to do, and with all the snow, there was no way he would be able to get to the courthouse or to the gym for practice. *Oh, why didn't this snow wait until next week, when all this was over with?* he thought as he flopped across his bed like a sack of potatoes.

But his dad had taught him long ago that worrying about things you couldn't change was a waste of time. He reached over, picked up the phone, and dialed the Patterson residence. It was eight thirty; Mr. Patterson should be at work by then, he knew. Cumberland Plastic Company was one of the few factories that did not close under any circumstances. If an employee could make it to work, that was fine, and if he couldn't, he couldn't, but Hank Patterson had a four-wheel-drive pickup, so a snow like that didn't faze him.

"Hello?" said the lovely voice of Julie's mom over the phone.

"Mrs. Patterson, can I speak to Julie, please?" Another thing his dad had taught him was to always be polite. He'd also taught him to always be prompt, but he was still working on that one.

"Sure, Tom, I'll get her for you," she answered.

As Tom waited for Julie to come to the phone, he thought about the Simpkins treasure. Was it gold, money, or maybe jewelry? Or maybe there was no treasure. "Most legends you hear about turn out to be false," he'd heard his mom say once. Maybe this was false—but there had to be something. The plates they had found with the codes had to lead to something—but what?

"Hi, Tom." Julie's sweet voice came over the phone, bringing Tom's thoughts back to earth.

"Hi, Julie. What do you think of the weather—beautiful, isn't it?"

"Well, they told us we were going to get some snow, and here it is! Say, Tom, I don't guess we'll be able to get to the courthouse today. Would you like to maybe get some of the gang together and go sleigh-riding at Mr. Tyson's place this afternoon?"

Tom wasn't really in the mood for sledding, but he figured it would take his mind off all the things that were clogging it up right now. "Yeah, that sounds like fun—I'll call Jason and Marques, and you can call some of your friends. What time do you think we should meet up there?"

Julie hesitated for a moment and then spoke up. "Let's make it one o'clock. Do you think Mr. Tyson will mind all of us kids coming up there on his place?"

"No, I don't think he will as long as we behave ourselves—but I'll give him a call just to make sure. Julie, why don't we go on over to the courthouse? If we can make it all the way over to Tyson's farm, we should be able to make it across town to the courthouse." Tom was determined to get to the bottom of the mystery—the Simpkins mine was somewhere in those hills overlooking Richfield, and a little winter storm wasn't about to keep him from finding it.

"Well, my mom said she heard on the radio something about the courthouse being closed because of the weather. I'll ask her again just to be sure."

"Just don't tell her why we want to go there," said Tom.

"Oh, I won't—I never was too good at keeping a secret, but I'm not letting this one leak out. Hold on a minute while I ask her."

Tom could hear Julie holler over the other end, and her mom yelled back something.

"Mom said the courthouse is open today; they just decided to postpone the trials until another date. Do you think we can get over there this evening before it closes?"

"I've got a better idea." Tom couldn't believe some of the ideas he'd been coming up with lately. "Why don't we go right now? The snow's letting up some, so we shouldn't have too much of a problem getting there—and besides, if we wait until after the sleigh ride, it may be too late, or the weather may be too bad. Do you think Jason and Melissa can make it?"

Not only were Jason and Melissa able to make it, but they were standing under the oak tree in front of the Simpkins house, shivering and huddling close together, by the time Tom and Julie managed to get there. "Whose idea was this anyway?" asked Jason through his deep purple lips. "We about got covered up by a snowblower just before you guys arrived."

"Oh, come on, Jason. Where's your sense of adventure?" Tom said. "You know what they say about treasure hunters: neither rain nor sleet nor snow."

"That's for the mailman," Melissa said with a laugh. "Oh, come on, Jason; this is going to be fun. And besides, I've seen you walk two miles through the snow for a jumbo burger at the Burger Hut." It was easy to see that Melissa was responsible for Jason being there and that it was not the other way around.

The four treasure hunters finally stopped their arguing, headed down Second Avenue, and turned right onto Park Boulevard, the street that would take them directly to Main Street and the Jackson County Courthouse. Since traffic was understandably light, the four walked through the middle of the street, where most of the snow had been cleared away, and except for dodging an occasional snowplow, they were able to make it to Main Street with surprising ease. They had decided to move the sledding party back to three o'clock instead of one, which would give them plenty of time to find out what they were looking for.

By the time the group reached the courthouse, they were covered with a white frosting of snow and were chilled to the bone.

"These people are gonna think we're a bunch of nuts, coming all the way across town through the snow to look at a bunch of maps and records." Jason was wearing a goofy-looking green toboggan with "Save the Whales" printed in a white band around it, so he looked like a nut anyway.

Tom led the others through the courthouse before finally coming upon someone who could help them. "Could you tell me where you keep all the old maps and records of Richfield dating back to around 1870?" Tom was talking to a pretty woman in her midthirties, who wore a three-piece suit. "It's for a project we're working on." Tom really didn't think he was lying. It was a project—not a school project but a project nonetheless.

The woman led the four to a large room filled with volume after volume of huge catalogues that resembled enlarged term papers. "I'd hate to have to check one of these books out—I'd get a double hernia just carrying it home," said Jason.

The girls giggled at his remark, but Tom was too busy with the woman to hear what Jason had said.

"These are all of the recorded maps of Richfield, dating back from the time Richfield became a town and continuing until the present time. I believe the volumes you enquired about are right over here." She pointed her long, slender index finger to a table on the right side of the room, next to the window. "Now, all we ask is that you please be careful with these maps—they are very old and therefore very fragile."

"Thanks, Mrs. Winters," Tom said. "That's a fine name for a day like today," he added in a whisper as the four sat side by side at the big table. "Now, what we're looking for is a map of Richfield dated somewhere between 1865 and 1875. And look at the hills surrounding the town—that's where the mine should be located." Tom was barking out orders like a drill sergeant—one with a high-pitched voice, of course.

The four searched through the maps, checking every section carefully. Mrs. Winters was right—the maps were fragile. Jason tore a small piece off one of the corners while trying to turn from one page to another. "Whoops!" He shrugged, swiftly cramming the torn corner into his coat pocket.

"C'mon, Jason; be more careful. Do you want to get us kicked out of here before we find out what we're looking for?" asked Tom.

"Sorry, pal. I didn't mean to," Jason responded as his face reddened.

"Look here, you guys!" shouted Melissa, causing the others to return their attention to the maps. Melissa's right index finger pointed to a small area in the southwestern corner of a Richfield map from 1869. "Here it is, you guys—right here!"

Sure enough, there it was—in print anyway: the Caroline Mine. "Good work, Melissa. You've found it," said Tom. "Only I can't make out any of the roads and markings on this map."

"Well, that's understandable considering it's a map of Richfield in 1869," said Julie with a look of concern crossing her face. "You know, I just thought of something. A lot of things have happened since that time—new highways have been built, tunnels have been cut into some of those hills, and they just finished that new road going up to Carver's Lake. For all we know, that mine could be under a four-lane blacktop by now."

Julie had a point, but they all agreed it was just as possible the

Caroline Mine was still up there, uninhibited by the progress of the times. "Let's ask Mrs. Winters. Maybe she'll know just where this part on the map is," said Tom.

He left and then returned a few minutes later with Mrs. Winters. Tom showed her the area they were interested in, paying close attention to keep his finger away from the heading "Caroline Mine." This was their secret, and it was going to stay that way—there was no sense in letting a stranger in on their good fortune.

Mrs. Winters wrote down the general directions on a Post-it pad and then proceeded to another table on the other side of the room. The four teens followed her, not knowing exactly what she was doing but anxious to find out.

Mrs. Winters could tell the kids were puzzled, so she decided to explain. "I marked down the general area of the map of 1869. Now I'll compare it to one of our present maps. This should tell us where the area is; who owns it; and, most importantly, which highway, if any, has been built on or near it." She grinned and winked at the four.

In the past few years, new roads had been coming up faster than new babies were being born. "If this pace keeps up, every citizen in Richfield will have their own highway," Tom had heard his dad jokingly tell his mom.

Mrs. Winters spent the next five minutes looking back and forth between her notes on the old map and the new map. Finally, she raised her head and directed her attention to the curious teenagers. "I think I've got it figured out. According to the deed entries in the old map you were looking at, this entire area was owned at one time by Joe and Charlie Simpkins." She paused to study their faces, noting that those names brought a certain raising of eyebrows. "In 1876, all of this land was reverted back to the town of Richfield because the Simpkins hadn't paid taxes on it for the required five-year period. The land was taken over by the federal government in 1975 and added to the national forest region of that area. According to the new map, this entire area was to have been a state park by now, but evidently, the funds haven't been allocated yet to begin construction."

"Well, where is this area located?" asked Tom.

Mrs. Winters studied the map for a couple more minutes to be sure and then addressed the teens again. "Well, kids, you see here"—she pointed to a spot on the map—"that Highway 41 runs right along the edge of the forest. There is only one road in this area, and that's the old Oak Ridge Road, which runs through the forest and on into the mountains on the western face."

Tom watched as Mrs. Winters moved her finger along the black line that represented Oak Ridge Road. *I wonder where the mine would be located along the road,* he thought to himself. He glanced over to the others, who were all looking at him—they'd had the same thought he had. "Mrs. Winters, would it be all right if we took this new map over to the table where the old map is? We need to do some comparisons."

Mrs. Winters approved their request but reminded them again to please be careful. Tom and Jason picked up the huge volume; carried it over to the other table, taking small steps to keep from dropping it; and then gently set it down next to the old one.

Looking at each map and taking notes, the four slowly began to zoom in on the exact location of the mine. The way their eyes moved back and forth, one would have thought they were watching a tennis match. No tennis match could have been as exciting, however. Tom traced Oak Ridge Road onto a white sheet of paper and then placed the paper over the old map. Since the maps were exactly the same size and the road on the map showed the location of each curve, it wasn't long before they pinpointed the location of the mine.

"The mine should be on the left of Oak Ridge Road right here at this horseshoe curve," said Tom. "I just hope that finding the mine in those woods will be as easy as finding it here on the map."

"It won't be," said Jason. "As much as that place has grown up, that mine is probably buried under a laurel thicket."

"But we're gonna find it. We've gotta find it!" Tom was getting excited. The others could tell it in his voice and see it in his eyes.

Julie took down all the information she thought they'd need and then joined the other three, who were bundling up for the trip back home.

"Let's stop at the Burger Hut; I'm getting hungry," Jason said, rubbing his stomach.

"The bottomless stomach strikes again!" Melissa laughed. But it was getting close to lunchtime, so the other three decided to follow Jason's lead.

After ordering four Jumbo Burgers, four large fries, and four large soft drinks, the four sat at the Burger Hut, eating and talking—but mostly eating.

Tom was afraid to talk too much about the mine. He was afraid he'd get his hopes up again. Every time he started dreaming about fame and fortune, something happened to dash those dreams like a pop bottle on a concrete floor. He also was too nervous to talk about the basketball game on Friday. The other three seemed to sense that, so the conversation centered mostly on school, the latest fashions, and the best way to get rid of zits.

Once the burgers, fries, and sodas were thoroughly consumed—Jason, who made it a point not to waste food, took care of what the others couldn't eat—the four bundled up again and headed for home. Tom had no sooner gotten home, however, than it was time to bundle up again for the sleigh ride.

All I get done is putting my clothes on and then taking them off, he thought to himself. *I'll be glad when summer gets here—then I can throw these old coats into the closet and leave them there for a while.*

The snow stopped at about four o'clock with an official reading of ten to twelve inches. Not only had Vince Tyson approved the sleigh-riding party, but he joined in on it and brought two of his grandchildren, who were visiting him. By the time Tom and Julie arrived, the entire hillside was covered with sleds and riders. "Wow, did we invite this many people?" he asked Julie.

"No, I guess word just got around. But the more the merrier, I always say."

In a flash, she picked up a ball of snow, hurled it at her unsuspecting boyfriend, and then took off just in time to dodge a snowball in return. The two ran up the hillside to join the others, having to dodge a sled coming down every so often before finally reaching the top.

They met Jason and Melissa on their way up—the huge car hood that Jason and Melissa were riding in, along with half a dozen more, swerved off its course, nearly plowing over the two helpless teens.

"What were you trying to do—kill us?" yelled Tom as Jason made his way back to the top.

Jason grinned his big, toothy grin at his buddy. "Look, old pal, if we'd wanted to kill you, we'd sure find an easier way than that. C'mon. You and Julie get on this thing; it'll give you the ride of your life," he said, pointing at the old car hood.

"Yeah, I bet it will. Who brought that thing anyway?" Tom asked.

"I did."

Tom turned to see Marques Hall, a tall, slim, good-looking black kid with a built-in smile that was always turned on. Tom wondered if Marques smiled in his sleep.

"I got it from my uncle's old Ford. Man, there's no sled this side of the Rockies that can keep up with this thing—it's got speed and plenty of room. There's just one thing it doesn't have."

"Steering!" all the kids around him said simultaneously.

Marques's grin just got bigger. "That's right. But who needs to steer? That's the fun part—taking off and letting it go wherever it wants to."

"But what if it wants to go into that big old pine tree down there?" asked Julie, pointing to a massive tree three-quarters of the way down the hill.

"Well then, you just jump off. No problem!"

"No problem, he says. Just try jumping off that thing while it's going forty miles an hour."

Julie was afraid, but Tom finally coaxed her into the old hood, and off they went, along with Jason, Melissa, Marques, and his girlfriend, Cindy Sheets.

Marques was right—Tom had never been on a ride like that one. To Tom and Julie, it felt as if the thing were going at least seventy or seventy-five miles per hour. Of course, it was only traveling about thirty, but when one was riding on a car hood, it felt as if it were going much faster. Every twenty feet or so, the hood would hit a dip, slowing down momentarily and throwing a ton of snow back onto the unsuspecting riders. Tom tried to hold on with one hand and wipe snow with the other, but as his eyes cleared enough to see, the hood would hit another dip, sending another barrage of snow into his face again. After the third dip, he just closed his eyes and rode it out to the bottom of the hill. Keith Jeffries told Tom at the end of his ride that they had just barely missed the big tree by about a foot. "I'm glad I had my eyes closed," said Tom. "I didn't even see the tree."

But Julie had. "Tom, don't you ever put me on that thing again! That thing just missed the tree by this much," she said, spreading her hands apart.

After Tom had calmed his girlfriend down, they spent the rest of their time on less spectacular but safer rides.

Vince Tyson built a fire on top of the hill, and the group roasted hot dogs and marshmallows until six thirty, when the group turned from a huge crowd of kids to a small group of weather-worn die-hards before completely thinning out by six forty-five. Tom and his three comrades were the last to leave. They bid farewell to Mr. Tyson, the best old man in the world, and headed through the gate that led to the main road. After they made it through, as they were shutting the gate after them, a big four-wheel-drive truck pulled up beside them.

"Hi, Tom. Megan told me you all were out here. Are you ready to go?" It was Kevin Sloan.

"Where are we going?" asked Tom.

"Well, to basketball practice, of course," said Kevin. "Don't you remember?"

"Yeah, I remember, but I thought with the snow and all …"

"Well, if you all can go to the courthouse and to a sleigh-riding party, you should be able to practice basketball."

Tom wasn't through with his questions. "But who's gonna let us into the gym? I was going to ask Mr. Short, but since we didn't have school today, I didn't figure he'd do it."

Kevin had an answer for that one too. "Oh, I forgot to tell you—I took the liberty of calling Coach Waters, and he said he'd be glad to let us into the gym. Not only that, but he said he'd stay to help us—he wants you ready for Friday."

"Not half as much as I want to be ready," said Tom. "Well, do you have room for us all?"

Kevin looked at the four and said, "Sure, if none of you has claustrophobia. Pile in."

Kevin drove them all to Tom's house, where they all called their parents to let them know where they'd be. Due to the bad weather, Wednesday's services were canceled at the Richfield Community Church as well as all the other churches in the county, which got Tom out of the sticky situation of telling his dad he couldn't make it to church. After the three made their calls, they piled back into Kevin's dad's truck—all five were in the cab, packed in like sardines—and headed toward the Richfield High School gym.

Richfield High was unusually dark on that Wednesday. Although it was a small school, RHS took great pride in its academic and athletic programs. There were probably as many trophies for academic endeavors in the school's trophy case as there were trophies for athletic achievement. Bright silver and gold trophies lined the case, showing Richfield victories in everything from football to debating and from basketball to science. There was even a huge trophy in the back denoting the Odyssey of the Mind team as the new state champions. Richfield was full of pride, full of tradition, and full of winners.

No one showed that winning attitude more than Coach Sam Waters. He wanted to see a new trophy in that trophy case—a trophy denoting the Richfield High junior varsity basketball team as the regional champs.

The coach had arrived at the school early and was standing in the dark hallway, looking into the trophy case, when he heard a vehicle pull up outside. He walked over to the door and peered through the frosty glass, straining to see if the truck was carrying the young teen responsible for his being there. As teenager after teenager piled out rubbing his or her sore, cramped legs and shoulders, the coach said to himself, "I'm sure glad Kevin didn't offer to pick me up; I don't think I could have survived a trip like that." But young muscles mended quickly, and in no time, Tom, Jason, and Kevin were on the court, warming up and doing layup drills.

"Okay, kids, let's get started," said the coach. "I want to get back home before my pipes freeze."

Coach Waters worked Tom hard; they practiced bringing the ball up court through a full-court press. They practiced setting picks and screens. Coach made sure Tom was familiar with all the rules, as well as all the defensive looks a team might show. Jason and Kevin were lots of help, posing as defensive players and giving Tom different obstacles—ones he would probably see during Friday's game against the Oak Grove Tigers, winners of the Hot Springs District. At 14–4, the Tigers were a formidable foe not to be taken lightly, and with all their starters healthy, they were favored in the local papers to win Friday night's game. How well Tom Parker played in that game would probably determine whether or not Richfield advanced to the finals—an unfair burden to place on the shoulders of a fourteen-year-old former benchwarmer.

Coach Waters didn't seem too concerned with his water pipes; he worked the three young men, especially his new point guard, until after nine thirty. By the time it was all over, their feet were dragging, and they were gasping for some fresh air to fill their burning lungs. "I've never been this tired in all my life," panted Jason, bending over halfway with his hands on his knees.

"Me neither," said Tom. "Look, guys, I really do appreciate this. You all have gone through a lot to help me. I just hope I can pay you back someday."

"You just win Friday's game, and we'll call it even," said Kevin, heaving for every breath.

Julie and Melissa sat in the bleachers, quietly chatting, while the practice session was in progress. "Do you think there really is a treasure?" asked Melissa. "I'm not trying to be pessimistic about this, but sometimes I wonder—you know, we're taking a lot of chances with this thing, and we may end up in a lot of trouble if we're found out. I just wonder sometimes if it's worth it."

Julie couldn't fault Melissa for her feelings—she'd had those same feelings more than once. "I know what you're saying, Melissa. Believe me, I do. It's all a big adventure right now, but I'm afraid that sooner or later, this thing is going to get out of hand, and we're gonna end up in jail—or maybe worse. I've heard my dad say he knew of some people who would kill to get their hands on the Simpkins treasure. I just hope we're not the ones who make that statement come to pass."

"Well, when are we going up to the mine?" asked Melissa.

"I guess we'll have to wait until some of the snow melts. We may be able to get up there Saturday morning," Julie replied.

"But how are we going to get up there? That's a long way off—we'd never be able to walk it."

"Tom's got that figured out; he's gonna get his dad to drive us up to where Oak Ridge Road turns off from Highway 41. We can then walk in from there. It shouldn't be more than a mile or a mile and a half. He said he's going to tell his dad that it's part of the project him and Jason are working on."

"What project?" Melissa asked.

"Oh, they're making it up as they go along. I just hope I'm

there when Tom has to explain it all to his dad; that should be fun to watch."

Melissa smiled. "I'd like to see that myself."

They'd heard on the radio on the way over that schools would be closed again on Thursday, so none of them were in a big hurry to get back home. Kevin promised Coach Waters he'd lock up, so the coach went on home to his family, leaving the boys to shower, change, and bundle up for the ride home. Each took his or her place in the truck, Tom with the gearshift in his leg, Jason with the door handle in his side, and the girls packed in on top of them. Kevin took Jason and Melissa home and then dropped Julie off at her house, leaving Tom as the last one to be escorted home. Having Tom alone at last gave Kevin the opportunity to ask the question that had been on his mind all evening. "Tom, why did you all go to the courthouse today?" Kevin noticed Tom shift a little and heard a bit of hesitation in his voice. Tom didn't like that question—it was obvious—but he did give Kevin an answer.

"Oh, me and Jason have a little project we're working on, and we needed some information at the courthouse, so we went down there—and Melissa and Julie went to help us. With the project."

After an answer like that, Kevin regretted having asked the question. There was something strange going on; he just couldn't figure out what it was. Why would four teenagers walk all the way across town in a snowstorm just to find out something for a school project? None of it made any sense, but it was their business, not his, so he'd leave it at that. "Well, here we are again," he said as he pulled into the driveway. "I promised Megan I'd come in and help her on a term paper. Look, Tom, I'm sorry about being so nosy just now. What you all do is your business and none of mine, okay?"

Tom had been bothered by Kevin's question, but that remark eased his mind a bit. "Okay, Kevin, no problem."

The two got out of the truck and waded through the snow to the freshly shoveled sidewalk, where they trudged, stomping the snow off their feet as they went, up to the front door and went inside.

"You boys are late; I was beginning to get a little worried about you." JoAnn Parker did most of the worrying for the Parker household.

Reverend Parker never let much bother him—and with good reason. "If I was the kind of person who worried about everything, I'd have been in a mental institution after my first year as pastor," he'd told JoAnn on several occasions. Being a pastor of a local church required two things—a kind heart and a tough hide—and Reverend Parker had both. He had put up with many coldhearted church members during the past ten years, as well as a few crybabies, as he called them, who wanted things done their way or no way. But he had weathered every storm without losing any of the love he had for those people. They were his flock, and he loved and cherished them, even though he had to straighten them out every now and then.

Tom and Kevin had finished shedding all their coats, gloves, toboggans, and scarfs by the time the preacher came into the living room. "Well, how did you guys do tonight, Tom?" he asked with a grin. "I'll bet you can almost beat Oak Grove single-handedly now, can't you?"

Tom hadn't thought his dad knew who they were playing or even cared, but James Parker did know, and he did care. He knew more about Tom's social life than he let on. He didn't want his son to think he was one of those nosy fathers always butting in on his personal affairs, so he let him think he wasn't watching—most of the time anyway.

"Well, I don't know if I can beat them by myself, but I sure hope I can help the rest of my team beat 'em," Tom answered with a grin almost identical to his father's. Tom was the spitting image of his father, as his granny Anders had said at least a thousand times. His square chin and dark eyes with long eyelashes—the envy of every girl—were a perfect match with his dad's, and although he was getting tired of people comparing him to his father, he had to admit there was a strong family resemblance.

Kevin and Megan retreated to her room to work on her term

paper; Mrs. Parker was in the kitchen, cleaning up; and Mr. Parker settled back to reading his Bible, so Tom slipped quietly into the den to play video games and just relax. It had been a long, hectic day, and he needed some time alone to kick off his shoes, lean back in the big old spongy chair, and settle his thoughts.

Unlike a lot of kids, who got so caught up in video games that they were stressed out before reaching the second level, Tom found playing those games kind of soothing—mainly because he didn't let those things get to him. If he won, he won, and if he lost, he lost. *Wouldn't it be great if I could treat Friday's game the same way as this video game?* he thought as he shoved the joystick to the right and pressed the A button. The only problem was, losing at this game only hurt one person—Tom Parker—but losing Friday's game would hurt not only him but also the team, the school, the town, and the district.

He tried to wash those thoughts out of his head—they were starting to make him nauseous. He moved his man around on the screen, maneuvering him through a cave, down the edge of a volcano, and finally through a tropical rain forest, where he was shot and killed by one of the Volton space mutants. "I've had enough relaxation for one night," he said to himself, reaching over and shutting off the TV and the game. He glanced at the clock: 10:45. It was too early to go to bed. Maybe there was an NBA game on.

Tom flicked the TV back on, changed to an all-sports channel, and sat back to watch. There was no basketball game on, though— just some crazy show about a bunch of guys racing camels through the desert. He reached for the remote, flicked the TV off again, and headed for his room.

Although he'd had a long, strenuous day, Tom couldn't get to sleep that night; there was too much to think about. The burden on him was just too much to deal with. No kid his age should have had to put up with that kind of pressure. He was having enough trouble just being fourteen years old without all the other stuff. But he knew if he could just make it through that week, then everything would be over with, and his life could get back to normal—at least as normal as it had been before. However, Tom couldn't see just how far from normal his life was headed.

When he finally did get to sleep, Tom had some more of his crazy dreams. In one dream, he was walking through a mine with Julie beside him, holding her hand, when suddenly, his flashlight went out. As he tried to turn it back on, somebody kept knocking his hand away from the switch. He finally got the light back on and shone it into the face of Julie—only to find that his beloved Julie had been transformed into a Volton space mutant with green hair, yellow fangs, and bright red eyes. He broke away from Julie's hold and ran through the mine, faster and faster, until the mine opened up into a big sports arena crowded with people. By then, his flashlight had turned into a basketball.

Coach Waters was standing on the sidelines, waving his arms and saying, "Shoot, Tom! Shoot! We're going to lose it all if you don't make this shot!"

Toby Miller was also there, waving his arms and saying, "Give me the ball, stupid! I'm gonna win this game!" Toby always seemed to invade Tom's dreams. He couldn't escape the guy, not even in his sleep.

Tom looked up at the scoreboard clock; only two seconds were left. He shot—but the ball wouldn't leave his hands. It was stuck there like glue. He looked at the clock again; only one second was left. He tried to shoot a second time; this time, the ball headed toward the basket—with him still attached to it. He floated through the air toward the basket with his right arm outstretched and the basketball still attached to his fingers. Closer and closer he came to the basket before finally slithering through the goal after the basketball, catching his feet on the net as he came through.

As he hung there by his feet, he saw Coach Waters run over to where he was. "I scored, Coach!" Tom said. "I won the game!"

Coach Waters growled, clenched his teeth, and yelled, "You shot the ball into the wrong basket, you idiot! You won the game for the other side!"

By that time, Toby Miller had made his way over, and he started punching Tom like a boxer hitting a punching bag. "I told you, stupid, 'Give the ball to me, and I'll win it!' Now look what you've done! You're a loser. A loser. A loser."

Suddenly, the net broke, sending Tom hurtling headlong to the floor below. Just as his head was about to splatter, he awoke with a jolt, with sweat dripping from his horrified face.

Man, what a dream, he thought to himself. Turning over in his bed, he looked at the clock on the nightstand: 6:30. He turned back over and tried to get back to sleep, but sleep wouldn't come, so he got up, dressed, and went downstairs.

EIGHT

"My, you're an early bird this morning." His mom was fixing breakfast. She had bacon frying in the pan, biscuits in the oven, and a fresh pot of coffee brewing. The smell of the food made Tom forget about his night and look forward to his day. "So how come you're up this early—do you have an appointment with somebody this morning?" she asked jokingly.

Tom smiled. "No, I just woke up and couldn't get back to sleep. Is dad up yet?"

"No, but I'm going to have to holler at him pretty soon, or he'll be late in getting to prison," she said. Reverend Parker had a standing appointment at the Jackson County Correctional Institute—a fancy name for a penitentiary—every Thursday morning from ten to eleven.

Tom laughed. "You're the only woman I know who would worry about getting her husband to prison on time."

JoAnn laughed too, realizing how funny her remark must have sounded. Just then, they heard shuffling upstairs.

"Well, Mom, it looks like you don't get to go upstairs and run him out of bed," Tom said with a wink and a smile. "Maybe next time."

Soon his dad came down the back staircase into the kitchen, and Tom couldn't help but laugh. "What's wrong?" asked Mr. Parker.

"Oh, I think it's a shame your congregation can't see you like you really are."

James Parker was standing in the stairway barefoot with his old bath robe tied loosely around him; one side was up past his knees, and the other was almost to his ankles. His hair, which was always perfectly in place at church, was sticking out on all sides, and his usually bright, sparkling eyes were a couple slits.

"You should go to church like that sometime—you know, let the people see that even the best of us have our bad sides." Tom laughed again.

James was too sleepy to laugh; he just flashed a crooked smile in Tom's direction. "Might not be a bad idea. Mm, boy, something sure smells good!"

"I'll have it ready by the time you make yourself presentable," JoAnn said.

Tom laughed again. "I hope it doesn't take you that long—I'm hungry."

James quickly showered, shaved, and dressed and was seated in his usual chair at the head of the table just as JoAnn was taking the last eggs out of the skillet.

After the preacher said grace, the three sat quietly eating the delicious breakfast JoAnn had fixed. For the first time in more than a week, Tom was planning on staying around the house for some much-needed rest. He felt as if he had been on an endless roller coaster for the past few days, and that day was as good a time as any to get off and take it easy for a while before he had to get back on and start his ride all over again.

James broke the silence, also breaking Tom's chain of thought. "Say, Tom, would you like to go with me to the prison? It'd be a good experience. I've told the prisoners about you, and I'm sure they'd like to meet you."

His dad's request surprised Tom, and he sat and stared for a second or two, groping for a reply. "No, Dad, maybe some other time; I really wanted to take it easy today."

"Okay, Tom, maybe some other time." James hadn't really expected a positive answer from his son, so he wasn't disappointed, but he still had hope that Tom would go with him sometime to see what a prison was like. More importantly, he wanted his son to meet the prisoners and talk to them. That way, he would realize what James had found out: they were just people—people who had made mistakes and given in to the tricks of the devil and needed the opportunity to get their lives back on track. Sure, there were some there who, if given a chance, would have gone right back and done the same thing over again—he knew that—but some could be reached, and Reverend Parker felt it was his duty to try to reach them. To the young preacher, the visits to the prison were not just part of his job; he was on a mission from God Almighty to spread the good news that Jesus saved, and that was what he intended to do. In the past few weeks, two of those prisoners had accepted Jesus Christ as Lord of their lives, and the number of prisoners coming to his services had grown from five to more than thirty-five. Jesus was reaching the prisoners through the fiery young preacher.

Coach Waters had scheduled a practice for three o'clock that afternoon, and except for attending the practice, Tom did just what he'd intended to do: he stayed home all day and rested. The sun was shining brightly that day, and although the temperature hadn't made it very far above the freezing mark, the deep snow was beginning to melt. By afternoon, the streets around Richfield were relatively clear, except for patches here and there. The snow movers were still busy at work, frantically trying to get the town in shape to open the schools back up on Friday, and it appeared their hard work had paid off, for the TV announcer said the Jackson County schools would be open tomorrow—much to the dismay of most of the kids.

Tom was ready to get back to school, get back to normal, and get the rest of the week over with. Sitting at home had given his body a rest, but his mind was still moving like a jet fighter in a combat zone. Barring any further snowfall, which the weatherman didn't expect, the snow should have melted enough by Saturday for them to make it to the mine—that was, if they could find it. "I wonder if it has caved in by now," he said to himself. "And if it hasn't, will it cave in on us while we're there? And if we do find the treasure, how will we explain it all?" He shook his head, trying to shake loose some of the wild thoughts tumbling around up there, hoping perhaps if he shook his head hard enough, they'd give up and leave him alone. The first big game of his life was coming up, and he knew he needed to concentrate on one thing at a time. He could worry about the mine after the game.

The practice session was one of the most grueling ones Tom had ever been to. Coach Waters worked the players so hard that when it was over, each player's tongue hung out like that of a hound dog on a hot summer day. After the practice, Tom and Jason sat in the whirlpool for an extra fifteen minutes, letting the hot, swirling water soothe their tired, aching muscles.

"I've never been through anything like that," said Jason of the practice. "He worked us harder than he did last night."

"Well, I guess he just wants us to be ready for Oak Grove; they do run that full-court press, you know."

About that time, the coach walked over to the whirlpool, leaned over the edge, and eyed the two young men. "Do you two want to have another drill session like last night—say, about seven o'clock?" He grinned. "Kevin told me he'd be glad to help you out again."

Tom looked at the clock on the locker room wall: 5:30. Then he looked at Jason. "Well, old buddy, how about it?"

Jason gave his best friend a tired smile. "Sure, I'll help; after all, I did promise to make a star out of you, and I can't back out now."

Coach Waters hadn't expected a response like that from the two, especially after what he'd just put them through. But it was a demonstration of what he had preached to his players through the years: "You can teach a boy how to run, how to dribble, and how to shoot, but you can't teach attitude! That's up to the individual." It looked as if Tom and Jason had the winning attitude. *With young men like this, we'll give that Oak Grove bunch a run for their money*, he thought. He stood there leaning on the whirlpool for a second or two with a big grin covering his face. "That's great! I'll see you at seven." Reaching into his pocket, he pulled out a ten-dollar bill.

"Here. You two go have a burger on me—just don't eat too much," he said, laying the bill next to Jason's clothes. "And be back here by seven—we've got a lot to do."

The two thanked the coach, climbed out of the whirlpool, and were clothed and on their way to the Burger Hut by six.

After dinner, Tom and Jason met Kevin and Coach Waters back at the school. "Well, boys, are we ready for our little workout?" Kevin joked.

"I'm ready to go home and collapse on the couch," said Jason. "We've already had one workout, and that's enough for me."

The coach overheard Jason's remark. "Well, Jason, I'll make a deal with you: you help us get Tom into shape, and after we win the regionals, I'll let you rest every evening until next year."

Jason grinned. "You've got a deal, Coach."

Thursday night's workout wasn't much different from Wednesday's, only it was more intense. Tom was taken through just about every situation a point guard could be in during a real game, and Jason and Kevin made things as rough on him as they could. Coach Waters couldn't help but smile throughout the night. The young freshman was looking better all the time. Sure, he was still making some mistakes, but his passing, dribbling, and ball handling were coming along great. *I just hope he doesn't buckle under the pressure*, he thought to himself. Unlike regular season games, the regional tournament was a gut-check time. The intensity doubled, and the pressure was almost unbearable. The coach had seen many kids with a lot more experience than Tom fold in a regional game. He just hoped his new point guard could handle it—and tomorrow night would tell.

The coached worked the three only until nine o'clock that night since school was open on Friday. They hurriedly showered and dressed and then loaded into Kevin's sports car, which he finally had dug out of the snow, and headed toward their homes for a well-earned rest. By the time Kevin pulled into the Parker driveway and turned off the engine, it was nine forty-five. Megan ran out to the car and opened the door for Tom to get out. "I've been wondering for the last two nights whether you're going steady with me or my brother," she said to Kevin with a smile.

Kevin leaned over and kissed her on the cheek as she sat down in the bucket seat Tom had just hurriedly vacated. "Aw, Tom's not my type; he wears his hair too short."

All three laughed, and Tom said his goodbyes and left the two alone for some serious necking.

James Parker was sitting in his favorite chair in the living room, reading the paper, when Tom walked through the door, rubbing his sore arms and legs. "Coach Waters must have put you through the wringer tonight, Tom," James said as he watched his son out of the corner of his eye.

"You're not kidding. He did," said Tom. "I've never been through anything like that." He proceeded to tell his dad the whole grueling story about the first practice session with the rest of the team and then the private session with Jason, Kevin, and the coach.

"Looks like you've been through quite a night," his dad responded.

"Well, I just hope it'll be worth it," Tom said with a sigh. "Dad, I'm worried about tomorrow night. I mean, what if I blow it for the rest of the team? I'd never forgive myself if I lost the game after they worked so hard to get there."

The preacher lifted his eyes from his paper and looked squarely at his son; he'd heard enough. "Now, Tom, I have always tried to teach you and Megan not to worry about things, and here you are, all torn up about a ball game. You just do the best you can, and everything will be all right—besides, no matter how important this game is, it's still just a game."

Just a game! Just a game? "Dad, it's not just a game; this is the most important game of my life!"

James hadn't meant to get his son so upset. "Okay, Tom, you're right. It is an important game—believe me, I know."

Tom knew his dad was right, as usual, but his little sermon

114

hadn't helped in calming his churning stomach. As he headed up the stairs to bed, Tom remembered that he needed to ask his dad something important. Heading back down the steps, he met his dad coming up. "Dad, I need to ask you a favor."

"What is it? If I can help you, I will."

"Well, uh …" Tom was stuttering again, a dead giveaway that he was trying to fake his old man out. "We need for you to drive us somewhere Saturday morning if the weather's good."

"Who's *we*?" his dad asked. His son's stuttering had aroused his curiosity.

"Oh, just m-me and Julie and Jason and Melissa." He was stuttering again.

"Where do you want to go?" He knew something was up; his son had been acting awfully strange the last few days.

"Well, uh, could you take us to where Highway 41 cuts off onto Oak Ridge Road? We're still working on our project, and we need to go up into the national forest to look for some things."

Tom's dad just stared at him for a few seconds, making him more nervous than he was already. "What things?" he asked. "You're being terribly secretive about this project, aren't you?"

Tom could sense that his dad was catching on to his act. He had come to understand something about his dad: Tom couldn't fool him for long. He always had a way of figuring his son out. Maybe it was a parent's intuition, but he could read Tom like a book.

There was another thing Tom had learned about his dad, though: what an understanding father he was. He looked his father straight in the eye, and this time, he didn't stutter. "Dad, I can't tell you about the project right now. I'll tell you about it after we get it all worked out—okay?"

James breathed a sigh of relief. *Well, at least he told me that much, whatever it means*, he thought to himself. "All right, Tom, you don't have to tell me about it. Just make sure you all don't get into any trouble." He was curious to know what the big secret was, but he trusted his son, and he figured he'd find out soon enough. "I'll take you all up there first thing Saturday morning."

Friday's school day came and went like a storm on a summer day. Tom spent most of his time in a daze. For all he learned on that particular day, he'd have been better off staying at home. Julie tried several times to calm her boyfriend down, but to no avail. In fact, there was nothing anyone could do to settle him down—not the teachers, not his friends, and especially not Coach Waters. Every time he saw the coach in the hall, his stomach did flip-flops.

"You're gonna be in the mental hospital before the game even starts if you don't straighten yourself out," Jason told his buddy.

"Jason, I don't think I'm gonna make it through this game; I've tried every way not to worry about it, but it just doesn't seem to do any good. Every time I get my mind off the game, I see the coach or one of the cheerleaders or even Toby Miller, and the fear starts creeping back again. And if we win tonight, it's a sure bet we'll be playing Hillside tomorrow night." Hillside, at 18–0, was playing the Cranston Blue Devils in the other semifinal game, and at 13–5, the Blue Devils didn't appear to be much of a challenge for the undefeated Panthers.

"Let's take it one game at a time, okay?" Jason told his friend.

Tom retorted, "That's easy for you to say."

Finally, the time Tom had been dreading ever since finding out about his starting role arrived: it was game time. The Falcons arrived at the Mayfield College campus, site of the Region Three tournament, at around six. The first game between Hillside and Cranston would start in half an hour, followed by the second game between Richfield and Oak Grove. Since they had the late game, the Falcons made their way into the packed sports arena to watch the first game.

An eerie feeling swept over Tom as he walked through the doors leading inside the huge sports complex. "I feel like I've been here before," he whispered to Jason. Of course, he knew that wasn't possible—he had never been to Mayfield College. But there was something about the place—something he'd seen somewhere before.

"Oh, come on, Tom. You're just nervous. Let's find us some good seats—I don't want to miss none of the action!" Jason yelled to him over the noise of the crowd as he made his way up the concrete steps leading to aisle upon aisle of soft, cushiony fold-down seats. "This sure beats those old hard bleachers, doesn't it, Tom?" he said. "I'd like to have a quarter for every splinter I've pulled out of my butt from those Richfield seats."

Tom smiled—he'd had his share of splinters too. Tom and Jason, along with three of the other players, found the best seats that were still empty and sat down to enjoy the show. Coach Waters had informed them to meet him at the entrance of the locker rooms at the start of the fourth quarter, so they knew they'd miss part of the game—not that it really mattered.

By the start of the fourth quarter, Hillside led Cranston by twenty points, and their coach was already pulling some of his starters. Keith Jeffries looked over at Tom at certain times during the game and just shook his head; those Hillside boys were as good as they had been billed.

Jason smiled at Tom with a twinkle in his eye. "If I were you, old buddy, I think I'd let Oak Grove beat us so they can go on to the next round—I sure wouldn't want to tangle with that Hillside bunch."

Tom was inclined to agree with his friend, even though he knew Jason was just joking.

"Well, it's almost high noon," Eric Martin said with a sigh, and the five got up from their seats and made their way down to join the rest of their teammates.

Tom thought about Eric's remark. "Yeah, it's almost high noon, and I feel like I'm gonna be the one who's gunned down in the streets—or, in this case, on the basketball court."

Jason laughed at his remark, thinking how glad he was that

he'd be sitting on the bench, watching the action instead of being out there in it.

The first game was nearly over by the time the Falcons had dressed, and according to a report from the scouts, Hillside had made it to the finals without any problem. Even the reserves were putting on a good show, keeping the Blue Devils from mounting any kind of late charge. Tom was sitting on the bench, listening to the crowd and trying to control his nervousness, when Toby walked up. He bent over Tom with a deep scowl on his face, his teeth clenched in hate. "Listen, Parker, this is just between you and me," Toby said. Jason was listening but pretended not to hear. "If you don't help me win that MVP trophy, I'm gonna give you the worst beating you've ever had. You got that?"

Tom nodded. "Yeah, Toby, I got it."

After Toby walked off, Jason looked at his friend with a stern expression. "You know that sooner or later, you're gonna have to face up to that bully, don't you?"

Tom sighed. "Yeah, Jason, I know, and it may be sooner than you think—I'm not going to lose this game for the rest of my teammates just to make Toby a star."

After the pregame pep talk, the players rushed out the door with a shout and headed down the tunnel leading to the gym floor. As they headed down the tunnel, they met the Hillside Panthers coming back. The Panthers were still yelling and exchanging high fives after a convincing 74–56 win over Cranston. A couple of the more outspoken Panther players pointed fingers at the Falcon players, taunting them. "We want you! You guys are dead meat!" Several of the Falcons were ready to respond, including Tom and Jason, but Coach Waters stepped in before any trouble erupted.

"Save it for the game!" he told his players. "Let's worry about Oak Grove right now."

As they reached the edge of the tunnel, Tom's thoughts came rushing back from a dream he'd had earlier. He knew he'd seen that arena before; it looked just like the place he'd seen in the dream in which he'd shot the basketball into the wrong basket. Terror gripped his throat, making it hard for him to breathe. His dream was coming true—most of it anyway. He was going to shoot the ball into the wrong basket, lose the game, and embarrass himself in front of three thousand people. Sweat popped out on his forehead, and his knees started shaking—he felt as if he were going to faint. But just then, a funny feeling swept over the young freshman—something he had never felt before. There was a peaceful calm slowly ebbing from inside, and a voice spoke to his mind: *Tom, it's going to be all right. Everything is going to be all right.*

"Did you hear that?" He suddenly turned to Jason.

"Hear what?" Jason asked. "I can't hear a thing over the noise of this crowd."

For a moment, Tom thought he had gone crazy. Maybe the pressure had finally pushed him over the edge. Yet there was something different about him—he wasn't afraid anymore. There was peace inside where seconds earlier there had been utter turmoil. *If this is what it feels like to be crazy,* he thought, *then I don't ever want to be sane again.* He followed his teammates out onto the court to the roar of the Falcon faithful.

Staring up into the cheering section, he got an unexpected surprise: sitting halfway up from the scorer's table were his parents, Jason's parents, Megan, Kevin, Julie, and Melissa. His dad caught his son staring at them with his mouth open in surprise, and he gave Tom a thumbs-up. James Parker had missed most of his son's games that season, but he wasn't about to miss this one. They had arrived just before the end of the first game and taken the last group of seats available in the Falcons' cheering section. James had watched the final two minutes of Hillside's rout of Cranston and thought about what a good team the Panthers had. After the final buzzer had sounded, ending the game, he'd spent most of the next few seconds scanning the crowd and thinking about how great it would be if people put as much enthusiasm into serving Jesus as they did into their sports. Then his eyes had caught the Falcon players standing in the mouth of the tunnel, ready to come out onto the court. He'd spied his son standing there as pale as a ghost with a horrified expression on his face. *Tom's having trouble coping with all this*, he'd thought. *Well, maybe I can do something about that.* Giving no thought to how out of place he looked or who might have been staring at him, James Parker had bowed his head and begun to pray.

Lord, I know that what I'm asking is unusual, but you did say in your Word that you love us more than we love our own children. That's why I'm asking you on behalf of one of my children: Tom Parker. Lord, please help Tom; calm his nerves, Lord, and give him the assurance that you're always there for him, just as you have always been there for me. Lord, I know this is just a game, but I believe that you care about everything that affects our lives, and right now, this basketball game is affecting my son's life. So I'm asking you to just help him, Lord—for his sake and for mine. In Jesus's name, amen.

He had finished his prayer and lifted his head just in time to see the Falcons take the floor, and he could tell by the expression on Tom's face that the Lord had answered his prayer. Although it appeared James was raising his eyes to view the ceiling of the arena, his view was directed somewhere much further than that. "Thank you, Lord," he said as a tear trickled down his cheek.

It was then that Tom stared up into the seats and saw them. "Go get 'em, Tom!" his dad shouted with his arms extended and his thumbs pointing upward. His son gave him his patented little crooked smile, waved at Julie, and went back to the layup drills.

After the usual introductions and the national anthem, the Richfield Falcons and the Oak Grove Tigers took the floor. Tom swallowed hard, took a few breaths, and walked to his position at the midcourt circle for the opening tip-off. He was still nervous, but the gut-wrenching fear he'd had in the tunnel was gone. He still couldn't figure out what had calmed him down, but he wasn't about to argue with something if it worked, and this had worked perfectly—whatever it was.

Oak grove controlled the tip and put up a quick shot for an early

2–0 lead. Keith Jeffries inbounded the ball to Tom, who took one step forward and was quickly surrounded by two Tiger defenders—it was the full-court press Coach Waters had warned him about and drilled him on so much during practice. Only now Tom couldn't remember anything the coach had taught him. He was panicking—he knew it, the coaches knew it, the crowd knew it, and more importantly, Oak Grove knew it.

Tom tried to jump over his defenders' heads to get off a pass, but all he got was an elbow to his head, which the referees didn't see. The ball was knocked out of his hand and into the hands of one of the Tigers, who scored an easy layup. Oak Grove was up 4–0 less than twenty seconds into the game. Tom was dazed for an instant, but he quickly gained control of his senses. If only he could have gained his composure that fast, the first half would have gone a little better—but he didn't. He made countless errors both physical and mental and saw his team losing control of the game before the first quarter was over. As the second quarter progressed, he did a little better—but not much. He made a few good passes and was improving on bringing the ball up the court through the Tigers' press, but by the end of the first half, Oak Grove led 31–21, and most of the blame could be traced to a certain young freshman point guard with the name Parker across the back of his jersey.

"You stink!" That was Toby's way of telling Tom that his play wasn't up to par. "My grandma could've played better than that."

Tom sat there silently, wishing Toby's grandma was going back out there for the second half instead of him. He did stink. Toby was the only one with guts enough to tell him, but he knew everybody else was thinking it—including himself. He had done his best, but that full-court press was hard to break, and the boys from Oak Grove had run it almost flawlessly so far.

As he sat with his head in his hands, wishing he could crawl into a hole somewhere, a friendly voice called out to him. "Tom, you're doing good, but you've just got to relax! Don't let their press get to you."

Tom looked up to see who the words of advice were coming from. It was Eddie Gordon, the man he was replacing, with his fractured arm still in a sling. Tom had always liked Eddie; he was a good basketball player and a good point guard, but Eddie was not the conceited type. He had worked a lot with Tom when he was a substitute, helping him with his dribbling and shooting but mainly his attitude toward the game. "Remember, Tom, it's just a game; you do the best you can and try to win, but the most important thing is to have fun, because if you can't have fun doing it, then it's not a game anymore." Tom remembered Eddie telling him that at the beginning of the season, but somewhere amid all the pressure to win and be a success, that truth had gotten shoved into the back of his mind. The sight of Eddie standing there brought it all back. His dad had echoed Eddie Gordon's words only last night: "No matter how big a game it is, it's still only a game."

Tom smiled at Eddie and then gave him a more serious look. "Eddie, do you remember what you told me at the beginning of the season? You know, about basketball being fun, and if you couldn't have fun doing it, then it wasn't a game anymore?"

Eddie smiled at his replacement. "You were listening after all," he said.

"Well, I listened, but I just didn't see what you meant by it—until now, that is," Tom said. "I have made this game so big that it's taken over me. I've created a monster out of an innocent game I have played all my life, and I'm letting it ruin my life, not to mention letting my teammates down."

Eddie looked Tom squarely in the eye. "Well, my friend, what are you gonna do about it?"

"Well, for one thing, I'm going to go out there and show them what Tom Parker can do"—he winked at Eddie—"when he's having fun."

"That's what I like to hear," Eddie said. "Now, get out there, and show them the real Tom Parker."

That was just what Tom did.

Richfield inbounded the ball to start the second half, and as they had in the previous half, Oak Grove started their trapping pressure defense, but this time, they were guarding a different player. He still had the same number on his jersey and the name Parker across the back, but it wasn't the same bumbling, clumsy klutz they'd had so much fun with in the first half.

Tom caught the ball, faked left, and then switched the ball to his other hand and took up the sideline like a freak before the Tigers had time to set their trap. In the confusion, the Tigers had three of their defenders on the other end of the court, which made it easy for Tom to throw a bullet pass to Marques Hall for an easy layup. The Tigers then tried to inbound the ball but were caught off guard by the full-court press of the Falcons—a little trick Coach Waters added at halftime. Eric Martin stole the inbound pass and whipped it to Tom at the foul line. Tom turned and shot. *Swish!* The Falcon crowd was on its feet, cheering; this was the Falcon team they'd come to see.

Oak Grove quickly quieted the Falcons fans with a score of their own, but again, Tom broke through the press, tossing a lob pass to Toby for an easy baseline jumper. Then he and Eric Martin trapped one of the Tiger guards, causing him to make an errant pass that Keith Jeffries turned into a quick layup.

Richfield kept picking away at the Tigers before finally taking the lead halfway through the fourth quarter. The same crowd who had booed Tom so much in the first half were now hailing their young hero, and none was cheering more than his father the preacher. When Tom hit a three-point shot late in the fourth to give the Falcons the lead for good, the crowd, the Falcon bench, and the players on the court erupted—except for one. Toby just looked at Tom and scowled. But Tom didn't notice; he was too busy taking high fives from Keith Jeffries, Eric Martin, and Marques Hall. *This is fun!* he thought to himself.

When the final buzzer sounded, the Falcons trotted off the court with a hard-fought, well-earned victory by the score of 55–52. Tom had thirteen points as well as eight assists and four steals, most of which had come in the second half.

Coach Waters congratulated his team but warned them not to get too excited about the win, because tomorrow night's game with Hillside would be their toughest test of all. Of course, Toby had to get his two cents in: "We almost didn't make it to Hillside because of Parker!"

Tom hung his head, but Coach wasn't about to let that remark go. "Yes, Toby, thanks to Parker, we dug ourselves into a hole, but thanks to Parker, we dug ourselves back out of that hole in the second half. You played a good half of basketball, Parker," he said to Tom. "Let's just hope that in tomorrow's game, you can put two good halves together—we'll need it if we're ever going to beat the Panthers."

Tom raised his head up and smiled. "I'll give it my best shot, Coach—you can count on it."

Coach's remarks helped to soothe Tom's nerves a little. It wasn't easy being ridiculed after he'd just played his heart out, but Tom considered where the ridicule was coming from, so it didn't bother him too much. Toby had had a bad game too, which was probably the reason behind his outburst; he wanted a scapegoat—someone he could lay all the blame on.

Tom and Jason quickly showered and dressed, trying their best to avoid Toby. Tom thought it would be better for the team—and himself—if he stayed out of the hospital until after the Hillside game. "Well, Toby's game tonight sure put a dent in his chances for that MVP trophy," Tom told Jason. "He'll be lucky if he makes it onto the all-tournament team."

Jason smiled and nodded. Toby had scored just twelve points and shot only five of sixteen from the field. Tom had done his best to get him the ball, not because he had threatened him with bodily harm if he didn't but because there had been times when he was open. But Toby had done just what he had done throughout the year: taken shots while being double- and triple-teamed. The coach had even threatened to pull him out of the game if he didn't start passing to the open man, but that hadn't helped. Toby was a one-man show—in his eyes anyway—and he wasn't about to change. The coach had left him in the game but had given Tom instructions to keep the ball away from him—which had infuriated him even more.

Thoughts of revenge went through Toby's young brain—thoughts he had entertained many times in the past. But he would wait to see how the next game went before he carried out his plot. He would wait to see if young Mr. Parker was willing to do things his way or not. *If he does, there'll be no problem, but if not, well, I just hope his preacher daddy has his insurance paid up*, he thought with a grin as he threw his equipment into his gym bag and stomped out of the locker room.

Tom and Jason had a few minutes to talk to their folks and the girls outside the gym before getting on the bus for the trip home. "Tom, you did great!" said his father, and all the others smiled their approval.

"Well, maybe in the second half, but I looked pretty bad in the first half," he said with a wink to his dad.

"Well, you were just nervous in the first half, but that's understandable—this was a big game for you."

It was then Tom remembered what had helped him so much in the second half. "You know, Dad, you were right in what you said last night: this is just a game. I had put so much importance on this game that I had forgotten that. But Eddie Gordon came up to me in the locker room at halftime and reminded me of that. While I was playing the second half, it was just like I was out in the backyard at the house, playing with Jason and some of the boys just for the fun of it. I had worried so much about this game that I let it get control of me, until I realized it was only a game and nothing more. Then I relaxed and was able to play the type of game I was capable of playing."

James Parker's eyes lit up, and he held his hands up toward heaven. "Praise the Lord!" he shouted, causing a few heads to turn.

Then he turned his attention toward his son. "Tom, I prayed that God would help you through this, and he did! Don't you see? Eddie didn't just walk up to you during halftime and give you that pep talk—he was sent from God. I prayed before the game started that God would help you through this, and he has."

Tom felt a funny feeling deep down inside. "Y-you said you prayed for me, Dad? When was that?"

"It was when you all were standing there in that tunnel, waiting to come out onto the court. I could see you were troubled, so I asked God to help you through this."

Tom couldn't believe his ears; that was the same time he had heard the voice calming him down and assuring him that everything was going to be all right. Maybe there was something to this God of James Parker's after all.

"Is anything wrong, Tom?" his mom asked, noticing he was in deep thought about something.

Tom's thoughts returned to the present. "Uh—oh, it's nothing," he said. He didn't want everybody to think he was crazy, so he kept the strange voice to himself. He figured his parents would probably understand, but the others would probably make an appointment for him at the mental hospital.

About that time, the coach yelled for the rest of the team to get on the bus, so Tom and Jason said their goodbyes, kissed their girls, and loaded into the bus along with the other stragglers who had waited until the last minute to board. Julie and Melissa loaded up with Reverend and Mrs. Parker and followed the bus back to Richfield High, where they picked up Tom. Jason's parents pulled into the parking lot a few seconds later, and Melissa climbed out of the Parkers' car to join Jason for the ride home in the Bennetts' car. After everybody was safely settled into his or her respective vehicle, they said their goodbyes again and headed out of the parking lot and toward their homes.

Kevin and Megan had gone to the game in Kevin's sports car, so they were waiting on the rest of the family at the Parker estate.

When his dad drove by Julie's house without stopping, Tom yelled out, "Hey, Dad, I think you forgot something!" but his dad just looked over at Tom's mom and smiled.

"Oh, did I forget to let Julie out? I guess we'll just have to take her home with us."

What his dad was doing didn't make any sense, but Tom figured that was just the way parents were—there was no use in trying to figure them out.

As they got closer to home, though, he realized what his dad's crooked little grin at his mom had been about, for in the driveway were the Bennetts' car, the Stewarts' car, and the Pattersons' car, along with Kevin's sports car. From their reactions, it occurred to Tom that everyone was in on this—whatever it was—except him and Jason. The two players were led up the steps blindfolded and through the front door of the house, where the blindfolds were removed. There was a big banner strung across the living room ceiling that read, "Congratulations, Tom and Jason!" in big, bold letters. This was a victory party. Tom's dad and mom had planned it and invited all the interested parties. Julie's parents were there, as well as Bob and Nancy Bennett and Melissa's parents, Charlie and Robin Stewart. They had meant to surprise the two boys, and from the looks on their faces, the boys were thoroughly surprised.

Tom was the first to speak. "B-but how did you know we'd win?" he asked.

"We didn't," said Hank Patterson as he shook the boys' hands. "Win or lose, we were going to have this party to let you know how proud we are of you." For the first time in his life, Tom felt comfortable around Julie's father.

Jason piped up. "Why didn't you wait until tomorrow night? Then you could have put up a banner that read, 'Congratulations, Regional Champs.'" Everybody laughed.

"Well, we can just have you guys another party tomorrow night," Bob Bennett said. "You know how I love parties." Everybody laughed again—it was easy to see where Jason got his craziness from.

The party lasted until around midnight, when the last car drove away, leaving the Parker clan to sort out the details of that hectic but successful day.

"Well, Tom, what did you think of your party?" his mom asked as they headed up to bed.

"It was great, Mom. I really appreciate it," he answered.

"Well, I want you to know, Son, that I am very proud of you tonight, and I'd be just as proud if the Falcons hadn't won."

His mother's remarks were still going through Tom's head as he got ready for bed. The warmth and love of a caring family made life worthwhile. Wealth and fame might have been nice to have, but all the money in the world couldn't give a person the feeling he or she got from a kind word or a loving hug. Tom had good dreams that night.

NINE

"C'mon, Tom. Get up. You wanted your dad to drive you somewhere, didn't you?" Tom's mother was trying to wake him.

Tom sat up in bed and looked out the window. The sun was coming up over the mountains, sending golden streams of light through his window and across his bed. It was going to be another beautiful day. There was still plenty of snow on the ground from the midweek storm, but the roads were clear, the air was clear, and for once in a long while, his head was clear.

"Now to go find that treasure," he said, throwing the covers back and slinging his legs out across the floor.

In a snap, he had showered and dressed and was at the kitchen table, wolfing down a plate of pancakes smothered in syrup. "Mom, you've outdone yourself again," he said as he soaked up the last bit of syrup with the last forkful of pancakes.

JoAnn turned from the stove, putting her hands on her cheeks. "Why, Tom, flattery will get you everywhere!"

He laughed at his mother's corny remark as he hurriedly got up from his chair and headed toward the basement door. "I have to borrow some of Dad's tools, Mom; I'm sure he won't mind."

He could hear his mom talking as he strolled down the steps. "Just as long as you take care of them and put them back where you got them—you know how your father feels about his tools."

Did he ever—he'd gotten a nice red spot on his rear end when he was eight for losing a ratchet. Nowadays people called it child abuse, but Tom knew it as a good old-fashioned spanking—one he'd deserved.

He got the tools he would need for his third—and hopefully last—big adventure: a shovel, a mattock, a hammer, a chisel, and an old mining light his grandpa Parker had given to his dad just before he died. The light was old and a little rusty, but it still worked, and the battery pack had been fully charged. He stuffed the light deep into his gym bag so no one would see it. He didn't want his parents asking questions, at least until after they had found the treasure. Then he would answer any questions they had.

As he reached the top of the stairs leading from the basement to the kitchen, the doorbell rang.

"Oh, hi, Julie. Come on in. Tom's in the basement, but he should be up any minute." JoAnn Parker was a kind and gentle woman. She always made Julie feel at home whenever she came to visit.

She and Julie were sitting in the living room when Tom walked in and dropped his tools onto the floor.

"Oh, hi, Tom." Julie's eyes lit up when she saw him. "Your mom and I were just talking about you."

"Something good, I hope," he answered.

"Oh, we were just talking about how much we enjoyed watching you play last night."

Tom's head was beginning to swell with all the compliments and praise. But he knew how meaningless last night's game would be if they lost that night. "I just hope you can say the same things about me after the Hillside game," he said with a touch of modesty. "Are Jason and Melissa going to meet us here, or were we supposed to pick them up?"

The ringing of the doorbell answered Tom's question for him, and he looked through the front window and saw the face of his goofy friend standing there with Melissa attached to his arm. Jason spied Tom looking out the window and made one of his funniest faces, which caused Tom to bust out laughing and say, "C'mon in, you two—and hurry. I don't want the neighbors to see what kind of strange people I allow in my house."

Melissa walked through the doorway first, followed by her crazy boyfriend.

"Hi, Mrs. Parker. Hi, Julie," Jason said in the same breath as he removed Melissa's coat and then his own.

"Hi, Jason, Melissa. Can I get you anything? I think I still have some pancakes and sausages left," JoAnn said. That was Jason's cue.

"Well, if it's no trouble, I'll have some; I'd hate to see it go to waste." Jason was a human garbage disposal. He'd eat just about anything to keep it from being wasted.

"Jason, did your dad ever give you the lecture about eating all the food on your plate because of the starving people in Africa?" Tom asked.

"No," said Jason.

"I didn't think so," replied Tom, winking at his mom, who smiled back. She went to the kitchen to get Jason's food together, leaving the four alone in the living room.

"Tom, do you think we'll be able to find the you-know-what?" asked Jason in a soft whisper in case anybody was listening. "A lot can happen to a place in a hundred years."

"I know. I've thought about that," whispered Tom, "and it'll probably be rough going through those woods with all the snow. I'm sure there's more snow up there than we have here, and it hasn't melted that much."

"Do we have everything we need in case we do find it?" asked Melissa.

Tom pointed to his gym bag. "There should be enough tools in there to get the job done. Did everybody bring a flashlight?" Everyone nodded. "Julie, did you bring the plate?"

"Yeah, I've got it," she said. "Boy, I sure hope we find this thing; I'm getting kind of tired of thinking up excuses for getting out of the house, and I know my parents are beginning to get suspicious."

The other three nodded—they knew where Julie was coming from, especially Tom. He'd told his folks more fibs in the last week than he had in the past five years.

Mrs. Parker interrupted their secret meeting. "Jason, your food's ready!" she yelled from the kitchen.

The other three followed Jason into the kitchen, where they talked some more while they watched him eat. He was almost through with his last bite of sausage, when Mr. Parker walked through the back door with a bag of groceries in each arm and his keys dangling from his teeth. After setting the bags down on the counter, he was finally able to put the keys back in his pocket, where they belonged. "Are you kids about ready to go?" he asked.

"As soon as I get down this last bite, Mr. Parker," replied Jason.

James smiled. When Jason had first come to visit them about six years earlier, James had told him, "Make yourself at home," a phrase Jason had taken literally for the past six years. But James didn't mind; he liked seeing a young boy eat—he just couldn't understand how Bob Bennett could afford to feed that boy without having to work two jobs.

While Jason finished his meal, the others loaded their equipment into the back of the old station wagon. James looked suspiciously at Tom's bag as he tossed it into the back. *I wonder how many of my tools he has this time*, he thought, *and how many of them he'll return with.* But as he had all the other times, he let it go—there was no use in asking his son a bunch of silly questions, especially in front of his friends. "C'mon, kids. Let's get going—I have to get to the hospital in half an hour for my visits."

The five loaded up. Tom and Julie sat in front with the preacher, and Jason and Melissa were in the back. Soon the old station wagon was winding its way down Second Avenue toward the intersection of Highway 41.

The old Oak Ridge Road was located in the southwest hills, about six miles from the Richfield town limits. The old, rough road, which was seldom traveled except by an occasional hiker or sightseer, wound its way through the Lewis and Clark National Forest, past Danson's Ridge, and into the Rocky Mountains before coming to an abrupt halt at Highway 68 on the other side. Tom had been on that road only once in his life, when he'd gone with his Boy Scout troop on a camping expedition into the mountains. As he got out of his dad's station wagon, though, it didn't look the same as it had back then. Snow covered the road leading up into the forest, with only one set of tracks in the snow, showing that a vehicle had driven that way.

"Are you sure you kids don't want to wait until some of this snow melts before going up in there?" James asked. But they were all in agreement—it was now or never.

Even though they were growing up, they hadn't grown out of that "I want it, and I want it now" phase. The four kids were after something—James didn't know what, but he figured it must have been pretty important for them to go hiking up into the woods through a foot of snow to get it.

"Okay, if you're determined to go up there, I'll be back for you in three hours," he said, as was part of their agreement. "Now, don't get too far away from the road; I don't want you all getting yourselves lost—you'd freeze to death before we could find you."

After his dad had driven off, Tom and the others busied themselves with getting all their gear together for the long, tedious trip, when a vehicle pulled alongside the four adventurers.

"Excuse me," said the driver, "but do any of you kids know where we can find Marsh Canyon Road? We seem to have gotten ourselves just a little bit lost."

The four just stood there staring for a few seconds before Jason finally spoke up. "You go on down Highway 41 for about four miles until you come to an old abandoned gas station. Turn right at the station, go about two miles, and turn left—that's Marsh Canyon Road."

"Thanks for the information," said the good-looking young guy at the wheel. "Say, if you all are going hiking, you picked a bad time of year to do it."

Jason piped up again. "Well, if you don't mind my saying this, you've picked a bad time of the year to be getting on Marsh Canyon

Road; that road will probably be mighty rough, even for a four-wheel-drive vehicle."

"Well, we're sort of the adventurous type—you know, living on the edge. Kind of like you four, going hiking up into the mountains like that."

Jason couldn't argue with that, so they said their farewells, and the vehicle pulled back out onto the highway. After it pulled away, Julie and Melissa spoke up at the same time: "A red Jeep!"

Tom didn't want everybody getting worked up over nothing, even though he was a little suspicious himself. "Now, we don't know if that's the same red Jeep we saw at the Simpkins house. Those guys look like travelers to me, so let's not go jumping to conclusions."

The others agreed, and they proceeded in getting their gear and heading up the path through the snow that the lone vehicle had made on Oak Ridge Road.

Meanwhile, the Jeep traveled around a sharp curve on Highway 41 before pulling off the road and turning around.

As the snowy road made its way through the vast expanse of trees, the already weary hikers slowly trudged along toward their destination. The snow itself was rough enough, and with all the tools he was carrying, Tom was beginning to wear out quickly. He and Jason were taking turns carrying the heavier tools, such as the mattock and shovel, and Tom was ready to be relieved of his duties for a little while. "Hey, Jason," he yelled to his friend, who was about twenty yards ahead of him, "how about carrying this stuff for a little while? I'm pooped."

Jason stopped and waited on the others to catch up with him. For once, he was anxious to go exploring. There were no haunted houses to break into up there—just an old abandoned mine. "How much farther do you think we have to go before we get to that horseshoe curve on the map?" he asked as he slung the two shovels and the mattock across his shoulder.

"I don't know—it shouldn't be very far from here, though. I'd say we've traveled at least a mile."

Actually, the four had only gone a half mile, but in knee-deep snow, distance was a little harder to measure. By the time they reached the sharply bending curve that marked their first milestone, the hikers were almost wishing they'd taken the preacher's advice to wait for the snow to melt. But they had come too far to turn back now, so they knew they must press forward.

"My legs feel like lead," said Jason as he dropped the tools into the soft snow.

"At least you can feel yours; on the last hundred yards, I had to keep looking down to make sure mine were still there," said Melissa.

"We can rest here awhile, but then we have to get moving—we only gave ourselves three hours, and we've already used up thirty-five minutes just getting up here." Tom was gasping for breath, as were the others.

They sat down in the snow just long enough to get their breath and their bearings.

"Now, according to the map I copied at the courthouse, the mine should be somewhere in that region," Tom said, pointing to a spot to the right of the roadway. There was a high, steep bank up from the road, which would give the kids a slight problem, but it leveled off at the top. Tom wasn't sure how far into the woods they'd have to go to find the mine, so he hurried the others, who reluctantly finished their rest as well as the candy bars Jason had brought along.

With Tom and Jason's help, the girls made it up the steep bank, and although they were covered in snow, they all seemed to be in pretty good shape.

"Okay, where to now?" asked Melissa, knocking the snow off her jacket.

"Let's all spread out about twenty feet apart," Tom said. "Look for anything that resembles a mine opening. Check in every thicket, around every cliff, and in every gulley. Don't pass up anything; that mine is here somewhere, and we have to find it."

The kids spread out, walking slowly, checking every rock and stump and making sure no mine was behind it or around it. The going was tedious as they pushed through the knee-deep snow, and the sound of one falling was heard from time to time. Yet on they trudged, as if their lives depended on it. There was no stopping and no turning back. They knew a fortune in gold could be up there in those hills somewhere, just waiting to be discovered, and they were bound and determined to unlock the mystery and find it.

After checking behind a large boulder to no avail, Tom looked behind him. Far below him, he could see Oak Ridge Road. It looked almost as small as it did on his crude drawing. He looked right to see Julie checking behind a laurel thicket, again to no avail. He looked to his left to see Jason picking himself up after falling headlong into a narrow gulley. Melissa, who was to the left of Jason, yelled over to make sure he was all right. "Yeah, I'm fine," he said, dusting himself off for the umpteenth time.

The hillside was getting steeper, and they were using up a lot of time. Tom knew if they didn't find the mine soon, they'd have to turn back. He knew the girls had hiked about as far as they could through the snow, and so had he and Jason. He yelled to the others, "I think we'd better go on back and wait till a better time! This is crazy—we're never gonna find the mine in all this snow anyway."

Jason was climbing up from the gulley and had almost reached the top, when he lost his footing and fell headlong again, this time covered completely in a snowdrift when he landed. The other three moved over as fast as they could, which wasn't easy in all the snow, to where Jason lay flopping around in the snowdrift like a hooked trout. "Jason, would you get up out of that gulley and stop playing around?" Tom said to his buddy.

"That's not a gulley!" Melissa yelled. "Look!"

Tom and Julie turned to where Melissa was pointing—the gulley led to a huge thicket of laurels. Tom strained to see behind the laurel thicket and then gasped for breath. Had his heart stopped beating? He couldn't tell, but he knew he wasn't breathing—he was too excited to breathe. There, barely visible behind the thicket, was an opening of some kind, almost covered by the drift. The gulley

Jason had accidently fallen into was not a gulley after all; it was a narrow roadway leading to whatever was behind the thicket.

"We found it!" Jason yelled at the top of his lungs, his body still covered in snow.

By that time, Tom and Julie had already moved around the thicket and were staring through the opening. It was a mine all right, but was it *the* mine? The opening had been boarded up, but most of the boards had fallen off, and the ones that hadn't were rotting away.

"How do we know this is it?" Julie asked Tom. "There are mines all over these hills."

"Let's dig around in the snow and see if we can find a sign or something—if not, I guess we'll just have to take our chances," Tom replied.

By that time, Jason and Melissa had joined them, and they started digging, which took a while, considering there was about three feet of snow to dig through.

Tom and Jason had almost reached the bottom, when Melissa glanced up over the mine opening. "What's that?"

Tom and Jason raised their heads, their brows dripping sweat. Over the mine opening, almost completely covered in snow, they could see a small, barely visible corner of wood.

They stopped their digging and tried to reach whatever it was over the mine, but it was too high for either of them. Jason put Melissa on his shoulders and hoisted her up. Straining every muscle she had, Melissa was finally able to rake the snow away from the board with the edge of one of the shovels. There before them was a wooden sign. The right portion was broken off, so all that remained were the letters *Caro*.

"It's the Caroline Mine! We found it!" said Tom, almost too excited to talk.

"Melissa, I sure wish you'd seen that sign earlier. Me and Tom almost broke our backs shoveling all that snow," Jason jokingly said to his girlfriend.

"Well, come on, you guys," said Tom. "We don't have a lot of time, and remember, this mine is over a hundred years old, so be careful—we don't want it coming down on us."

Jason knocked one of the boards covering the mine loose with his dad's pick, making an opening large enough for them to crawl through. After making sure they all got through safely, Tom turned on his mining light and shone it around. The Caroline Mine was narrow, only about six feet wide, and the walls and the roof were braced at five-foot intervals with large wooden beams obviously made of oak. It was evident that after his brother's death, Joe had reinforced the mine to make sure there were no more disasters. There was evidence of a small cave-in about twenty feet into the mine, but there was plenty of room to get by. The mine appeared safe enough to Tom but not to Chicken Little. "Look there at that cave-in, Tom," said the frightened voice of his troubled friend.

Oh no, here we go again, thought Tom to himself as he turned to calm the boy down—again. "Jason, that cave-in could've happened fifty years ago; there's nothing to worry about. Besides, you should have known there'd be a slight bit of danger involved in this."

Jason swallowed hard, trying to regain his composure. "Sure, Tom, I thought about that; I guess it's always easier to face the danger when it's in your mind than when it's right in front of you."

Tom understood; he was scared too, but tried not to show it. "Yeah, Jason, I know what you mean. Well, come on. Let's figure this thing out."

Julie took the second plate from her front coat pocket and held it up to the light. "Let's see here. 'Caroline'—we've got that. Now 'In-35.' We all assumed that must mean 'in thirty-five paces.'"

Tom stepped back to the edge of the mine entrance and started stepping forward. "One. Two. Three." Suddenly, his toe caught on something, sending him reeling forward. He held his arms out just in time to catch his fall, and his hand hit something cold and hard.

"Look, guys." Jason shone his light at the floor of the mine. "It's a miniature train track." Actually, it was a track for mining cars to carry the excess dirt and rock out of the mine.

Tom got up, checked both hands to make sure he wasn't bleeding, and repositioned his light on his belt. "Well, now that we've solved that puzzle, let's get on with our thirty-five paces."

Slowly, counting as he stepped to make sure he got it right, Tom walked into the mine with the others following in single file. Julie was next, followed by Melissa, and Jason brought up the rear—his favorite place. They were careful not to make any sudden moves, for fear of triggering a cave-in. Their breaths came in short, even puffs, and their steps were short and steady. They felt for humps or rocks before setting each foot firmly down.

"Twenty. Twenty-one. Twenty-two." Tom kept pacing with the numbers coming from his mouth in short whispers. "Twenty-seven. Twenty-eight. Twenty-nine."

Jason was excited; he wasn't as scared in the mine as he had been in the house, but he was terrified nonetheless. This was something new to him; the closest he had ever come to an adventure was when he and Tom had explored the old cave at the Tyson farm, but they'd found only a couple bats and some crickets hanging upside down from the ceiling with their antennae tickling Tom's and Jason's bare backs as they walked underneath. This could be different. *There might be bats or crickets in this mine, but there also might be gold in this mine!* His heart started beating faster as he counted along with Tom.

"Thirty-two. Thirty-three. Thirty-four. Hey, Tom, you quit counting. Where's thirty-five?"

"Right here's thirty-five, Jason."

Jason shone his light in Tom's direction, and the beam stopped on an old cart sitting on the tracks. "Okay, here's thirty-five. Now, where do we go from here?" Jason asked Julie.

"According to this plate, we're supposed to go down fifteen paces."

They all looked around—there was no shaft leading down and not even a hole in the floor.

"Well," Tom said with a sigh, "what do we do now?"

A thought entered his mind—one he didn't like entertaining.

Maybe 'Caroline' on the plate didn't refer to the mine. Maybe it had something to do with the house or, worse yet, the towers. Julie and Melissa didn't seem as upset as Tom, though they were a little disheartened.

Jason didn't seem upset at all; he had found a toy to play with. He climbed inside the old mining car, his eyes aglow, and started tinkering with the levers that controlled it. "Oh man, I've always dreamed of riding one of these mining cars through a lost mine— you know, like that movie we saw last summer. I'll bet this thing can go ninety at least."

Tom didn't feel like putting up with Jason and his toys. "Come on. Get out of that thing, Jason. We may as well go on back down and wait for my dad; it looks like we blew this one," he said, disgusted with the way things had been going. "If I could get my hands on that Joe Simpkins for five minutes, I'd wring his neck! He's just toying with us. I'll bet he's looking down on us right now, laughing at the four little fools he's been stringing along. Jason, I said get out of that thing, and let's go!"

Jason got up and began crawling out of the old cart. "Hey, man, this doesn't mean we're gonna go back into that old house, does it?" he asked. Now he was disappointed. Upon seeing the old mining car, he had forgotten what they were there for. His mind had been absorbed by that four-wheeled contraption of bolts and steel, which had been rusted by time but was still in relatively good shape. Now it dawned on him that this had been another wild goose chase, without even a plate to show for all their troubles. As he slowly crawled out of the old cart, being careful not to rip his pants on the jagged edges of metal, his left foot pressed against the lever, knocking it loose from its rusty latch and pushing it forward.

Suddenly, the four heard a rumbling sound coming from deeper inside the mine. "It's a cave-in!" shouted Tom, grabbing Julie's arm and pulling her away toward the outside. "C'mon, Jason! Get Melissa, and let's get out of here!"

Melissa had the beam of her flashlight centered on the source of the rumbling noise. "Tom, Julie, look at that!" she cried. At a spot on the floor about thirty feet from where the mining car sat, a crack was developing, getting wider and wider. Suddenly, the floor dropped away at the crack and into the darkness below. "Jason, get out of the cart—hurry!" Melissa shouted—but it was too late.

The old, rusty mining car lurched forward into the blackness caused by the cave-in. Rolling downward on the miniature track, Jason hung from the car, still in the position he'd been in when it started rolling, trying to get his balance and get back in the car before it picked up any more speed.

For a second or two, it appeared Jason was going to have the ride he'd been talking about earlier. Yet no sooner than it had started, the car came to an abrupt halt, hurling Jason through the air like a pitcher throwing a baseball.

Tom, Julie, and Melissa held their breath for what seemed like an hour. Had the cave-in swallowed up their friend and companion?

When they finally started breathing again, the dust stirred up by the cave-in made it impossible to get any good air into their lungs. Coughing and shining their lights through the dust, straining to see a trace of their friend, the three began yelling into the murky blackness. "Jason! Jason, can you hear me?"

There was no sound.

Tom shone his mining light into the hole as the dust slowly began to settle, but still, there was no sign of Jason. He wondered what would make the ground open up like that; in all the cave-ins he'd seen on TV, the roof had collapsed, but he'd never seen a floor collapse before. But right now, what had caused the cave-in wasn't what was bothering him. Terror gripped his heart. Somewhere down in that hole was his best friend. Was he alive, or was he dead? If he was alive, he could be hurt badly. Until the dust settled, though, there was nothing any of them could do.

Melissa continued to yell through the blackness in hopes of getting some kind of response. Still, they saw and heard nothing. In a moment of panic, she turned to Tom with a look of sheer terror.

"I'm going down in there to get Jason out!" she cried, and she turned and started to step into the opening.

Tom and Julie grabbed her arm and held her back. "Melissa, it's not going to help anything if you fall into that hole and get hurt too," Tom said. "It's gonna be hard enough getting one injured person out of here without making it two."

Julie looked at Melissa. "Tom's right, Melissa; I know how you must feel, but getting yourself hurt or killed isn't going to help Jason. We've just got to wait a few more minutes for the dust to settle, and then we'll be able to get down in there to check on him, okay?"

Melissa finally settled down and waited with Tom and Julie for the air to clear enough for them to explore the opening and find Jason.

After about five more minutes, the air was clear enough for the three to move over to the opening, and they were amazed at what they saw. What they had thought was a cave-in hadn't been a cave-in at all. Only one end of the thirty-foot section of floor had dropped—the end opposite the mining car. The floor next to the mining car hadn't given way; it had stayed in place. The drop had created a ramp about thirty feet long, causing the car to roll forward and stop when it hit the bottom of the ramp.

Tom shone his light around the area where the car had been previously. "Hey, girls, look at this."

The girls fixed their gaze on the beam of light, which was centered on the floor—there were two large hinges holding up that end of the floor, while the other end had dropped. The ramp hadn't happened by accident—somebody had rigged the floor to give way.

Just as Tom knelt to get a closer look at the hinges, he heard a low moaning sound coming from the bottom of the ramp. "Jason, is that you?" he yelled into the opening.

"Oh, my head" was the answer he received.

Everyone breathed a sigh of relief, especially Melissa. She took off down the ramp, feeling the wall with her free hand to make sure she didn't stumble. "Jason, are you all right?" she asked her boyfriend. "We were so worried about you."

By that time, Tom and Julie had forgotten about what had created the ramp, and they were making their way behind Melissa to the bottom.

Jason was sitting in a small room, rubbing his head, with an expression of pain on his face. "Man, what a ride," he said as he looked around to see where he was. His flashlight had busted at the end of his trip, so he had to wait until the other three got down with their lights before he could find out what had stopped the car so abruptly, what he had bumped his head on, and whether he was in a room under the mine or had died and gone to the outer darkness he'd heard Tom's dad preach on.

Melissa ran over to Jason, wrapped her arms around his neck, and almost knocked him down again. "Oh, Jason, I'm so glad you're not dead," she said, planting a kiss on his dirty forehead.

"So am I, Melissa," he said, "but where in the world are we? What is this place anyway?"

By then, Tom and Julie had reached the bottom. "Jason, believe it or not, this is our 'Down-15'!" Tom exclaimed. "I counted the number of paces as I walked down this ramp, and right here"—he shone his light at a spot just in front of the mining car—"is number fifteen." Tom laughed as he walked over to his fallen friend. "Jason, I'm never gonna make fun of you and your imagination again."

"Why is that?" Jason asked. He was still having trouble figuring all of this out, and the nasty bump on his head wasn't helping much.

Tom proceeded to explain. "Well, Jason, something in the mining car triggered some sort of mechanism in the mine, which caused this one end to give way, creating the ramp. Understand?"

Jason shook his head. "Not really," he said.

Tom said, "Well then, Jason, let me ask you this: Did you push one of those levers while you were getting out of the car?"

Jason's eyes lit up. "Yeah, I pushed a lever over with my foot as I was crawling out of that thing. That's when the floor dropped, and I took my ride."

Tom walked over to the mining car, shining his light all around to see if he could find what he was looking for. "Aha! Here it is!" he exclaimed. He shone his light on a thin metal cable leading from the mining car up to where the floor had given way. "You see, Jason, when you pushed that lever, it tightened this cable, triggering some kind of mechanism that brought this end of the floor down." Tom smiled and shook his head. "I've got to hand it to Joe Simpkins; this guy was a genius—who else would have thought up something like this?"

Jason's eyes lit up again. "You mean to tell me the treasure is down here?" He had forgotten about his headache and was up on his feet in an instant. "Okay, gang, what are we waiting for? Let's solve the rest of this code and get this gold—or whatever it is."

Julie produced the metal plate from her coat pocket again and continued reading the inscription. "Okay, now we go left ten paces."

To make sure he got it right the first time, Tom double-checked the fifteen paces down the ramp, ending up in the same position he had before. Taking his time, he then turned to the left and paced off the necessary ten paces according to the code. "Now what?" he asked Julie.

She looked at the plate again and then at Tom. "Well, it just says, 'Down.' There's no number on this one."

Tom shone his light in Jason's direction. "Well, Jason, do you feel like digging?"

Jason smiled. "Are you kidding? For a treasure in gold, I'd dig with a teaspoon if I had to."

Using Jason's pick, Tom's mattock, and their shovels, the boys dug feverishly for about ten minutes, creating a hole the size of Granny Parker's old wash tub. The dirt was hard but not very rocky, so they had little trouble in their digging. Tom checked his watch and discovered they had only fifty-five minutes left before their rendezvous with his dad, so he knew they would have to hurry.

If only Joe had given them some indication of how far down they needed to go, it would have made things easier. But for all they knew, this thing—whatever it was—could be ten feet down. Jason was determined to find this treasure, however. Tom had never seen his friend work so hard.

"C'mon, Jason. Slow down. With that nasty bump on your head, you shouldn't be straining yourself like that. I'll bet you're—"

Tom didn't get a chance to finish his sentence. Jason's pick had struck something solid only a few inches from the bottom of the hole. Excitedly, the two went to work clearing away all the excess dirt from their find. The girls held their breath again, and every light beam was aimed at the bottom of the hole. As Tom cleared away the last remaining handfuls of dirt, every eye strained in the darkness, hoping to be the first to see their treasure—but what they saw didn't look much like a treasure.

Tom reached down and picked up their prize, the reason for all their work and trouble: a small metal box approximately twelve inches wide, eighteen inches long, and four inches deep. Rust had nearly eaten up what remained of the metal, but it was still intact and still secured with an antique lock also covered with rust. He looked up at his friends with a wave of disappointment covering his face. "Well, gang," he said, "I don't know what it is, but one thing's for sure: it's not gold."

Jason's dreams shattered again. How many more times was this old dead miner going to lead them around like blind rats in a maze? He looked at Tom with sad eyes and sighed. "Well, let's open it up and see what it is."

Tom set the box down a few inches from the hole and reached for the pick. After he hit the lock three times, the rust finally gave way, and the lock fell to the ground. Then, using the flat end of the pick to pry with, he was finally able to break the strong grip the rust had on the box, and the lid sprang open.

Looking inside, the four saw a rectangular object wrapped in cloth. As Tom removed the cloth from the object, they noticed that it was a book of some sort, and upon further investigation, Julie read the words on its cover: Holy Bible. It was a Bible—just a plain old everyday King James Version. *I'd cry if I wasn't a teenager,* Tom thought to himself. Looking at Jason, he could tell his friend was trying to hold back tears as well.

"A Bible!" Jason yelled. "Is that all our secret treasure is—a Bible?"

By that time, Julie had picked the old Bible up and was flipping through its pages. "Hey, look here, you guys. There's a marker here." The others looked at the Bible, which was marked about two-thirds of the way through by a piece of red ribbon already half rotten.

"So it's marked—big deal," Tom said as he rose and started getting his tools in order. "C'mon, gang. We've got forty minutes to get down out of here and catch my dad; I'm not hanging around here one more minute."

Ignoring Tom's remark, Julie turned to the page in the Bible that was marked and shone her flashlight onto it. There were two verses of scripture underlined in the book of Matthew, in the sixth chapter. "Tom, I think I've found out the last part of the codes," she said, looking down at the Bible. "Listen to these two verses." She proceeded to read from Matthew 6:20–21, adding her own emphasis:

> But *lay up for yourselves* treasures in Heaven, where neither moth nor rust doth corrupt, and where thieves do not break through nor steal; for where your treasure is, there will your heart be also.

Julie moved her light from the verses she had just read and shone the beam onto the faces of her three friends, who had confused looks on their faces. "Well, don't you get it?" she asked. Realizing they didn't, she proceeded to explain. "Don't you see? The term *lay up* on the first plate didn't have anything to do with basketball or bricklaying. If you put the term *lay up* on the first plate with the 'for yourselves' on the second plate, you have 'lay up for yourselves,' the start of Matthew 6:20."

Melissa spoke up. "You mean to tell me that the treasure people have been looking for all these years has turned out to be the treasure in heaven that these Bible verses talk about?"

Julie sighed. "Yes, that's what it looks like; I guess Joe Simpkins must have gotten religious in his last days, and this was his message to any would-be treasure hunters that heaven is where you find your real treasure."

Tom picked up the biggest rock he could find and hurled it across the room; it ricocheted off one of the walls and back against the mining car, making a terrible clanging noise. He was mad. "I just can't believe it!" he yelled at the top of his lungs, too upset to even think that all the noise he was making might cause the mine to cave in. "We've spent all this time and trouble breaking into a house and wading through knee-deep snow to this stupid mine, and what do we come up with? A sermon in an old Bible! I could've saved myself the trouble and gone to church so my dad could preach to me. This Joe Simpkins must have been the craziest man who ever came out of these hills!"

Julie, who had been listening intently to her boyfriend's tantrum, finally spoke up. "Tom, I don't think Joe was the one who was crazy—I think it's us. I mean, here we are, running around in weather like this. Jason nearly got himself killed on that mining car, not to mention all the lies we all told our parents to keep our secret—and for what? So we could find this treasure that turned out not to be a treasure at all. No, Tom, Joe Simpkins was the smart one—it's us. We're the crazy ones."

Heading back out of the mine, feeling lower than a snake's belly in a wagon rut, the young teens walked along, not talking. Julie brought the Bible along. She said maybe they could sell it to a museum—at least that way, they could get a little something for their trouble.

By the time they made it back down to Oak Ridge Road, they'd noticed that another set of tire tracks were present. A second vehicle had taken the chance and tried to make it into the mountains, but from the looks of the disturbance in the snow, whoever it was had decided to turn around and head back down. The four made it back down a lot easier than they had made it up, mainly because the journey was almost all downhill. They were still ten minutes late, however, and Tom's dad was waiting on them.

Seeing their glum expressions as they got into the car, James could tell they hadn't found what they were after. "Looks like things didn't go too well for you guys," he said.

They all shook their heads. "No, Dad, things didn't go well at all," Tom answered. James pulled out onto the highway and headed toward home, carrying a gloomy group of teens with him.

The ride to the Parker house was quiet. None of the kids felt like talking, and James was afraid to say anything, for fear of getting an earful from his son, so he kept his mouth shut until they reached the house. As he pulled into the driveway and shut off the engine, though, he gazed around at the forlorn looks and couldn't keep quiet any longer. "Look, you kids, I don't know what this is all about, but you'd better pull yourselves together—especially Tom and Jason. You've got an important game in just a few hours, and you'd better be prepared for it."

The little speech seemed to shake the teens up some, and they sat there for a few seconds staring at each other. "Dad's right," Tom said. "We've got to snap out of this; tonight's game is the biggest game of my life, and I've got to be ready for it."

As James got out of his car, he thought to himself, *It's good to know that the old man is right about something.* Most teenagers seemed to think they knew it all, so it was comforting when they took an adult's advice about something. He had gotten so used to his son telling him how wrong he was about everything that it was reassuring to hear him say, "Dad's right."

JoAnn Parker was sitting on the couch in the living room, watching TV and mending a tear in Tom's favorite shirt, when James walked through the front door, grinning from ear to ear. "What are you so happy about?" she asked her husband. "You must have gotten the board to approve that new fellowship hall you've been wanting for so long."

James walked over to the where his wife sat, leaned over, and planted a kiss on her cheek. "No, it's nothing like that. I just gave the kids some advice, and believe it or not, they took it."

JoAnn's eyes got bigger. "You're kidding!" she exclaimed. She too had had her bouts with her two teenagers, so she was surprised to hear that one of them actually had agreed with a grown-up. "Well, what was it all about?"

James sat down next to his lovely wife and relayed to her the whole story of the trip. When he came to the part about picking them up after their trip, he paused and frowned. "You know, honey, when I saw the kids coming out of those woods, I couldn't believe it—they had dirt and mud all over them. And Jason looked like he'd taken a bath in a pigpen. And that's not all—he had a big bump on the side of his head. He tried to hide it, but I saw it." He paused again for a few seconds and then continued. "What I can't understand is, how did they get so dirty traveling through the woods in knee-deep snow?"

"Maybe they found a cave and went exploring," JoAnn said.

"Well, I guess that would explain it, but what would they need all those tools for? Tom took one of my shovels and a mattock, and Jason took a shovel and a pick."

This time, JoAnn frowned and then looked curiously at her husband. "Couldn't you get Tom to tell you what this is all about?"

James shook his head. "I tried to find out the other night, but Tom would say only that he'd tell me all about it after it was all over with—whatever that means."

The two shut up as the four teens walked through the front door. They had perked up slightly but only because they knew they had to. They all said their hellos to Mrs. Parker and then proceeded to take off their soiled outer clothing. Jason looked like a little dirty-faced boy at the market whose daddy had brought him along just because he wanted to come. He headed upstairs to the bathroom to wash off, while Tom and the girls headed to the kitchen for a snack. James looked over to JoAnn, who was curiously waiting to hear more. "I'll have to tell you the rest of it later," he said with a smile as he picked up his newspaper. He knew his wife hated to be cut off in the middle of a story, but he couldn't take the chance of the kids overhearing.

In a few minutes, Jason came down the back staircase, looking cleaner than he had when he'd gone up—but his expression wasn't much better. They were all disappointed in their "treasure."

"Julie, did you look through that Bible to see if there were any plates like the other two we found?" Tom asked in a whisper. He didn't want his mom and dad to hear.

"Yes, I looked all through the Bible—three times, to be exact—but there's nothing else in there. Those verses are the only ones I saw underlined too."

Jason was starting on his second sandwich by then. One thing was for sure: the disappointment hadn't spoiled his appetite. "So I guess the treasure hunt is over," he said, reaching for the pickle jar. "I suppose I'll have to send back the red sports car I ordered, as well as the four Super Bowl tickets."

Tom smiled at Jason's remarks, but he wasn't in the mood for any humor right now. He had been certain before that day began that he would be rich by the time it ended. He had visualized a TV news crew at the mine as the four came out with their treasure chest full of gold bars, and he'd imagined all the reporters and newspaper people asking him how it felt to uncover the infamous Simpkins treasure. But it was not to be. There was no gold, publicity, picture in the paper, or spot on the talk shows. Their big adventure was over, and they would have to go back to their normal everyday lives. Tom wondered, though, after all the four had been through, if life would ever get back to normal for them.

After Jason and Melissa left, Tom and Julie went up to Tom's room for a few minutes to sort everything out. Tom knew he had to pull himself together before game time. This was to be the biggest game of his life, and he had to be ready both physically and mentally. Yet at that moment, the game seemed unimportant and uneventful. They had discovered the secret of the century, and it had led them nowhere. All the trouble, lies, and secrets of the past week had produced two plates and an old Bible—some treasure!

"Julie, do you think there may have been something we missed—maybe at the house or in the mine? I just can't make myself believe that this Bible is the lost Simpkins treasure."

Julie looked lovingly into the eyes of her boyfriend. "I know, Tom. It seems crazy to me too, but we did the best we could—the plates gave us the directions, and we followed them to the letter. C'mon. Let's try to forget about this, at least until after tonight's game—remember what your dad said."

"Yeah, I remember, but it's gonna be rough to keep my mind on the game with this hanging over my head."

The two continued to talk, with Julie trying to steer Tom's mind away from the treasure. They talked about the game, how hard Mr. Thorndyke's history class was, and how much they cared for each other.

Meanwhile, James and JoAnn were downstairs, continuing their conversation. "Well, I told the kids to straighten up and forget about whatever it was that had them depressed—and believe it or not, they listened," James told his wife.

JoAnn was a little puzzled. "Well, I can't understand what this project, or whatever it is, is all about. Those kids have been acting very strange lately—especially that kid of ours."

James smiled. He knew what his wife meant. "I understand, honey, but we're just gonna have to trust him and give him some space. Whatever he's doing, it hasn't gotten them into any trouble—yet. Until it does, the two of us are going to have to trust him. Tom's not a little boy anymore; he's a young man, and we can't hover over him. We'll have to wait until he's ready—then he'll tell us."

TEN

Julie left for her house at four o'clock, giving herself enough time to get ready for the game. As much as Tom loved her company, he was glad she had left. He needed a few minutes to get his thoughts in order before he too had to get ready. The Falcons were huge underdogs for that night's game, according to the paper—a fact that didn't surprise Tom or anyone else. He knew that if he didn't play well that night, it wouldn't matter much. After all, no one was expecting him to—no one, that was, except Tom.

He had always pushed himself in everything he did—that was the Parker way. He knew what he had to do that night, but he wasn't sure he was ready to do it—that was what was bothering him. All the cheers and ovations of the night before would quickly be forgotten if he wasn't able to come up with at least as good a performance. He was worried about the game, which was a comfort of sorts—at least his mind was on the game now instead of that Bible. He wondered how much trouble he'd have with Toby; whether he'd be able to guard Luke Dotson, Hillside's hotshot guard; and how disappointed his parents would be if he fell on his face.

He didn't have time to do much worrying, though, as he heard his mom yelling at him from the bottom of the stairs. "Tom, it's almost time to go to the school, so you'd better be getting ready!"

The players always had to board a bus at Richfield High and travel together to the away games; it was school policy. Plus, it gave the coaches a chance for a little extra coaching along the way. Tom had a feeling the fifty-mile trip from Richfield to Mayfield College would be the longest ride of his life. Of course, if they lost, the ride back would be even longer.

As Tom pulled his bike into the Richfield High parking lot, he spotted Jason heading into the front of the school, where the rest of the team was assembled. As usual, Tom was the last to arrive, though to save time, he'd ridden his bike instead of walking. "Hey, Jason, wait up!" he yelled.

Jason turned to face his friend, displaying a large white bandage across the left side of his forehead. "Hi, Tom!" he yelled. "My mom made me put this patch over my cut in case somebody hits me in the head. Of course, if I get hit in the head in this game, it'll probably be by a flying box of popcorn." Jason had perked up a little since Tom had seen him last.

"What did you say to your folks about the bump on your head?" Tom asked.

"Oh, I just told them I fell in the snow and hit it on a rock. That's not really lying—I did fall in the snow, and I did hit my head on a rock, just not at the same time. So are you ready to whip up on those Panthers?" He smiled, winking at Tom.

"You bet I am!" Tom returned Jason's wink with one of his own. Of course, as much as he wanted to beat those big-headed braggarts, he felt Richfield didn't have much of a chance.

Tom was right; the bus ride was one of the longest he'd ever taken. Every one of the players seemed to be on edge—except, of course, for everybody's favorite egomaniac. "We're gonna pound them guys into the ground!" Toby yelled, thumping his fist against the back of one of the seats. "That is, if Parker gets me the ball!" His fiery eyes cut a path across the bus to where Tom was sitting.

Tom paid no attention to Toby's remarks but did glance up to see Coach Waters, who was taking in the conversation. The coach stood up in his seat to face the players—one in particular—and gave an unusual talk.

Sam Waters had been in that situation many times before, so this game was nothing new to him. Yet he had never coached a more arrogant, self-centered kid than Toby Miller. He'd coached Toby last year, but it had been different then; Toby had been only a role player, so his head hadn't started to swell. But this year, Toby was a starter and their leading scorer. His ego was moving along at a much higher level than his scoring average, though, and the last few games, Coach sensed that it was getting out of hand. He knew that if he didn't do something, that night's game could easily get out of hand also.

"Guys, I wasn't going to say anything until just before the game, but now I feel like something needs to be said. If we're going to win this game, it's going to take an all-out effort on the part of each and every one of you—but as a team, not as a bunch of hotshots who want to single-handedly beat Hillside." The coach sent a fiery look in Toby's direction—even more intense than the one Toby had given to Tom. "Toby, I'm talking to you now. The rest of the team can listen, but it's you I want to get this one thing across to: if I hear you make any more remarks like the one I just heard, your name won't be on the MVP Trophy; it won't even be in tonight's lineup. Is that clear?"

Toby swallowed hard, nodded, and settled shamefully back into his seat. Tom hated to see anybody get chewed out, even if he deserved it, but at least the coach's little speech should shut Toby up—for a little while anyway.

The Mayfield College gym was filling up fast. The people of Region Three loved and supported their schools, especially the football and basketball programs. Large banners hung across the front of the huge sports complex, displaying phrases like "Go Falcons!" and "Tear 'em up, Panthers!" Tom had been nervous before, but his stomach was doing flip-flops now. Jason sat calmly in his seat while his buddy squirmed from one side to the other. "Boy, Jason, I wish it was you starting this game instead of me."

"Oh, you'll do fine—just remember how you whipped Oak Grove last night," Jason answered.

"Yeah, but there's only one difference: Hillside is not Oak Grove. They're the best team in the state, and I'm gonna be guarding one of the best players in the state," said Tom. "Boy, I'll sure be glad when this is over with; I think I'm breaking out in a rash."

By the time the Falcons were dressed out and heading down the long tunnel to destiny, the crowd had swelled to capacity. Tom heard a deafening roar just before they made it to the tunnel entrance. The Hillside Panthers had taken the court, and their fans were showing their approval. Tom took deep breaths, trying to loosen up and, more importantly, gain his composure. Then it happened, just as it had happened the night before: an overwhelming peace flooded Tom's mind and body.

This time, he knew what it was: his dad was praying again. He looked up into the rows and rows of seats, scanning every section before finally spotting James Parker with his head bowed, looking out of place among the screaming mob. "Thanks, Dad," he said under his breath. Then, looking upward, he mouthed, "And thank you, God."

There must have been something about this God, and Tom was going to find out—but right now, he had a game to play.

The Richfield crowd roared its approval as the Falcons made their way onto the gym floor and went through their warm-up drills. Tom took a couple glances at the Panthers' side of the gym. There he was—Luke Dotson. It was easy to see why the young man had been named first team all-state. His easy, fluid motion, ball handling, and shooting touch made him an all-around player capable of scoring thirty points and dishing out a dozen assists all in the same game. He'd accomplished that feat a couple times that year, and if Tom didn't do his job, he'd do it that night as well. *Oh, how I wish Eddie Gordon's arm wasn't broken and he was guarding Luke instead of me*, Tom thought. He turned his gaze to the Falcon bench, where Eddie, whose arm was still cradled in a sling, sat watching the action.

Eddie caught Tom's glance, gave him a thumbs-up, and yelled, "You can do it, Tom!"

"I wish I was as sure of that as you are!" Tom yelled back.

After the player introductions, the national anthem, and

last-minute pep talks by both coaches, the teams took the court for the opening tip-off. Coach Waters hadn't said much to Tom during his pep talk, just to do the best he could and try to slow Luke Dotson down. "I know you won't be able to completely stop him—just try to contain him and slow him down," Coach had told him.

As Tom walked onto the court, he felt another wave of serenity flow over him. It was not unlike what he'd felt in the tunnel, only this feeling was even stronger. He sensed a presence unlike anything he'd ever felt before. *If this thing isn't from God, then this place must be haunted*, he thought to himself as he found his place around the half-court circle.

Tom reached out to shake the hand of Luke Dotson as he awaited the tip-off. "Good luck," he said to Luke in a calm tone that surprised even him.

"Yeah, good luck to you too—you're gonna need it!" Luke replied. It appeared Luke's success had gone to his head.

I wonder if he's any relation to the Miller family from Richfield, Tom thought as a smile crossed his face. A remark like that would have destroyed him on any other night but not that one. Tom Parker was out in the backyard again, having fun with his friends, and win or lose, he was going to give it his best shot. Neither Luke Dotson nor any other player on the Hillside team was going to shake his confidence, not on that night.

Hillside controlled the tip, sending the ball in Luke's direction. Tom moved over quickly on defense, staying so close to his opponent that the two looked like Siamese twins. But as quick as a flash, Luke faked Tom to his right and then moved to the three-point stripe and nailed a three-point jumper. As the ball swished through the net, Luke looked over at Tom with a sneering grin. "There's plenty more where that came from," he said mockingly as he headed back up the court to set up on defense.

Tom wanted to say, "Not if I can help it," but he figured that would only add fuel to the fire, so he kept his mouth shut and turned to receive the inbound pass from Keith Jeffries.

Moving quickly up the court, Tom whipped a pass to Eric Martin, who in turn found Toby in the corner. This was Toby's moment in the sun, and of course, he was going to make the most of it. He turned and popped a baseline jumper over the two defenders who were trying to guard him. It appeared at first as if the game was going to be a contest between the two hotshots, Dotson and Miller, the two whose egos had fully surpassed their playing abilities. But as the crowd settled down to watch the two-man battle of skills, another player entered the picture—a player who had been riding the bench only a week ago.

Tom stole the inbound pass and whipped a pass under the basket to a wide-open Marques Hall for an easy layup. Tom then tightened up on his defensive pressure, causing Mr. Dotson to take a bad shot, which Marques Hall rebounded and sent quickly up court. Tom took off like a shot to the other end of the court, took the pass from Eric Martin, and hit a three-point shot over the outstretched arms of Luke Dotson.

Luke's eyes widened as he looked into the face of his opponent. *They told me this guy was gonna be a pushover*, he thought as he turned and waited for the inbound pass. Tom was playing with the poise and confidence of a seasoned veteran. The young man who was supposed to be the weak link in the Falcon chain was proving to be the spark his team needed to defeat the Panthers.

But Hillside hadn't gone through the season undefeated by rolling over and playing dead. The Panthers gained their composure, and by halftime, they had built a ten-point lead, 38–28. Statistically, Tom had held his own against the superstar Luke Dotson. Their point totals were even, with each scoring twelve points, and Tom was only one back in the assist column. Right now, though, the points and assists didn't mean anything to young Parker. The Falcons were behind—and not only that, but they were behind a team that had maintained a reputation for getting big leads and increasing them. He knew the second half could be worse than the first if they didn't find some way to stop Hillside's potent offense and penetrate its sticky defense.

Coach Waters gazed at the players in the locker room, as if pondering what words he could say to them that would work the miracle they needed to pull the game out. Tom was seated next to Jason, his uniform drenched with sweat, panting for every gulp of air he could take into his burning lungs. It was easy to see that the young man was giving his all to win the game. Jason sat there as fresh as a daisy, disturbed that his team was trailing but realizing he would probably have no chance in helping to pull this one out. "Tom, you're doing great, man," he said to his teammate. "You're keeping up with that hotshot Dotson, and that's something nobody thought you'd do—not even me."

"I just wish we weren't so far behind; the way Hillside plays, a ten-point deficit is gonna be very hard to make up." Tom had barely gotten his statement out before Coach Waters addressed the team.

"Men, we're going to have to tighten up on defense if we ever hope to win this game. Toby, you're gonna have to take away the baseline from the Mullins kid. Eric, you and Tom continue to stay in Dotson's face. You've contained him pretty good in the first half, but you've got to keep up the pressure—he's capable of taking over the game if we let him."

The coach didn't have to tell Tom about Luke Dotson. He and Eric had played their hearts out, and all they could do was slow the young superstar down.

The coach continued. "Now, guys, I want you to remember this: the game is not over, not by a long shot. We still have a half of basketball to play, and we can win this game—that is, if you want to win bad enough. Now, let's get out there and win this game for the Falcons of Richfield High!"

As the players headed toward the locker room door with a mighty yell, Tom went over Coach Waters's talk in his mind. He'd heard Coach's remark about winning for the Falcons of Richfield High at the start and the half of every game that year, yet this time, it sounded different. He didn't know if the coach had said it in a different tone this time or if maybe he'd just listened a little bit better than he had in the past. One thing was for sure, though: this time, it made him even more determined to try to win the game. That old Bible was completely out of his mind—for now.

From the start of the second half, the Hillside team looked as though they were going to turn the game into a rout. Blake Mullins blew past Toby along the baseline for an easy layup, and James Hayden, the other guard, hit a short jumper over the outstretched fingertips of Eric Martin. It was then that disaster struck for the Falcons. Tom was bringing the ball up the floor, glancing up at the scoreboard as he went: 42–28. Suddenly, he spotted a wide-open Toby in the right corner. Lobbing the ball over Luke's hands, he placed a perfect pass into the hands of his egotistical teammate. What happened next surprised everybody on the court, on the bench, and even in the stands: Toby passed up a wide-open baseline shot and, putting the ball on the floor, headed toward the basket. The only problem was, Blake Mullins was standing there, all five feet eleven inches and 185 pounds of him, creating an obstacle between Toby and the easy layup.

"Shoot it, Toby; you've got the shot," Tom said under his breath.

No sooner had he gotten the words out than he saw Toby collide with his opponent, sending both players crashing to the floor. To make matters worse, Toby came up swinging, and he caught an unsuspecting Blake Mullins off guard with a wicked right cross to the chin. The referee, who had already called a charge on Toby, moved in quickly to break up the fight. Blake came up and lunged toward Toby, only to have some of his teammates grab him and hold him back.

Marques Hall had caught Toby by the arm and was restraining him, when the ref blew his whistle, slinging his arm toward the sidelines. "Okay, Miller, you're out of the game!"

When Toby heard that, he went berserk; he pulled himself from Marques's grasp and ran toward the ref, shouting obscenities as he went, with his fist clenched, looking as though he were ready to shove the whistle down his throat.

Tom tried to grab Toby, but it was no use; Toby slung him aside like a rag doll and continued his quest—only to find himself standing face-to-face with Coach Waters. "Toby, get to the showers—now!"

At that point, Toby knew it was over; there would be no more fighting—not that night anyway. Toby shouted a few more hostile phrases over his shoulder as he proceeded to the locker room.

By the time the smoke had cleared, Hillside had a free-throw opportunity via the technical foul, plus the ball. Coach Waters called a much-needed time-out before the foul shot to get his team together. As boastful as Toby was, he was still the Falcons' best player, and it would be a whole lot tougher to win without him. Coach now had an important decision to make: Who was going to replace their fallen star? He gathered the players around him and, looking over the situation carefully, made his decision: "Bennett, you go in for Miller."

Jason's head twisted around so fast he nearly pulled his neck out of its socket. "You want *me* to go in for Toby, Coach?" he whimpered. "Are you sure?"

"Don't argue with me, Bennett; get your warm-up jacket off, and report to the scorer's table. Now, boys"—he was back to calling them boys again, as Coach didn't think he should call a team that was losing by fourteen points men—"it's going to be a lot tougher without Toby in there. Just give me all you've got, and I'll be proud of you, regardless of the outcome. Parker, I want you to take more shots than you have been taking. If we're gonna catch up, we've got to open up their defense, and the only way to do that is with the outside shots. Hall, I want you to help Bennett on defense, especially when Mullins gets the ball. We can still win this game—it's not over yet. Now, let's get in there and show those Panthers what we're made of."

Blake Mullins calmly sank the free throw, and Hillside lined up to take the ball inbounds. Tom looked at Jason, who was obviously nervous. One minute he'd been relaxing on the bench, and now he was in the game. This would be his one chance to prove himself, but Tom was sure he would rather have let somebody else have the glory. Besides, the bump on his head was beginning to bleed a little through the patch. Entering the game was not something Jason Bennett was looking forward to. Tom looked toward his friend and mouthed, "Calm down." Jason nodded and moved into position to guard Blake Mullins.

Hillside inbounded the ball in Luke's direction, and suddenly, a small, skinny arm reached in to knock the ball from Luke's outstretched hands. Before the Panthers could react, Tom Parker raced down the court for an easy layup. It was evident that young man, win or lose, was going to fight all the way to the end. The Falcon crowd roared its approval; it was one of the few chances they'd had to cheer all night.

As quick as a flash, Tom set up on defense and slapped away another Panther pass—right into the hands of Jason Bennett. Jason quickly faked Blake Mullins out of position and went up for a soft jump hook shot. *Swish!* The crowd erupted again. The lead was down to eleven points now, and it seemed the Falcons weren't going to be routed. The Hillside coach called for a time-out. Tom looked at the score-board: 43–32. The game was still in their grasp.

Tom then looked at Jason with a wide smile sweeping across his face. "Where did you learn that shot?" he asked, referring to the jump hook.

"Aw, I used to practice that shot all the time," Jason said with a quick grin. "It's the only shot I have that won't get stuffed back in my face by that Mullins kid."

"How's your head feeling?" Tom asked.

"It's okay. Hurts a little bit, but I think I can make it," he answered.

The coach's advice was just to keep up the pressure and not give Hillside any open shots. The Falcons seemed to take the advice pretty well too, for they kept chiseling away at the Panthers' lead.

At the end of the third quarter, the score was 49–42, and midway through the fourth, they had narrowed the deficit to 56–51. Both crowds were going crazy. The Panther faithful were pleading with their team to hang on, while the Falcon supporters were yelling for their team to catch up.

Luke Dotson hit a jumper, putting the lead back up to seven, but Tom nailed a three-pointer at the other end, cutting the lead to four points, the closest they had been since early in the game.

The most amazing thing about the Falcon comeback was that it was being led by two benchwarmers. Tom and Jason were playing their hearts out, which inspired the others on the team to play better. The loss of Toby hadn't hurt the Falcons at all—in fact, it had helped them. They were playing as a team, a close-knit unit, a well-oiled machine, and it looked as if Hillside didn't have the equipment to shut the machine down.

With two minutes to go in the game, Hillside led 62–59, and Tom was gasping for breath. He'd played almost the entire game, a feat he was not accustomed to in the first place, and that was taking its toll on the youngster. James, JoAnn, and Megan Parker were cheering on their young heroes, along with Julie, Melissa, Kevin, and, of course, Bob and Nancy Bennett. This was the time when all of the players on both squads would have to reach down deep inside for that extra something—that little pocket of energy kept stored away for such a time as this. The game was going to be won or lost depending on which team wanted it the most. The last two minutes of a game were a test not of skill or ability but of endurance, stamina, and, mainly, desire—the desire to run down that errant pass or go after that rebound, no matter how much your legs hurt or your thumping heart told you not to.

The rest of the game meant nothing now; as far as the Falcons were concerned, the score was 3–0, and they had to make up that deficit no matter what it took. This was their time—their moment to show how much guts and determination they really had—and the next two minutes would tell whether they had it or not.

Luke brought the ball up the court slowly, trying to keep it away from the outstretched arms of the little pest who had already made six steals. He whipped a bullet pass to James Hayden, who brought it over the time line before returning it to his teammate. Luke then put the ball on the floor, moving swiftly toward the basket. Tom moved over quickly to cut him off but was too late. The ref blew the whistle, signaling Tom for a blocking foul—his fourth. If he made one more foul, he'd be out of the game, so he knew he'd have to take it easy from there on in.

He breathed a sigh of relief when Luke, who normally was a good free-throw shooter, was only able to sink one of his foul shots. Jason rebounded and sent a quick outlet pass to Keith Jeffries, who whipped the ball up court to Marques Hall. Marques squared up for a jump shot, only to be fronted by Blake Mullins, who had anticipated his move. It was then that Marques spotted Jason out of the right corner of his eye, racing down court like a thoroughbred. The ball left Marques's hands, bounced one time, and landed in Jason's hands. Jason, still in full stride, raced to the basket, laid the ball softly off the glass, and watched it swish the net strings as it went through.

The Falcon crowd came to their feet almost in unison and let out a deafening roar that shook the rafters. Tom could only stand there with his mouth hanging open. He had always thought Jason had the potential to be a good basketball player, but he'd never seen his friend play at this level before. As Jason ran past grinning from ear to ear and holding out his hand for a high five from his buddy, all Tom could do was shake his head and slap Jason's outstretched hand. He couldn't get his jaws to shut long enough to smile back at Jason, and there was no use in trying to say anything—the words wouldn't come out.

Jason hadn't said anything to Tom, but his unbelievable level of play was something he couldn't understand either. He had been like a bowl of jelly when he'd first walked out onto the court, but when Tom had mouthed the words "Calm down" to him, he'd felt a peace and serenity he had never felt before. It was as if, in a moment of time, someone had opened him up and removed every doubt and fear he had ever had. In a basketball game, confidence played as big a part in how well a player performed as talent and ability. That was the one category that had eluded Jason Bennett. He knew he had a certain amount of talent, but he lacked the confidence it took to put his talent into action. But for now, Jason had almost a supernatural abundance of confidence. The question was, where had it come from?

With one minute left to play, the score was 63–61 in favor of the Panthers. Luke brought the ball up the court, all the while being harassed by the Falcons' newest star. Tom's lungs were burning, the sweat running from his forehead stung his eyes, and his right calf was cramping up on him. Still, he came after the Hillside hotshot, who by then was showing a lot more respect for his young counterpart.

Forty-five seconds remained; Hillside was looking for a good shot, all the while letting the time on the score clock wind down. The Panthers were still in shock over losing their big lead to a team without their star. But the game was still theirs to win—or lose.

Suddenly, Luke spied Blake Mullins on the baseline. He whipped one of his precision passes just past Tom's outstretched fingers, and the ball rocketed into Blake's chest, almost knocking him out of bounds. Blake quickly regained his balance and drove toward the basket. All Tom could do was watch. If Mullins hit this shot, the game would virtually be over. With only twenty-five seconds to go, it was inconceivable that the Falcons would be able to get two more scores.

Marques Hall tried to cut off the Panther forward but was too far out of position. Mullins maneuvered down the baseline until he was about five feet from the basket and then left his feet. The ball was nestled in his right hand with his left hand steadying it from the side for an easy layup. The ball slowly left Mullins's fingertips, floating, spinning, and sailing toward the basket—the final nail in the coffin for Richfield.

Suddenly, another set of fingertips appeared from out of nowhere, slapping the ball away just before it reached the rim. Jason Bennett had stretched all five feet eight inches of himself to block the shot, sending it in the direction of a dazed Marques Hall.

Tom's mouth flew open again, his eyes widened, and he almost fainted. In the meantime, the Falcon crowd had gone berserk. The left-side stands were a sea of red, standing, cheering, clapping, and high-fiving, and some were even dancing. The Falcons still had their chance to do what nobody expected them to do—except maybe Coach Waters, Tom, Jason, Marques, Keith, Gary, Eric, the rest of the team, the Falcon faithful, and, of course, Reverend James Parker, who was clapping the loudest of all.

Marques Hall called for a time-out. As Tom walked off the court, he glanced at the clock: eighteen seconds left to fulfill their destiny. He made his way with the others to the bench, eyeing an excited Eddie Gordon as he walked by.

"Still having fun?" Gordon laughed.

"Ask me again in eighteen seconds," Tom replied.

The five starters sat on the bench, facing Coach Waters. "Now, men"—they were men again—"we've got eighteen seconds to get the ball in bounds and get off a good shot; that's plenty of time if we do it right. Hall, you try to get the ball to Parker or Mercer. Now, if you can get a good shot, go for three," he said, referring to a three-point shot, "but if not, try to tie it up. And whatever happens, I want you to know I'm very proud of each one of you."

Back on the court, Tom glanced through sweaty eyes to the row of seats in which his family sat. Eighteen seconds were left out of the longest two hours of his life. He saw his dad smiling, waving, and giving him the thumbs-up—in short, acting like a kid again for the first time in a long time. He was proud at that moment to be part of the Richfield Falcons, and he was letting everybody see his school pride.

Tom's attention returned to the game. Marques Hall was ready to inbound the ball. Tom took his place with most of the others around the foul circle, waiting for the ref to blow his whistle and hand the ball off to Marques. The whistle blew, and as the ball touched the fingertips of Marques, Tom took off like a shot toward the half-court circle. The only problem was, Luke was with him stride for stride. Mr. Dotson was upset about being upstaged by this newcomer—especially in the one game in which it was supposed to have been his turn to shine. But he was determined that Little Mr. Parker would not steal his spotlight—now or ever!

Eric Martin ran toward Marques to receive the inbounds pass just in time to avoid the five-second violation. As the ball nestled into Eric's hands, the clock started ticking.

Eighteen seconds. Seventeen. Sixteen.

Eric passed to Jason on the baseline, but finding no daylight, Jason whipped it back to Eric.

Fifteen. Fourteen. Thirteen.

Eric dribbled to the top of the key, careful to keep the ball from the outstretched arms of James Hayden, the Panthers' top defensive player.

Twelve. Eleven. Ten.

Tom had finally succeeded in eluding Luke's iron grasp, and he ran to the right side of the three-point line. Eric, glad to be rid of the ball, bounced it to Tom, who was once again smothered by the pesky Panther star.

Nine. Eight. Seven.

Tom passed to Gary Mercer on the baseline. With no open shot, Mercer passed the ball right back to Tom.

Six. Five. Four.

Tom looked around to Eric—he was smothered by Hayden. Jason was smothered by Mullins inside. This was going to be Tom's game to win or lose. The young star in the making was going to have to prove right then and there if he had what it took.

The crowd on the Panthers' side yelled, "Stop him!" while the Richfield faithful, almost in unison, shouted, "Shoot! Shoot! Shoot!"

Three. Two. One.

Tom knew he was behind the three-point line, but with Luke in his face, he had to make a fade-away jumper, one of the hardest shots there was. He wheeled around, left his feet, and eyed the basket.

The whole time, young Luke Dotson was eyeing Tom Parker. Luke left his feet soon after Tom and, sticking his right arm in Tom's face, dared him to be the hero.

As the ball left Tom's fingers, just barely missing Luke's outstretched hand, the final buzzer sounded. The clock was on zero as the basketball started its climb into the electrified air of the stadium. Up, up, up it climbed before hovering for what seemed like an eternity, and then it began its descent to either drop into the hoop of glory and honor or bounce off the rim, taking with it Tom's—and Richfield's—chance for victory.

By the time the basketball started its downward trajectory, Tom was on his back. He never saw the shot—Luke Dotson was shadowing his view as he almost came down on top of Tom. There was a huge roar. Tom couldn't tell which direction it came from. "Come on, Luke—get out of the way! Somebody please tell me something!" Were the Panther faithful or his beloved Falcons dancing the victory dance right now? What had happened?

His question was soon answered by his best friend. Jason ran over to his pal, screaming, "Tom, you did it! You did it!"

After jerking Tom to his feet and hoisting him, with the help of Marques Hall, onto his shoulders, Jason carried the dazed young warrior, tired and bruised, across the gym of Mayfield College to the delight of the screaming red throng.

Tom looked at the scoreboard: Richfield had 64, and Hillside had 63. His tired face formed the crooked smile that was his trademark. He had done it, or better yet, they had done it. They had accomplished a feat that no one had believed they could accomplish—no one, that was, except that small group of tired, battle-weary teenagers; their coach; and their fans. They had beaten the mighty Panthers of Hillside High.

The next few minutes were a blur as the players cut down the net, with Tom making the final cut and then waving the net over his head as a soldier would have waved a flag. Victory was theirs—this was their moment to bask in the glory. The team members celebrated—except for one.

Toby Miller sat in the Richfield locker room, his face almost as red as the uniform he still had on. *This was* my *night to shine! I was gonna be the MVP, the hero—my name was gonna be on the front of the sports page tomorrow,* he thought in disgust, hurling a towel across the room. Through the thick concrete walls, he'd heard the roar of the crowd at the final buzzer, and for a second, he'd wondered who had won—but he really didn't care. Had Richfield won without him, he'd be the joke instead of the hero. Hurriedly, he changed his clothes and headed out of the locker room before the rest of the team made their victorious entrance.

Tom was in a daze. Had this really happened, or was he just dreaming? The young freshman was grasping the bottom of a beautiful trophy. No, it wasn't the championship trophy; it was the most valuable player trophy, the one given to the best player in the tournament—the one Toby Miller had already made room for on top of his dresser. As shocked as Tom was to receive it, everyone agreed he was the one who deserved it. Tom had taken the starting role just a few days earlier, and he had led his team to one of the most stunning upsets of the decade.

Camera bulbs flashed in his face as he looked over the adoring fans. He knew that he alone didn't deserve the trophy. His teammates had also played their hearts out, and Coach Waters's brilliant coaching had been instrumental in their victory. But the one he wanted to share in the glory was whoever or whatever had given him the incredible calmness and peace to settle him down during the most stressful time of his young life. *Whoever you are, this is for you,* he thought, raising the trophy high into the air. For an instant, he felt another hand helping him hoist the trophy over his head.

The bus ride home proved to be more jubilation. Coach Waters spent the entire time trying to console Toby, the only one who wasn't celebrating. Tom made it a point to stay as far away from his enemy as he could. No one told Toby about Tom winning the MVP trophy, but Tom knew he'd find out about it sooner or later. "I'll really have to watch my back from now on," he told Jason.

"Yeah, he'll be after you more now than ever," Jason said. "You know that sooner or later, you'll have to face him, don't you, Tom?"

"Yeah, I've thought about that a lot. I just hope it's later—much later!"

The bus arrived back at the Richfield High School parking lot around eleven o'clock to a surprisingly large crowd of loyal supporters roaring their approval as the bus pulled off the highway.

"Man, you'd think their voices would have been gone by now," said Marques Hall, still drinking it all in.

Gary Mercer leaned out the window as the bus made its way past the jubilant spectators, slapping hands with about a dozen who were on his side of the bus. By then, the rest of the team had stood up—except Toby—and were peering out of the bus as well. As the bus came to a halt, they made their way to the front and then, one by one, exited to more celebration. The town of Richfield had little to celebrate, but this was their night, and they weren't about to stop until they got it out of their systems—which, for some, wasn't until several hours later.

The Parkers, Bennetts, Pattersons, and Stewarts all headed to the Parker house for a victory party, as promised to Tom and Jason the night before. It didn't last too long, only until around one o'clock, because James Parker needed to get in bed. Tomorrow was Sunday, his busiest day of the week. None of them got much sleep, though—they were too keyed up from the past few hours.

When Tom did finally go to sleep at around three o'clock, he dreamed he was back at the Mayfield College gymnasium. In his hand was a basketball. There were three seconds left on the clock, then two, and then one. He shot. The ball hovered for a second before dropping softly back down, tickling the net as it went through.

Suddenly, Tom saw a man standing under the goal, dressed

in white. He couldn't see his face because of the radiant beams emanating from him, but he heard a voice—a voice so powerful it shook the walls of the coliseum. "You will have greater victories than the ones you have just had!"

That was all he said; then he disappeared as quickly as he had come.

When Tom awoke that morning, he pondered what, if anything, the dream meant. He was about to find out.

ELEVEN

James and JoAnn Parker headed for church on that beautiful Sunday morning. They were surprised to have their young son and his girlfriend riding in the backseat. They had told Tom that he could sit out that service due to all the excitement from the night before, and any other time, he would have loved to lie in bed just a little bit longer, but something wouldn't let him. He had to find out what the supernatural feeling he'd had during the games was. He also had to know if his dream meant anything or if he was just coming back down from a huge adrenaline rush he had been on for the past week. If the answer wasn't in church, he'd look elsewhere, but he had questions, and he needed answers.

He held tight to Julie's hand all the way to church. On the seat beside him sat a one-hundred-plus-year-old Bible.

The church service started as most church services did. There was an opening prayer, followed by a hymn. The song from the hymn book was selected, and Tom settled back, prepared for the usual boring two hours. He thought about the two-hour span last night—the greatest two hours of his young life, the two hours that had changed his life. But when the singing started, something was different. Tom listened to all the words, taking them in and meditating on them. One of the lines from the song talked about the cleansing power of Jesus. Did Tom need to be cleansed from anything? He was a pretty good kid most of the time, and God would look over his faults—that was what God was like, wasn't he? Another line spoke of "the love of Jesus, even before we knew him."

What did he mean? Tom had always known who Jesus was—he'd been taught that all his life. Another line was about the victory that came from knowing Jesus. What was that victory? All he'd ever seen from Christians was a life of constantly giving things away and missing out on all the good stuff just to please that God of theirs. That was no victory—to him, it was prison.

Yet these people seemed to be happy—truly happy. All of them, especially his parents, had something deep inside that allowed them to come through the worst of circumstances with smiles on their faces and a glow in their hearts. What separated them from all the other religions? And what did Jesus have to do with it?

"The choir sure does sound great this morning, doesn't it, Tom? Tom?" Julie's voice jolted Tom back from his daydream.

"Oh yeah, it sounds great," he finally responded.

"What were you thinking about?" asked Julie. "You seemed to be a million miles away."

"Oh, it was nothing—just religious thoughts. I figure since I'm in church, I'll think church thoughts," he said with his usual crooked smile. They both turned their attention to the last verse of the song before joining the teenage group downstairs for Sunday school.

Even Sunday school was different on that particular morning. Tom actually paid attention to Mr. Allen, their Sunday school teacher. Jim Allen couldn't understand what had gotten into young Mr. Parker. He was attentive and even asked questions. All this was coming from a kid who only last Sunday had fallen asleep in class and fallen out of his chair. *I don't understand it, but I like what I see,* Mr. Allen thought. *Maybe his newfound stardom is causing him to open up. Well, whatever it is, praise the Lord for it!*

Julie could also see a change in Tom. *He sure never acted this interested in religion before,* she thought. *Well, maybe it's just another of the many phases he is going through.*

The Sunday morning worship service also went through the usual routine: an opening prayer, one choir song, the offering, and then another choir song. But for once in his life, Tom wasn't bored out of his mind. Something was happening to him, something he didn't understand. He was nervous, scared, excited, and anxious all at the same time. The two songs the choir sang that morning seemed to penetrate his heart like a broad-headed arrow from a hunter's bow. Then the last song ended, and it was time for his father, Reverend James Parker, to come to the pulpit.

Reverend Parker remarked on the basketball triumph of the night before, singling out Tom as the MVP. The congregation applauded, causing Tom's face to turn three shades of red. When the applause settled down, Reverend Parker asked the congregation to turn to a certain passage of scripture in their Bibles.

"Where did he say to turn to?" Tom asked Julie with his thumbs on the old King James Bible, ready to open it.

"I think he said Matthew chapter six, verses twenty and twenty-one."

Sitting across from them, JoAnn Parker nodded, confirming Julie's reply. Slowly, Tom turned the pages of the old Bible, taking care not to tear any of the pages, until he came to the scripture. He stared down at the page with a look of bewilderment on his face. Those were the same verses Joe Simpkins had underlined in that old Bible more than one hundred years earlier!

"What in the world is going on here?" he whispered to Julie, who also had a surprised look on her face. "This is starting to get kinda spooky." They both shrugged it off as coincidence and proceeded to listen to the preacher.

"In verse nineteen of this chapter, Jesus tells us, 'Lay not up for yourselves treasures upon earth where moth and rust doth corrupt, and where thieves break through and steal.' This verse tells us that earthly treasures are only temporary—they may be here today and gone tomorrow. But look at verse twenty." Tom's dad was getting excited; Tom could tell because his voice was getting louder and louder. "'But lay up for yourselves treasures in Heaven, where moth nor rust doth corrupt, and where thieves do not break through nor steal.'"

Tom wondered how you could lay treasures up in heaven when you were still on earth, but his dad continued.

"Jesus came to this earth to die on a cross. He became the supreme sacrifice for you and me so we could be forgiven of our sins. All those who repent of their sins, believe in their hearts, and confess to Jesus that God raised him from the dead, according to Romans 10:9, shall be saved. Jesus also lets us know that heaven is going to be our true home, and the things we put up there will never fade away. All the glory, all the prizes, and all the splendor of this present world do not last. All that will last is what you give to God. But the first thing you have to give him is yourself."

Tom could feel a thumping in his chest as his dad continued his message. Something was going on inside him, something he couldn't understand. All of a sudden, his life didn't seem like much at all. His dad was right—the awards he'd won the previous night would soon be sitting on his dresser, collecting dust. Sure, the memories would linger on, but for how long? Just until the next Richfield team won the next tournament. He needed something better, something that would last longer than what he had. But would he find it in Jesus? He needed to hear more.

"Verse twenty-one tells us, 'Where your treasure is, there will your heart be also.' We will follow after our treasures, whether they are earthly or heavenly treasures. The reason most people in this world have never accepted Jesus Christ as their Savior is because their hearts are after worldly things. They seek fame and glory, but as we have all found out, fame, glory, and money will never lead to true peace or happiness. Only Jesus can give us that. In John 14:27, Jesus tells us, 'Peace I leave with you, my peace I give unto you; not as the world giveth, give I unto you. Let not your heart be troubled, neither let it be afraid.' If you want to have true peace and joy in this world, you will only find it by accepting Jesus Christ as Savior of your life. Give your life to Jesus, and he will fill your heart with such joy and peace you will never doubt it. His precious blood, which was shed on the cross, will cleanse you from your sin, and you will become a new creature in Christ, according to 1 Corinthians 5:17. This verse also tells us that 'old things are passed away; behold, all things are become new.' But you have to take the first step."

At that point, Sister Clark started playing a song softly on the piano. Tom had heard the song many times, but this time, the thumping in his heart grew stronger. He looked down at his hands—they were clutching the seat of the pew so tightly his knuckles had turned white. He felt a tear trickle down his face. What was happening to him? He was coming apart at the seams.

C'mon, Tom. Snap out of it, a voice seemed to tell him. *If you give in to this stuff, all your fun will be over—you'll have to be like all these others, spending your dreary life here in this dreary church with all these dreary people. Do you really want that?*

James Parker continued speaking. "This song says to come as you are. That is how Jesus wants you to come—just as you are. Only he can clean up your life and remove your sins. A good life won't do it; coming to church won't do it—only Jesus can do it. He can do for you what you can't do for yourself. Would you come now and give your life to Jesus? I promise you you'll never, ever be the same again!"

Tom looked at Julie; there were tears running down her cheeks. The message had gotten to her too. Tom wanted to get up and walk down the aisle to give his heart to Jesus, but he couldn't move—the conflict inside him continued. Part of him just wouldn't let go.

Reverend Parker said something then that released the fear in Tom's heart: "If you will take the first step, Jesus will take it from there. Try him and find out."

That was all it took. Tom grasped Julie's hand and looked into her big tear-stained eyes. "I have to go up there," he said.

Wiping the tears from her eyes, Julie nodded to Tom. "Me too."

Together the two stood up and moved along the pew, past his now weeping mother, out into the aisle, and down toward the front. By then, Tom's father was weeping too, with his hands high in the air, shouting, "Thank you, Lord! Oh, thank you, Lord!"

His dad was right again, as usual. As soon as Tom stepped out into the aisle, the conflict ended. He was determined to give Jesus his heart and soul—his everything. He'd heard his father say one time that getting saved wasn't like walking slowly into the water; it was like diving right in. Well, he was ready to take the plunge. There was no turning back. He was now on the high dive, ready to plunge headfirst into the unknown.

Reverend Parker met two sinners at the altar that day. All sinners coming home were special to him, but obviously, these were just a little more special than usual. He read the scriptures from Romans telling Tom and Julie what they needed to understand in order to be saved. Then he asked them to pray with him the sinner's prayer. As Tom prayed, his tears flowed; the words, with sniffles, came out as he cried out to God, the only one who could help him now.

Then, suddenly, it happened: there came that peace again, only now it was stronger. Tom could feel his burdens lifting away. He felt a ton of troubles, worries, and bottled-up resentment lifting from his shoulders. There at that altar, Jesus came into the hearts of the young man and his girlfriend. Their stony hearts were turned to flesh. Their tears came like a river that morning. Tom had always been embarrassed for people to see him cry, but now he didn't care. He had come home, where he belonged. Peace flooded his troubled heart, and all at once, the troubles vanished. The same thing was happening to Julie. There at that altar, they laid their old sinful, grief-stricken lives down and became new creatures. Unseen by human eyes, Jesus Christ, the Lamb of God, stood among them in that little church. The Holy Spirit opened their hearts, and Jesus entered—they had found true victory in Jesus Christ!

Tom felt the way he had the night before, only a thousand times better. The tears just wouldn't stop, even after he rose from the altar, and he hugged everyone there. His dad, not usually one given to emotion, was practically dancing with joy. JoAnn was the first to get to Tom and Julie, and she hugged them both for quite some time, weeping, praising God, laughing, and doing a bit of a dance herself.

The occasion was, as always, a time of celebration, and that little church knew how to celebrate. Best of all, there were two more that day to join in the celebration. Right now, basketball didn't mean anything, their feelings for each other weren't important, and the Simpkins' treasure was the furthest thing from their minds. All that mattered was Jesus, the greatest treasure of them all!

As they headed home after church, Tom felt on top of the world. They stopped at the Burger Hut for lunch, but he couldn't eat much; he was too happy and excited to eat. Julie didn't eat much either. James and JoAnn just grinned and winked at each other. The feeling was new to Tom and Julie, but his mom and dad knew it—they still felt it, even after all those years.

After lunch, they dropped Julie off at her house, but she told them she'd come back to the evening service, and she was going to get her mom and dad to come too if she could. When Tom got home, he called everyone he knew to tell them all about the morning miracle. Jason couldn't understand Tom's drastic change. Only days earlier, he'd heard Tom complain about all the religious stuff his family was involved in, and now he was involved in it too.

The Sunday evening service was wonderful. Tom worshipped and adored his newfound Savior, singing his praises with all the voice he had, and when his dad preached, he hung on every word, drinking it all in like cold ice water on a hot summer day. He had found the answer he was looking for, and it wasn't in the church building, the people, or the singing. The answer was in Jesus Christ, or better yet, the answer *was* Jesus Christ!

His sister, Megan, who was already a Christian, could tell the change in her little brother. Oh sure, she would still pick on him— that was what big sisters did—but it would be different now. Tom would need all the love and encouragement that all young Christians needed. She knew that Satan would challenge his newfound freedom. The devil, she knew, never gave up—he would come against Tom and Julie more now than ever, trying to make them doubt their salvation and tempt them in an even greater way. But Megan knew that 1 John 4:4 (KJV) was true: "Greater is he that is in you than he that is in the world." Tom and Julie had help now—a greater help than they could ever imagine.

Tom said goodbye to Julie after the church service, with both deciding to turn in early that night. Julie had come with her mom and dad, who, though they did not receive what she had received, enjoyed the service. They all said their goodbyes and headed to their respective houses after one of the strangest and greatest weekends any of them had ever had.

TWELVE

But lay up for yourselves treasures in heaven. Treasures in heaven. Treasures in heaven! Tom sat up in bed with a jolt, a strange expression covering his face. "That's it! It has to be!"

It was Monday morning. Tom had just awakened to a new revelation. He quickly reached for the phone and dialed the Patterson residence. Julie's soft voice on the other end sounded even lovelier that morning. But Tom didn't have time for that right now. "Julie, I think I might have another clue about the Simpkins treasure."

"I thought we all agreed to give up on this treasure hunt—besides, I'm not sneaking out again. Now that I'm a Christian, I've got a responsibility—and so do you!" Her newfound life was taking root.

"I know, Julie; you won't have to slip out. Let's just meet at the Simpkins house after school this afternoon. If this turns out to be nothing, we'll forget the whole thing, okay?" Tom was learning some lessons that all Christians learned when they first got saved. First of all, young converts were changed on the inside, but they still had work to do on the outside—with the help of the Holy Spirit, the Word, and, of course, stronger brothers and sisters in the faith. Second, the devil was still the devil, and he loved to prey on young converts most of all. Even though Tom was born again, the Simpkins mystery wouldn't let go. He had to find out if his new idea was right or not—and that meant going back into the Simpkins mansion.

That Monday at Richfield High School wasn't the usual Monday. There was a special morning assembly honoring the new champions. Toby Miller was understandably absent, so Tom's biggest problem wasn't a problem—not that day anyway. Tom received a standing ovation when he was introduced. Red-faced and grinning from ear to ear, Tom acknowledged the happy crowd's approval. He modestly waved his right index finger, signifying the Falcons as number one. After the assembly, the rest of the day went pretty normally, except for the occasional high five or back slap between classes.

Tom told Julie, Jason, and Melissa of his plans. Although hesitant at first, they all agreed to do it, yet this time, it was Julie who caused the most resistance. "Tom, I don't think it is right to go back into that old house again; we shouldn't have done it the first time." But Tom was persistent, and she finally gave in.

The clock read 3:15. In only fifteen more minutes, they'd be out of school and heading for the mansion. A little voice kept telling Tom he'd get in big trouble if he did this, but he ignored the little voice and kept making his plans. He would learn—sometimes the hard way—to listen to that little voice as the years went on, but for now, his adrenaline was overclouding his good judgment. He just couldn't stop after going this far. The thought of giving up after all the time and trouble they'd spent looking for the treasure was out of the question. Tom was ready for another challenge—at least that was what he thought.

At the 3:30 bell, Tom hurried out of seventh-period English, down the hall, and out the door to meet Julie, who was waiting on the steps. They met up with Jason and Melissa a few minutes later in the parking lot and slowly headed out toward the Simpkins mansion, walking along Mayfair Boulevard to the intersection of Second Avenue. The group didn't talk much—they should have been used to venturing into the unknown by now, but they weren't. The thought of going back inside the house, even in broad daylight, had them all scared to death. "I hope this is the last time we have to do this," said Jason.

"Don't worry; it will be," Julie said. She gave a stern look to her young boyfriend. *I shouldn't be doing this*, she thought as she strolled up the sidewalk. Her grandma Patterson had told her a long time ago, "It doesn't matter who thinks up the trouble; if you go along with it, it may as well have been your idea."

The group didn't realize that even though it was light now, it would probably get dark before they made it in and out of the house—it was still winter. And if they did find the treasure, it would probably take much longer to get it out. They had all called their parents and told them they would be a little late in getting home—a normal occurrence for all of them—but just how late they didn't know.

Finally, the group reached the corner of Pine Street and Second Avenue, and there it was, looming like a huge monster of granite, ready to open its giant oak mouth and swallow them up. Even though this had been his idea, Tom was just about ready to chicken out himself.

The four stood there for a few seconds, staring up at the massive structure and trying to build up some courage. Jason swallowed hard, putting his hands on his legs, which were shaking uncontrollably. "Well, it doesn't look like anybody's home—let's just come back later. How about next year?" Even in the face of danger, Jason was always the comedian.

Tom turned to his friend with his crooked grin. "C'mon, Jason. Let's have one more big adventure before our parents find out and ground us for life."

"Or worse," Melissa said. "If the cops find out, we'll end up in jail."

Jail! That was something none of them had thought about much until that moment. Would this adventure be worth going to jail over?

"Tom, I sure hope your big idea pays off," said Jason, "because if it doesn't, I just may help Toby Miller beat you up!"

"Did somebody call my name?"

Cold chills ran all over Tom as the hair stood up on his neck again. All four kids whirled around to face the inevitable: there stood Toby with an evil smirk on his face. Tom could see the hatred in his eyes, something he hadn't noticed before.

"Well, well, well, if it isn't the superstar Tom Parker—the one who stole my MVP trophy away from me!" His yellow teeth gleamed as he sneered at Tom. "I'll tell you what I'm gonna do, Mr. Parker. I'm gonna just take all my frustration out on that stupid-looking face of yours."

This was it—the moment Tom had dreaded all his life yet the moment he knew he had to face.

"Toby, why don't you go on home and leave us alone?" Julie said, trying to help Tom avoid what would probably be a serious beating.

"Aw, is Tom's widdle girlfwiend twying to help him out again?" snarled Toby. "Well, your girlfriend can't get you out of it this time, Parker."

"I'm not trying to get out of anything, Toby." The calmness in his voice surprised Tom—even the hairs on his neck had gone down. "I've been running from you for too long. I should have faced you a long time ago instead of running away, but I'm here now!" Tom's days of running were over. Win or lose, he would face his foe. This was the day he stopped running. This was to be the start of a whole new way of life—a life not filled with constant fear and a life in which he would face each adversary head-on, realizing where each one came from: Satan.

As Tom stared squarely into the eyes of hatred that day, he noticed something else he'd never noticed before: loneliness. Here was a heart crying out. Tom looked at his foe in a different light. Instead of fear or hatred, he looked upon him with sympathy. "Toby, I'm not scared of you anymore, but I really don't want to fight you. Can't we just talk this over and try to be friends?"

Tom meant what he said, but Toby had been stewing over this thing for too long. "Listen, Parker, you've talked long enough. Now's the time to fight." Toby hadn't been labeled the class bully since kindergarten by talking things over. He had fought his way through every obstacle in his young fifteen-year existence, and that day would be no exception. "Now, prepare to take your beating like a man."

Toby lunged toward Tom with all his force. His right arm came right at Tom's face with his huge hand balled up in a fist, ready to make good on all the threats of the past years. There was no way out for Tom Parker. He had to stand and take his beating from the big bully—or did he?

As Toby's fist came forward, ready to do its damage, Tom suddenly ducked under the blow. Caught off balance by his opponent's surprising maneuver, Toby's large body went sprawling past Tom. He stumbled off the sidewalk, down the bank, and—*splash*—into the Simpkins mudhole.

Tom turned his head just in time to see Toby take his turn in the mud. *Serves him right.* The thought came into his head, but just as quickly, another thought entered his mind—a thought that wouldn't have been there a couple days earlier. *Tom, what are you thinking? Toby needs help. C'mon. Help him out of that mudhole—be the friend he so desperately needs.*

Toby was getting his bearings back and was coming up out of the mud, ready to take another swipe at the little pip-squeak responsible for this. Yet as he turned to face Tom, his body and face covered in mud, a hand reached out for him.

"Here, Toby. I'll help you out."

"Tom, what are you doing?" Jason stared in disbelief at his friend's gesture. "If you try to help him out, you'll end up back in the mudhole, maybe for good this time."

The other three had reeled with laughter as Toby plowed face-first into the huge pond of muddy water, but the laughter stopped as they realized Tom's most foolish maneuver yet. Reaching out a hand to Toby was the same as giving a hand to an alligator or a shark. Only Toby didn't lash out at Tom—he extended his muddy hand to Tom, who helped pull him out of the mud.

"Toby, I'm really sorry this happened." Tom still couldn't believe the words were coming out of his mouth. "But I really meant what I said earlier. I don't want to fight you, but I'm not running from you anymore. If we have to square off at each other every day for the rest of our lives, so be it. And I didn't take that MVP trophy from you—you lost it with your temper, just like you've lost everything else. But if the trophy means that much to you, you can have it."

The other three gasped; they hadn't thought Tom would give up that trophy for anything or anybody, especially Toby. "For you see, Toby, I found a treasure yesterday that is greater than anything else on earth. His name is Jesus. And you can have him too if you'll just ask him to forgive your sins and come into your heart."

The Toby of an hour ago would have grabbed Tom by the throat and strangled the life out of him. But this wasn't the Toby of an hour ago. Deep within the cold, hard black chambers of his heart, a tiny spark flickered. Tom's words had gotten to that lonely individual, and for once in his life, he actually listened to someone. He listened to, of all people, Tom Parker, his most hated foe.

Tom wasn't sure because of all the muddy water on Toby's face, but he thought he detected a single tear running down his cheek.

"I'm sorry, Tom, for all the trouble I've caused you over the years," Toby said as Tom and Jason helped him back up the bank onto the sidewalk. "You're right—I brought all the trouble on myself. I guess it was always easier to blame you than to take the responsibility myself."

Julie, Jason, and Melissa couldn't believe the transformation that had taken place in Toby. All three expected him to revert back to the Toby of old and break Tom's neck, but no more punches were thrown, and no more heated words were exchanged. Toby walked slowly toward home, shivering from the cold, soaking wet and covered with mud. Yet his heart was a little warmer than it had been. He turned back toward the four and gazed at his newfound friend. "Hey, Parker, does your dad still preach at that little church out on the highway?"

Surprised yet hopeful, Tom replied, "Yeah, Toby."

"Well, I just might see you there this Sunday." There was a creaking sound as Toby used mouth muscles he hadn't known he had to produce a broad, happy smile.

"I hope so." Tom smiled back. "Service starts at ten."

THIRTEEN

It was amazing how fast the teenage mind could change. No sooner had Toby gotten out of sight than the four teens were working their way toward the back entrance of the Simpkins mansion. Tom and Jason climbed through the window into the study and then helped the girls through, being careful not to cut themselves on the glass. The footprints were still on the floor, only now it seemed there were more sets of them. Tom quenched Jason's anxiety attack with a quick observation: "The extra footprints are the ones we left the other night. There's nobody here now, just as there was nobody here then."

The explanation seemed to satisfy Jason, who glanced at his watch—it was 4:30. "C'mon. Let's get this over with before it gets dark. I told my dad I'd be home by five thirty, and he'll kill me if I'm late."

Quickly, the four moved to the door of the study and, with a slow groan, opened it. Moving down the hall through the cobwebs and the musty smell, which hadn't changed from the days before, the four proceeded to the huge living room at the front of the house. Light from outside shone through the cracks in the windows, giving them an even greater look at the massiveness of the frontier castle. They saw their red-eyed monster, the huge staircase, and the lamp the cat had knocked over, which was still lying on the floor where it had landed. The huge chandelier made even more sparkling figures, which danced across the wall. Yet all the beauty and splendor could not distract the four from their appointed mission.

Tom held his breath, and as he let it out, he whispered, "There it is."

Jason, his hand still in a viselike grip on Melissa's hand, murmured, "Yeah, there it is."

The four made their way across the long floor of the living room and stopped at the fireplace on the right wall. The room was dimly lit, even though it was still daylight outside, so Tom flipped on his flashlight and shone it slowly around the opening of the fireplace and then slowly upward until it reached its destination. There, in all its brilliance, was the painting of the creation by Michelangelo. Tom's heart beat faster, and his breath came in short bursts. "Okay, let's see if there is treasure in heaven or not."

After moving one of the chairs from the dining room, Jason stepped upon it—not because he wanted to but because he was the tallest. He moved his hands slowly across the vast painting, spraying dust into the air with every swipe of his hand.

"Careful there, Jason. The dust is getting in my eyes," said Melissa, trying to wipe the dust from her eyes with her left hand while fanning away the remainder with her right. "Treasure or no treasure, I don't want to leave here blind."

"Sorry, Melissa. I'm doing the best I can," replied her boyfriend. "You'll have to move a little bit farther away from the fireplace."

"Have you found anything yet?" Julie, who had been quiet up until that time, spoke up. "We'd better hurry up—it's starting to get darker outside." She was right; the sunbeams that had been filtering through the cracks and dancing off the chandelier only a few minutes ago were almost gone, and a pale, dim light was the only remnant of that Monday evening.

Jason moved across the painting at a faster pace, especially after being reminded of the impending darkness. "I can't find anything up here t—" His voice dropped off as his hand stopped on a certain section of the painting. Moving his right hand back and forth across a ten-inch portion of the painting, Jason looked down at the others with a funny expression on his face.

"Well, Jason, are you gonna tell us what's wrong, or do we have to play twenty questions?" Melissa asked.

"It may be nothing, but right here behind God, there is a place that's kinda sunk in." He moved his hand across the spot he had mentioned, and the surface of the painting moved in slightly as his fingers moved across the canvas.

"How hard would it be to get the painting down?" Tom asked.

"Not too hard," replied Jason. "If you get one side and I get the other, we should be able to lift it off of whatever it's hanging on."

The light outside had already begun to fade out. All flashlights were on now, creating ghostly shadows whenever they moved. Tom and Jason got another chair for Tom to stand on, and together they lifted the huge painting from the two large wooden pegs holding it to the wall. "Man, this thing weighs a ton," squawked Jason with a noticeable look of strain on his face.

The two nearly dropped the painting—it didn't weigh a ton, but it was heavy, and because it was so big, it was hard for them to get a good hold on it. But they finally got it under control and lowered it down to the girls waiting on the floor, who leaned it against the granite fireplace. As quick as a flash, every light headed straight to the spot Jason had found earlier. It looked as if someone had removed one granite block in that area, chiseled the cement off it, and then put it back in.

Tom was getting more excited, but he remembered all the other chases from the previous week. *If this is another plate or another Bible,* he thought to himself, *I'm giving up on treasure hunting for good.*

Jason just wanted to get the whole thing over with and get out of the Simpkins house forever. "Okay, Tom, let's see what's back there."

The time was 5:15, and by then, the last shadows of daylight were fading from the scene. Jason reached up and began to shift the huge stone from its resting place. Even though the fireplace stones were smaller than the stones in the chimney outside, it still took a considerable effort on his part to get it to move. Besides that, reaching over one's head didn't give a person much leverage.

Tom wanted to help, but there wasn't room for both of the boys, so Jason was left to maneuver the stone out of its socket.

Slowly, it moved—first one side and then the other. Jason had to rest his arms every few seconds to relieve the tension produced by having them over his head. "My arms haven't hurt this much since I helped Vince Tyson put up hay last summer." He winced.

"Here, Jason. Let me work on it some," said Tom.

Jason gladly stepped down, allowing Tom to work and his arms to rest.

Julie and Melissa were getting impatient—it was already later than they had said they'd be home. "How much longer is this gonna take?" Melissa asked. "I just know my dad is having one of his fits right now."

"Mine too," said Julie. "C'mon, Tom—hurry."

But it wasn't a job he could rush. The stone was about halfway out now, and Tom had to move to the side of it to keep it from falling on his head when it did turn loose, which made his progress even slower.

Finally, with Tom on one side and Jason on the other, the two zigzagged the enormous stone to the edge, where it dropped with a thud to the floor below. The light beams from Melissa's and Julie's flashlights went to the granite block, which rolled a couple times before resting on its side, and then straight back to the ten-by-twelve-inch opening made by its absence.

By then, everyone's heart had nearly stopped beating. Tom strained to see if anything was inside the opening, but he couldn't see anything. He was almost afraid to look, having been disappointed all the other times. *I don't think I can take another disappointment,* he thought to himself.

"Hey, Tom, we're gonna have to find something taller than these chairs." Jason had interrupted his daydream. "Let's hurry—we're fifteen minutes late as it is."

The tone of Jason's voice told Tom that he wasn't as excited as the others. He was expecting disappointment this time. He'd gotten his hopes up all the other times—with the chimney, the cellar, and the mine—but not this time. He was ready to get the mystery over with, get out of the haunted mansion, and never set foot in it ever again.

Julie and Melissa felt pretty much the same as Jason. All the wild goose chases they'd been on the past week had led them nowhere, and all they had to show for their troubles so far were two plates, a Bible, and a peck of trouble.

Finally, the four maneuvered a large chest over to the fireplace. Jason, being the tallest, climbed upon the chest and reached down to take one of the flashlights. At times like that, Tom didn't feel so bad about being short. He'd had to reach his hand inside those unseen places all the other times, and now it was Jason's turn. "C'mon, Jason. Stick your hand in there, and find out what's in there."

"Okay, Tom, don't rush me."

Tom couldn't help but smile; only five minutes before, Jason had been pushing him to hurry it up.

Finally, Jason got up the nerve to slowly reach inside the opening. Cringing at every inch, as if expecting to have one of his fingers gnawed off, he stuck his arm in almost up to his elbow—and then he gave the others the look they'd grown all too familiar with. With a sigh, he whispered to the group, "It's another plate!"

Even though their expectations weren't high, a look of disappointment showed on every one of their faces. Julie was the first one to break the silence. "That's it!" She threw up her hands in surrender. "I say we go home, forget we ever heard of this, and get on with our normal lives!"

All the others were inclined to agree. By that time, Jason had pulled out the plate and climbed down off the chest. Out of curiosity, the four shone their lights on the plate to read the newest—and last, as far as they were concerned—message:

You've found it. Congratulations.

"We've found it? Found what?" asked Jason. "All we've found

is another plate—there's no gold in there. After finding the plate, I felt around behind it, and all that was there was the wall of the chimney! I was right the first time: Joe Simpkins was a practical joker, and this here is the punch line—only right now, it feels more like a punch in the face!"

The other three took turns looking at the plate, and then, one by one, the beams of the flashlights headed in other directions—except for one beam. Melissa, who had not said much—with Jason around, she usually didn't get many opportunities—slowly analyzed the plate, turning it over and then back while looking at one end. "Hey, you guys, look at this!" she yelled excitedly.

"Aw, come on, Melissa. Throw that thing into the fireplace, and let's get out of here," Jason said. "If I leave right now, maybe I'll just be grounded for half my life."

"No, Jason, I'm serious—I think I've found something."

The others reluctantly gathered back at the fireplace around the youngest teen.

"Okay, what is it?" asked Tom, expecting more clues that would probably lead nowhere.

"Look here at the notches at the end of this plate," Melissa said, aiming her flashlight at one end.

There were small notches cut into the metal—but what were they there for? "It's possible Joe just used the end of a sheet of brass that had already been used before," said Julie.

"But what if he meant to do this?" Melissa was unrelenting. "The plate does say, 'You've found it.' Maybe these notches hold the key to finding it."

"The key! Melissa, you're a genius!" Julie said. "These look like notches in a key!"

"But if this is a key, where is the lock?" Jason was still skeptical. He started walking toward the hallway leading to the back entrance. "I'm getting out of this place—do any of you want to come with me?" he said, shining his flashlight in their direction.

He received no answer—the other three were busy combing

the fireplace wall, looking for anything that resembled a lock. Of course, Jason was too scared to walk from the front of the house to the back by himself, so eventually, he threw up his hands and joined the others. "Okay, I guess we're all in this together. 'Live as a team; die as a team,' I always say." The living part didn't bother him; it was the dying part that made his knees knock together.

Julie and Melissa took the lower portion of the fireplace, while Tom and Jason surveyed the upper part with the help of the two chairs they had used earlier. By then, it was 6:15 and pitch dark outside. They should have been concerned about the police seeing the beams of their flashlights through the cracks, but they weren't. They should have been thinking about how worried their parents must have been, but they weren't. They should have been thinking about all the danger they were in, but they weren't. All their thoughts were on finding whatever the plate said they were supposed to have found. Nobody liked to be congratulated for something he didn't do. If Joe Simpkins was congratulating them for finding something, they wanted to find it!

"I think I've got something here." Tom spoke up in a loud whisper. "Look here along this line of concrete." The others zeroed in on Tom's find: there appeared to be a crack of some sort running straight down the line of concrete, through the staggered block below, and then through the next line of concrete.

"It's just a crack in the concrete and blocks, showing that the house has settled," said Jason. "I mean, one-hundred-year-old houses do eventually get cracks after so long."

"I've never seen a crack that straight made by aging," said Julie—and she was right. The crack looked as if it had been sawed using a straight edge.

Melissa, who was exploring the area around the crack, let out a startling yell, causing the already scared teens to nearly jump out of their skin. "This is it!"

After finally gathering their composure, the others shone their beams to see what had made her squeal: there was a small, round area cut into one of the blocks. It was about an inch and a half in diameter, with a horizontal slit running down the middle. Beside it was another crack the same as the one Tom had found. The four teens had been on an emotional roller coaster for the past week, and they were heading for the highest loop.

Julie, who had put the plate in her pocket, nervously got it out and put it into the slit—it fit perfectly.

Jason grasped Melissa's hand and held it tightly—not from fear but from excitement. Tom was standing on the other chair with his fingers crossed and a look of expectancy on his face.

Julie turned the key counterclockwise—nothing. The key stopped at the nine o'clock position.

"Turn it the other way," said Tom.

"Okay, I'll try." Slowly, she turned the key back to the twelve o'clock position and then to three o'clock. The key stuck again momentarily, and then, with a little more effort, she proceeded to turn it to six o'clock, then nine o'clock, and then back to twelve o'clock. *Click!*

"What was that?" asked Jason excitedly.

The crack next to the keyhole had opened. The cement on the top and bottom gave way, causing it to move. It was a door, approximately thirty-six square inches, cut into the block.

Julie grasped the open end, straining to open it farther, but she couldn't get it to budge. "Get up here, Jason, and open this thing!" she yelled. "It's stuck."

Julie climbed down from the chair, and Jason climbed up, almost in a single motion. Grasping the edge of the door with both hands, he pulled with all his might. The door started moving. Cement that hadn't budged in more than one hundred years slowly scraped against granite as the door opened. It moved slowly at first and then easier as the cement gave way. When he'd made an opening of around eight inches, Jason yelled to Melissa, "Come here, and shine the light in!"

Melissa quickly walked under the door and shone the beam of

her light through the small opening. "I can't see anything yet," she said, straining her pretty eyes at the opening.

"Here. Give me the light," said Jason. Melissa handed him the flashlight, and he slowly shone the beam into the darkness.

The light of a thousand fireflies bounced back into his face as his eyes got bigger, and his knees began to buckle. Tom thought his friend was going to pass out again. Whatever he'd seen had taken all the color from his face—Tom could see that even in the dark. Jason climbed down from the chair and then sat down in it, trying to regain his bearings.

"Man, what is it?" asked Tom. "You look like you've seen another ghost."

Jason lifted his head, gave Tom a weak smile, and said with a shaky voice, "Not a ghost—just a treasure!"

Excitedly, the other three tried to climb up onto the one chair at the same time, which was impossible. They then moved the two chairs together, throwing a still-bewildered Jason onto the floor. Their three lights shone into the opening, and they were almost blinded by what shone back at them. There in the little vault of granite and cement sat bars upon bars of the substance that many killed for, that separated the rich from the poor, and that was the monetary standard for some countries: gold.

They couldn't believe their eyes. They had finally found the treasure that had baffled treasure hunters for more than a century. The four wet-behind-the-ears teenagers had unlocked one of the mysteries of the ages and had become rich in the process.

It was hard for any of them to keep their bearings. Their hearts raced; their breath came in short gasps; and their knees, like Jason's, almost buckled under them. After a few seconds of struggling to regain his composure, Tom spoke first. "I can't believe it. We found it."

That was all he could manage to get out before falling off the chair, almost on top of Jason, who was still on the floor. Tom sat down on the floor beside Jason, trying to get a grasp of what had just happened. This was unbelievable—they had just become teenage millionaires.

"Hey, guys, how are we gonna get this gold out of here?" Julie brought Tom back out of dreamland. "We're going to have to sit down and think this thing through. I mean, we can't just carry out all of this gold, and even if we could, there's no way we could carry gold bars into the bank and exchange them for money—somebody might get suspicious."

"That's right. I never thought about that," said Tom. "I guess we'll just have to close the vault again, take the key, and hang the painting back up until we can think of a plan, because if anybody found out …"

"I'm afraid somebody has already found out, Mr. Parker."

Tom and the others nearly jumped out of their skin. Who was that? Where had that voice come from? Was it another ghost—maybe the ghost of Joe Simpkins?

All four turned suddenly, shining their lights in the direction of the voice, not knowing who or what to expect.

"Well, well, well, we meet again, Mr. Parker. And how are you this evening, Mr. Bennett? I hope all is well with your young companions." The man nodded to the two girls.

For a few seconds, none of them recognized the tall, lanky man standing about ten feet behind them. Then Jason spoke up. "Hey, it's the guy in the red Jeep!"

"Very good, Mr. Bennett; I thought you might have forgotten me," the man said. Then, turning around, he motioned for his partners, who were lurking in the shadows. The teens saw three men. Each held a pistol pointed directly at them. "Now, if all of you will cooperate, there won't be any need for us to use these—they're so noisy, you know."

"Yeah, we know," whimpered Jason.

The lead gunman motioned the four teens closer together, and they gladly cooperated. "I want all of you together, where we can keep our eyes on you," he said, but in the darkness, with just the flashlight beams, it was hard to keep an eye on them even when they were clustered together. "Now, I'm going to tell you why we're here. You see, Mr. Parker, we've been following you kids around ever since we spotted you at the chimney last week. You see, we've been searching for the treasure too—as a matter of fact, we were watching you from the north tower that night, and every day since then, we've followed you around. You see, Mr. Parker, the plate you found in the chimney was actually the second plate. We had already found the first plate. Only we found it the hard way. We did an in-depth study at Northwest University on the Simpkins treasure, and after six months of hard work, we finally found the link in an old newspaper leading us to the north tower and the first plate." He reached into the pocket of his jacket and took out the thin brass plate. "This plate was to lead us to the second and third plates—the ones you kids accidentally stumbled upon." A sinister smile crossed his lips. "At first, we wanted to shoot you four and take the plates, but now I'm glad we didn't, for you see, you kids led us right to the treasure, and you did all the work. All we needed to do was wait and let you junior treasure hunters do your job—and I must say, I'm impressed at how quickly you found the gold. I've got to admit, the way you guys looked coming back from the mine that day, I figured you would have given up, but you pressed on and found the treasure—which may be the last thing you'll ever do!" He cocked the hammer back on his pistol.

Tom's blood ran cold in his veins at that moment. As he looked at his friends and fellow treasure hunters, he could tell they were thinking the same thing he was: this was it. They'd taken one step too many. In their haste to find the treasure, they'd failed to see the obvious sign of trouble before them: the same red Jeep conveniently showing up at each adventure. Now it was over. Instead of living to enjoy their newfound wealth, they were going to be gunned down in cold blood, and someone else was going to enjoy the riches they had worked so hard to find.

"Y-You're not gonna just shoot us—are you?" Even brave little Melissa was as scared as the rest at that moment.

"Well, honey," the man replied, "if we shot you, there'd be an investigation, and something might turn up linking us to the crime, so what we're gonna do is let you end it all yourselves. You see, you four treasure hunters were prowling around along the ledge outside the north tower, when suddenly, the ledge gave way, causing you to fall to your untimely deaths—at least that's what the papers will read. Now, come along with us—we're going up to the north tower."

In that huge haunted house, the towers were the only places the four had been unable to make themselves search. Now, it was kind of ironic that the sinister north tower was the place where the last journey of their young lives was to happen.

The other three started moving toward the door leading up to the tower, but Jason couldn't budge—he stood there frozen like the statue with the red eyes.

"Mr. Bennett, are you going to come along with the other three, or are we just going to have to shoot you right here?" The crooks were losing patience with the young coward.

The threat seemed to snap Jason back to reality. He hurriedly ran to catch up with the others; then the four proceeded toward their impending doom.

As the creaking door opened up to the spiral staircase, the young teens slowly looked upward to the top of the north tower. Jason looked at his best friend and then at the three men with the pistols. His voice quivered as he spoke, yet not in a frightened way but in a solemn, remorseful tone. "Tom, it looks like this is it. I just want you to know that you've always been my best friend. We've been through a lot together. I didn't quite understand what you told me yesterday—you know, about finding Jesus and all—but I want to ask you: Do you think Jesus would save me if I asked him? I mean, it looks like I'm just asking him because I know I'm gonna die. What do you think, Tom?"

Tom could hear the muffled sobs of his friend and of Melissa, who was listening to their conversation. By that time, the group was beginning to make their way up the spiral staircase.

Tom kept looking forward, trying to maintain his balance, as they crept along the side of the tower. "Jason—and you too, Melissa—I have to admit I'm new at this salvation thing, but in my dad's message a few weeks ago, he said there was a thief dying on the cross next to Jesus. This thief asked Jesus to remember him, and I believe Jesus told him that he would see him in Paradise. So if Jesus forgave a man dying on the cross with him, I'm sure he will forgive you. I want you both to say the prayer my dad said with me and Julie yesterday."

One of the gunmen was getting irritated. "You'd better say your prayers, for it won't be long before you meet your Maker."

Ignoring his remark, Tom proceeded to lead Jason and Melissa in the sinner's prayer. He couldn't see their faces, but by the sniffling he heard from them both, he knew that both of them meant what they were praying.

"I'm ready now for whatever awaits me," said Jason, no longer the fearful coward Tom had known. Melissa agreed with her boyfriend—the feeling in her heart let her know that everything was all right between her and God.

As they neared the top of the tower, an unusual calmness came over young Tom Parker, much like the calmness he'd experienced during the basketball games. He remembered a passage of scripture his dad had quoted many times during his many messages: Psalm 23, a psalm he had been required to memorize in one of his Sunday school classes from his youth. As the four teens slowly walked up the narrow steps of the spiral staircase leading to the top of the north tower—and their imminent doom—he spoke, beginning softly and getting a little louder with each step: "The Lord is my shepherd, I shall not want."

Suddenly, Julie and then Jason and Melissa joined their young friend as they climbed: "He maketh me to lie down in green pastures; he leadeth me beside the still waters. He restoreth my soul; he leadeth me in the paths of righteousness for his name's sake. Yea though I walk through the valley of the shadow of death, I will fear no evil; for thou art with me: thy rod and thy staff they comfort me. Thou preparest a table before me in the presence of mine enemies; thou annointest my head with oil; my cup runneth over. Surely goodness and mercy shall follow me all the days of my life; and I will dwell in the house of the Lord forever."

By the time they had finished the entire psalm, the four brave teenagers and their captors had reached the one lone window at the top of the tower—a window that opened out onto a ledge that wrapped itself around the tower's outer wall like the brim of Grandpa Parker's hat. Tom noticed a hole in the wall where one of the granite stones had been removed. *If only the gunmen had found the second plate before we did*, he thought, *then we wouldn't be in this mess.* He was having regrets, just as the other three were. *Why did I have to see the shiny reflection in that chimney? And why did I have to get all treasure happy—I should've left it alone.* Greed in the heart of man had led to a multitude of untimely deaths through the ages, and it looked as though he and his three friends were going to add to that list.

"Okay, folks, it's time for you to join this Lord you've been babbling about all the way up the stairs." The first gunman motioned with his gun toward the window.

Tom was the first to climb through the window. "I'm the one who got us into this mess; it's only right that I be the first to go," he said as he put his right leg through the window.

"Don't worry, Mr. Parker," said one of the other gunmen. "When we get you all out on that ledge, we'll make sure you're the first to go—over the side, that is."

Slowly and reluctantly, the other three followed Tom through the window and into the cold February night air.

The ledge around the north tower, as well as the other three, was made of solid oak boards milled from one of the many forests that surrounded Richfield, built by Joe Simpkins as a lookout to protect the castle. Armed guards had been posted 24-7. It was only about four feet wide, with one thin hand rail that ran around the outer edge. As solid as the ledge had been when first added to the towers, time and the elements had taken a toll. Many of the boards were loose or gone, as was much of the railing. As Tom stepped out onto the ledge, the creaking of the oak boards let him know he had to step with care—it had been many years since anyone had walked on that ledge, and now there would be four, walking toward their doom.

The first gunman forced the last remaining teen through the window and calmly stepped through to join them on the outside. "We're going to have to take a stroll around to the other side," he said with a scowl. "The rail has already fallen off here—we have to make it look like the boards accidentally came loose when you leaned against it, in case there's an investigation." The three men weren't about to take any chances. It had to look like an accident, or they wouldn't be spending any of the money—they'd be spending the rest of their lives in prison.

As they inched their way around the tower with their backs pressed against the cold granite, the teens had to step carefully to avoid falling through one of the many cracks in the old ledge. At one point, Jason's leg fell through a crack that had opened up when one of the rotten oak boards gave way.

"Careful, Mr. Bennett," said the gunman. "I wouldn't want you to lose out on all the fun your young friends are going to have shortly."

Jason pulled his leg back through the crack and checked to make sure he wasn't bleeding, which was foolish because he'd be bleeding in a few minutes anyway.

Even though they all felt they were ready to die, they weren't ready to go at that time. *I've got so much to live for*, thought Tom, but he knew it would take a miracle to get them out of the predicament they were in—and he hadn't yet learned how to pray for a miracle.

But all of a sudden, the miracle they desperately needed happened!

FOURTEEN

The one gunman had followed the teens out onto the ledge while the other two stayed behind, one to guard the window and the other to guard the gold. As the five slowly crept around the wall of the tower, all of a sudden, there was a loud creaking noise, followed by the sound of boards breaking away. They all turned around to see what the noise was—just in time to see the gunman disappear out of their sight.

"He fell through!" yelled Jason as he turned back to face the others. Jason had been bringing up the rear of the caravan, with the pistol pointing into his back, ready to go off at the slightest movement. Now the gun wasn't there, and the man wasn't there either.

Tom eased by Julie and Melissa until he was standing next to an excited Jason. They shone their flashlights through the hole, expecting to see what was left of the gunman sprawled out on the ground below, but that wasn't what they saw. There, hanging from the edge of the hole, were two sets of fingers barely clinging to the broken edge, which looked ready to give way at any moment.

"Please help me," a feeble voice cried from below the ledge. He was no longer the smooth, confident young man who'd wielded his pistol so foolishly at the teen quartet. His gun was somewhere on the ground below, and he was helplessly pleading for any help he could get. He who had been ready to take four lives was now desperate for someone to save his.

"We have to help him!" yelled Tom as he put his flashlight

down and reached through the hole to grab the man's arm. The old Tom probably would have lifted the man's fingers one by one and happily watched as he plummeted the remaining fifty feet to his well-deserved death. Only this wasn't the old Tom; this was a new creature in Christ, with a heart to match.

Jason quickly joined Tom, reaching through the opening, grabbing the man's other arm, and pulling with all his might. Though the gunman wasn't a large man, Tom and Jason had trouble pulling him through the small opening. The creaking of the boards surrounding the opening let them know they didn't have much time. "This thing could give way at any minute," said Jason.

"We'd better hurry, or we'll all be killed," Julie said. "I wonder where the other two men are; I know they must have heard all the commotion out here." Suddenly, Julie's question was answered almost before she got it out of her mouth.

In the blackness of the night, a bright light shone up from below to where the young people were, piercing the darkness like a lighthouse beacon. Julie and Melissa shaded their eyes with their hands to keep from being blinded. Just then, they heard a bullhorn and saw blue lights flashing from every direction.

"This is the police!" a voice shouted from somewhere below. "Lay down your weapons, and put your hands in the air!"

"We can't right now!" Jason yelled back with a strain in his voice. "We're trying to save this guy!" He and Tom strained with every muscle they had to lift the man through the opening, but he wasn't helping much by thrashing his legs, which were dangling in the air.

"C'mon, mister—quit thrashing about!" shouted Tom as he tried to get a better hold on the man's coat sleeve.

"We're sending some people up to help!" said the voice from the bullhorn.

"I wouldn't do that if I were you; this ledge could give way at any minute!" Melissa said.

They all knew she was right—they were running out of time. Yet even with the danger they were facing, none of the teens were going to abandon this helpless man to save themselves.

Slowly, inch by inch, the two young men were able to raise the man back up through the hole as the oak boards continued to crack all around them. They saw his head first and then his shoulders, followed by his midsection and, finally, his legs and feet. As he stood facing his saviors, a smile of gratitude came across his lips. "Thank you for saving me," he said with a tear in his eye.

"You're not saved yet!" shouted Tom. "We're gonna have to get off this ledge before it gives way!"

As the five made their way around the ledge toward the window, the creaking and groaning of the wood grew louder. Just then, Jason shouted, "It's breaking loose!"

The old boards were cracking all around them, and they could feel the supports below them coming loose from their anchors. "Hurry! We gotta get to the window!" Tom shouted as he grabbed Julie's hand.

There wasn't time to step lightly, so the four teens, along with the freed gunman, made a dash around the tower ledge, dodging holes as they went, until they finally came to the open window. Suddenly, two arms reached out and grabbed Melissa, forcing her through the window. Seconds later, the arms reached out for Julie, pulling her through to the other side. Tom, who was bringing up the rear, could hear the ledge on the other side of the tower giving way and crashing to the ground below. The arms reached for Jason and then the gunman, leaving Tom on the ledge alone. Just as they reached out for Tom, the ledge under him dropped away.

FIFTEEN

As if in slow motion, Tom began falling, dropping like a stone toward the ground below. As he fell, his life flashed before him. He saw his mom and dad in images of his childhood. He saw himself and Megan playing games in the backyard. Images of the days before suddenly flashed by: the playoffs, the winning shot, the Caroline Mine and the runaway mine car, the treasure in gold they'd found only to lose it in an instant, the ledge falling out from under him, and his descent into death and the unknown.

All of a sudden, two hands reached down and grabbed Tom's arms, jerking him to a sudden stop. "Hang on, Tom! I've got you!" a voice cried from above.

If this is an angel, it sounds a lot like Dad, Tom thought to himself. Looking up in the darkness, he saw the image of his dad, James Parker, who was halfway out the window, stretching as far as he could to hold on to his only son. His hands grasped Tom's coat sleeves, and he strained with all his might to keep his grip.

Tom now knew what the gunman had gone through earlier while Tom and Jason tried to pull him up—only this time, he was on the other end, helpless and dangling almost fifty feet above the ground with his legs thrashing violently, as if that would do anything to move him even the slightest bit upward.

"Calm down, Tom!" shouted his dad. "I'm not going to let go of you!"

As Tom looked up into the face of his father, a peace came over him. He could barely see his father's face, as the spotlight was shining on the other side of the tower, but he could sense the look of determination he'd grown accustomed to: Reverend Parker was not going to let go of his son.

Tom's legs quit thrashing. He put his feet against the walls of the granite tower. He felt for even the smallest crevice to put his toe into so he could thrust himself upward.

James strained to lift Tom up while some of the others inside the window held on for dear life, trying to make sure the good reverend didn't fall. Slowly, the young teen was lifted up, helping as much as he could by putting his toes in between the granite blocks and pushing himself up. By the time he reached the edge of the window, Tom could look inside and see all the ones helping in the rescue. His mom was there, holding on to James's belt. Jason, Julie, and Melissa were grabbing other parts of his clothes and hanging on with all their might. It was the most beautiful sight in the world. Even the gunman was there, holding on to Jason as Jason held on to the preacher.

Finally, they lifted Tom up far enough that he could grab hold of the windowsill and pull himself through to safety. His dad wasn't about to let go of Tom's coat sleeves, though, until he made sure he got through the window safely.

All the rescuers let out a huge roar as Tom was pulled through the window. No sooner had he gained his composure and stood on his feet than his mother wrapped her arms around him, nearly squeezing the breath out of him. "Oh, Tom, I'm so glad you didn't fall," she said as she squeezed him just a little tighter.

"Mom, I can't breathe." That was all Tom could get out.

JoAnn loosened her grip—a little. By that time, Julie, Melissa, and Jason had joined in, hugging their young friend and breathing sighs of relief.

Finally, it was his dad's turn. As James reached out to take hold of his son, there were tears in his eyes. He hadn't realized until just that moment how close he had come to losing him. "If you ever pull a stunt like this again, I'll push you over the ledge myself," he joked. "By the way, you're grounded for the rest of your life."

"Sounds fair enough," said Tom. He was so relieved to be standing safely inside the tower instead of hanging from the outside that he was willing to accept any punishment his mom and dad dished out.

When they all got back down to the bottom of the spiral staircase, they heard sounds coming from the huge living room. Tom counted at least a dozen cops there as he walked through the door. There were also a few news reporters who had been tipped off to all that was going on. He saw the other two gunmen sitting on the couch in handcuffs, dejectedly looking at the floor. The sheriff came over to the other gunman and started reading him his rights as one of the deputies put handcuffs around his wrists and then led him over to where his friends were.

The reporters, who had been checking out the opening over the fireplace, instantly directed their attention to the four young treasure hunters, rushing over to the young teens with cameras rolling and microphones ready. "How did you find the gold?" one of them asked.

"Did you know these other men were after the treasure too?" asked another, not giving any of them time to answer the first question.

Tom and Julie tried to answer one reporter's question while Jason and Melissa tried to answer the other one. None of them were used to this type of publicity, and it was a little overwhelming.

Just then, the sheriff yelled for them to come over to the fireplace, under the section where the gold had been found. As the four slowly strolled across the room to where the sheriff was standing, thoughts of doom went through the mind of each one. "Well, this is it," said Jason. "Wonder how many years we'll get for this."

"I don't know," answered Tom. "Maybe we'll get out in time to draw our Social Security." He chuckled nervously, knowing in his heart that this was no joking matter.

"Do you kids have any idea how much trouble you have caused?" The sheriff spoke in a gruff tone of voice. "Not to mention the fact that you could have been killed!"

Tom had known Sheriff Etter his entire life. He was a big man. More than six feet tall and weighing around 250 pounds, he had deep-set eyes and a granite jaw and sported a few scars to show that he'd been in a scuffle or two during his many years in law enforcement.

"What I should do is throw the book at you." He scowled, but then a big grin came over his face. "But it wouldn't look too good on me if I locked up the ones responsible for finding the Simpkins treasure. I will have to charge you with trespassing, though. I can't just let you get off with nothing."

"How much time will we have to serve for that?" asked Jason nervously.

Sheriff Etter laughed. "You won't have to serve any time for that; it will only be a fine since it's a misdemeanor—but I'm sure you'll have no trouble paying for it with the money you get from the gold."

Their eyes widened as big as saucers. "You mean we get to keep it?" said Tom.

"You found it, didn't you?" the sheriff said with a chuckle. "Besides, the townsfolk would string me up if I didn't give the gold to its rightful owners. You solved the riddle, and you found the gold—that makes it yours!"

A huge cheer broke out in the crowd as Tom, Julie, Jason, and Melissa shook Sheriff Etter's hand and then proceeded to hug each other; their parents, who had all shown up by that time; and then the reporters, the deputies, and everyone else in the room.

Tom had just one question left—for his dad. "How did you know we were here?" he asked with a puzzled look.

His dad flashed the big grin he was famous for all over Richfield. "Tom, you're about as subtle as an elephant stomping through the mud. I've had my suspicions from the start, but I wanted to give you the benefit of the doubt. However, when you were so late in getting home this evening, I sensed that something was wrong, so I called around the neighborhood until I finally found someone who said they'd seen the four of you going into the mansion. Then I called Sheriff Etter and told him we'd meet him here and get to the bottom of this. I'm glad we got here when we did, or you'd be in that pile of rotten wood at the base of that tower right now." Then he gestured with his index finger toward the ceiling. "Somebody was looking out for all of you!"

"I know he was, Dad," Tom said. "I want you all to know how sorry we are to have caused all this trouble." He looked at his young friends. "But once we got started, we couldn't stop. We just had to see where all these clues would lead us." Julie, Melissa, and Jason all nodded in unison.

His dad shook his head as he glanced over at the sheriff. "I've got to tell you, I don't think I could have let it go either," he said.

"Sheriff, look at this."

Sheriff Etter swung around to face one of his deputies, who had a small wooden box in his hand.

"I found this inside the hole where the gold was."

The sheriff took the box from the deputy and then turned it over a couple times, trying to find a way to open it. He saw a small flap of leather protruding from the edge of the box. With a gentle tug, the top of the box opened. All eyes in the room, as well as a few cameras, strained to see what was in the box and find out why it had been hidden away in the vast treasure of gold. The sheriff reached in and took out a rolled-up piece of parchment faded by time and tied around the middle with a small red ribbon. The ribbon broke in his hand as he tried to untie it, and the small scroll unrolled, showing a hand-printed document of some kind.

"It's a letter," said the sheriff as he held his flashlight up to get a better look.

"What does it say?" yelled many of the anxious participants as well as some of the curious bystanders.

The sheriff asked for some extra light, and a couple of his deputies gladly obliged. He then strained his eyes at the letter and read:

> Greetings to you in the name of the Lord. If you are reading this letter, it is safe to assume you have found my gold. I congratulate you, for you are now the proud owner of a fortune that will probably

last you through your lifetime. I want to let you know my story. I'm sure those of you who will read about me would like to know about my sudden disappearance from Richfield.

You see, after my brother, Charlie, was killed and I discovered the gold, I did everything I could to buy some happiness in my life. That's the reason I had this house built. I used the finest materials to build the house, and I sent all over the world for treasures to fill it. Yet with all the wealth I accumulated, there was always an empty spot in my heart.

But in the spring of 1877, I found what I was missing. In a little church in Oak Grove, I bowed on my knees and asked Jesus into my heart. Not long after that, I felt the call of God to become a missionary and to reach others for Christ. As I write this, I'm preparing to catch the next stage to San Francisco, where I will sail to Africa. I plan to live out my days ministering the gospel to anyone who will listen.

The riddle you just solved, including the Bible verse that was part of it, was my way of letting you know that the only real treasures are the ones we lay up in heaven. This gold will not buy you lasting happiness—only Jesus Christ can do that. The gold is yours to do with as you wish, but don't expect it to solve all your problems, because it won't. I found out that a life lived for Jesus Christ is the only way you can have true peace and happiness.

Yours in Christ,
Joe Simpkins

Sheriff Etter gently rolled up the letter, placed it back in the wooden box, and closed the lid. The crowd stood there in stunned silence for what seemed like an eternity. In one night, two of the greatest mysteries the town of Richfield had ever known had been solved: the disappearance of Joe Simpkins and the location of the golden treasure. TV cameras continued to roll as little by little, the people came out of their trances and started to mill around. News reporters faced the cameras once again as they tried to gather all the information they could for their eleven o'clock news broadcasts. The four heroes again tried to answer the barrage of questions put to them by the reporters, as well as by family members and bystanders. Sheriff Etter told the teens he would have a couple of his deputies guard the gold until the next day, when they could have it removed by armored car to the nearest treasurer's office. As far as they could tell, there were around one hundred bars of pure gold, weighing in at about twenty-seven pounds each, worth between $15 million and $20 million.

As Tom attempted to answer one of the news reporter's many questions, he glanced over to the couch where the three gunmen were still sitting, looking dejectedly down at the floor. "Sheriff Etter!" he yelled across the room.

The sheriff, who was busy answering questions of his own, held up his large hand as if to say, "That's enough questions," and walked over to where Tom was standing. "What is it, Tom?" he asked.

"What's going to happen to these guys?" Tom asked, pointing in the direction of the guys on the couch.

As the sheriff looked over at the three young men, he sighed and softly said, "Well, we'll be charging them with trespassing and armed robbery as well as attempted murder—after all, they were planning on forcing you four off the tower ledge at gunpoint."

Tom glanced over at his three friends and then back to the sheriff. "Can you just wait a few minutes while I talk it over with them?" he asked as he motioned to Julie, Jason, and Melissa.

The sheriff nodded in agreement. "Make it quick, though. We need to wrap this up—it's getting late."

Tom hurried over to the others, who gathered around him in a small huddle. As Tom talked, they all nodded in agreement. With Jason, Tom's idea seemed to take some coaxing—especially from Melissa. Then the four made their way over to Sheriff Etter, who was with the three young men.

"We've talked it over and have decided not to press charges," Tom said.

Everybody's eyes grew wide, especially those of the three young prisoners. The one who had led them out onto the ledge spoke first. "You mean we don't have to go to prison?" he said with a nervous sigh of relief in his voice.

"Not unless the sheriff has some other charges against you!" said Melissa.

Sheriff Etter took out his keys and proceeded to take the handcuffs off his prisoners. "I'll have to charge you with trespassing like the others, but otherwise, you're free to go."

The crowd let out another cheer as the young men took turns hugging everyone, especially their four deliverers. "I don't understand. Why would you just let us go?" said one of the lookouts. "We were ready to kill you four in order to have that gold to ourselves."

"That's right," said the second lookout. "I can't believe you're not pressing charges—if it were me, I'd be sending you all up the river for a very long time."

Tom addressed the three former convicts. "You know, if it was a week ago, we would probably feel the same as you—but something happened that has changed our minds. You see, we all have had an experience that is greater than finding this gold—we met Jesus Christ!" The way Tom spoke, with boldness and authority, reminded some in the crowd of his father. "I believe God had a hand in helping us find this treasure, as well as in rescuing us from the tower ledge. God has a special purpose for all of us, but we have to give ourselves to him in order for him to fulfill that purpose." He reached forth his hands to the young men, who were listening intently to the young witness, as he spoke with just a trace of a tear streaming down the corner of his eye. "We can help you to meet Jesus if you'd like."

There on that old couch in the old living room of the old mansion, the four young adventurers knelt with the three young gunmen, seemingly oblivious to the commotion going on around them, and led them to the cross, where Jesus wrapped his loving arms around them and brought them into the family of God.

By that time, James and JoAnn Parker had come over, and they helped the three understand what they needed to do—but it didn't take much. They were ready! Tears flowed as each of them said the sinner's prayer and let Jesus come into his heart. Tom heard a few sniffles from other parts of the room as well. *This is your night, Jesus,* he thought as tears continued to run down his face.

By the time Tom and the rest had left the Simpkins mansion, it was after eleven o'clock. They were tired but too excited to sleep. The four teens had talked it over and decided to share the gold with the three gunmen, who were Mayfield College kids, as they'd found out at the mansion. Part of the money would be added to a program that had been started years ago but had reached a dead end due to a lack of funds: the Save the Simpkins Mansion Program. Now there would be enough money to restore the mansion to its original splendor and also make it a tourist stop and museum in memory of the Simpkins boys. The museum also would tell the story of the great treasure hunt.

It was after midnight when they said their final goodbyes. As Tom climbed into bed, his mind raced over every detail of the past few days, including the tournament, the gold, and the near-death experience on the tower ledge. Yet the memory he dwelled on the most was the moment when Jesus Christ had become his Savior, Lord, and Master. It was a moment he would never forget. As he slowly drifted off to sleep, the words "Thank you, Lord" rolled softly off his lips.

SIXTEEN

Twenty-Five Years Later

Tom and Julie were happily married and had three kids of their own—two daughters and a son. Tom was now the mayor of Richfield, and he and Julie were the owners of a computer software company. James Parker was still the pastor of the Richfield Community Church, although he was preparing to retire by the end of the year. His replacement was to be none other than Toby Miller, the former class bully. After Toby's turn in the Simpkins mudhole on that fateful day, the words of young Tom Parker had rung in his ears all the way home. He had gone to the church that following Sunday, and Jesus had been there to meet him. All the bitterness and resentment had been washed away that day along with all his sins, and he had become a new creature in Christ. He had gone on to become one of the best basketball players, as well as one of the best citizens, Richfield had ever known. He and Tom both had gotten into Mayfield College on basketball scholarships, where Toby had gotten a degree in engineering. Then he'd gone to seminary, where he'd received an advanced degree in theology. He had worked at Tom and Julie's company for the past fifteen years but would be resigning soon to take over the reins as pastor.

Jason and Melissa also had gotten married, and to everyone's surprise, Jason had gone on to the police academy, where he'd graduated with honors, and he was now the sheriff of Richfield, having replaced Sheriff Etter.

"Talk about irony," Tom had said to Julie as Jason was sworn in. "The biggest chicken I ever knew has become the new sheriff."

"Of course, with Melissa as one of his deputies, he'll have plenty of help," Julie had said with a grin.

The couple also had three kids—two sons and a daughter.

When Vince Tyson and later his wife, Gladys, had passed away, their kids had put the farm up for sale. Tom and Jason had bought the farm and divided it into two equal tracts: one for Tom and Julie and one for Jason and Melissa. Jason had let Tom have his choice because he'd known he would want the one with the most trees.

The Simpkins mansion was a masterpiece. Every part of it had been restored in intricate detail. Even the ledges around the towers had been replaced. Volunteers helped to take care of the multitude of tourists who visited the mansion each year. It was the biggest tourist destination in that part of the state. Tom, Julie, Jason, and Melissa volunteered in their spare time, and James and JoAnn planned to help with the museum after they retired.

As for the gold, some of the money from the sale of it had gone into trust funds for the four teens; some had gone to the college kids, who all had bought new red Jeeps; and the remainder had gone into restoring the mansion. A few bars had been left untouched in the old vault and added to the museum as a reminder of the mine and the two miners, the mansion, and the treasure hunt.

As Tom sat on the branch of the huge oak tree that stood on the east end of his property, he couldn't help but reminisce about the life he'd had. He thought about Julie and his three children. Natalie had graduated from Richfield High with honors and was getting ready to attend Mayfield College along with Tyler Bennett, Jason and Melissa's son. Ava was a freshman at Richfield High, and Adam was in the seventh grade. Tom thought about how happy he and Julie were together and how much he loved doing things with his family. He thought about the land he now owned and how much he had always loved roaming the hills of that beautiful country farm. He thought of his mom and dad, how proud he was of them, and how happy he was for them in their upcoming retirement. He thought of Toby Miller and the drastic change in him—a change that even Tom never would have imagined. He thought about all that had transpired during the fateful two-week period that had changed his life forever, as well as the lives of his friends.

But the one thing he thought about most was the wonderful Sunday morning twenty-five years earlier when he and Julie had walked down the aisle of that old country church with tears streaming down their faces and given themselves to the only One who could truly change their lives forever. The treasure they'd found on that glorious day far exceeded anything they had found before or since. It was a treasure not measured by monetary standards or acquired by any means known to man. It was a treasure unlike any of the ones found in history books or archaeological magazines. It was a treasure even greater than the one they'd discovered inside the wall of the Simpkins mansion. It was a treasure they would take with them forever on earth and beyond. It was truly a treasure of the heart.

Printed in the United States
By Bookmasters